Y0-EBA-004

Thy Sting, Oh Death

THY STING, OH DEATH

John Keith Drummond

ST. MARTIN'S PRESS
NEW YORK

THY STING, OH DEATH. Copyright © 1985 by John Keith Drummond. All rights reserved. Printed in the United States of America. No part of this book may be used or reproduced in any manner whatsoever without written permission except in the case of brief quotations embodied in critical articles or reviews. For information, address St. Martin's Press, 175 Fifth Avenue, New York, N.Y. 10010.

Design by Kingsley Parker

Library of Congress Cataloging in Publication Data

Drummond, John Keith.
    Thy sting, oh Death.
    I. Title.
PS3554.R75S8   1985   813'.54   85-10056
ISBN 0-312-80419-9

First Edition

10 9 8 7 6 5 4 3 2 1

Alla Cara Maestra

NORMA DI TANO

(1906–1978)

La Vergine degli Angeli vi copra del suo manto, e voi protegga vigile di Dio l'Angelo santo . . .

—"La Forza del Destino"

Floor plan — Bessermann House, First Floor

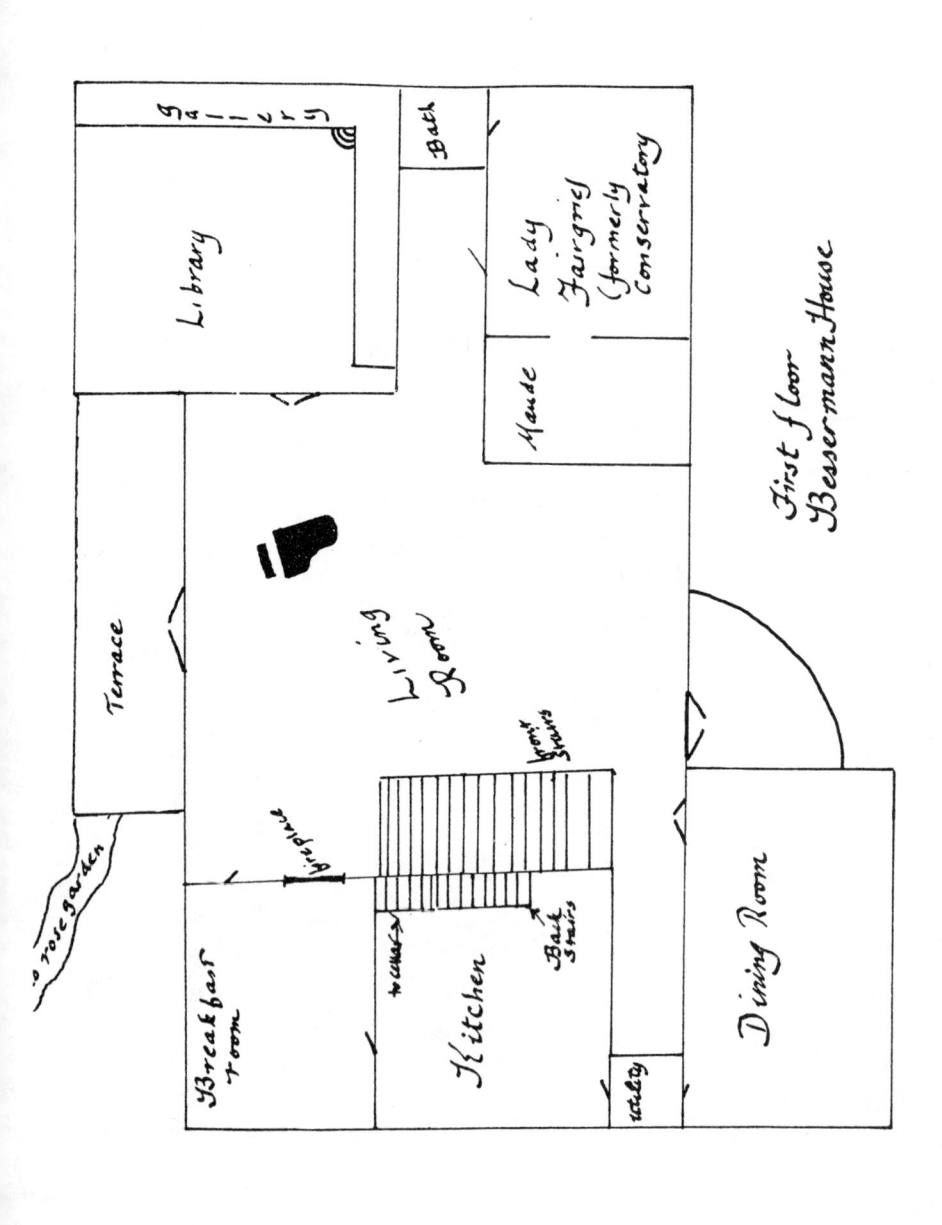

- Library
- Gallery
- Bath
- Maude
- Lady Faryres (formerly Conservatory)
- Terrace
- to rose garden
- Living Room
- Breakfast room
- fireplace
- Kitchen
- Front stairs
- Back stairs
- Dining Room

First floor
Bessermann House

2nd Floor

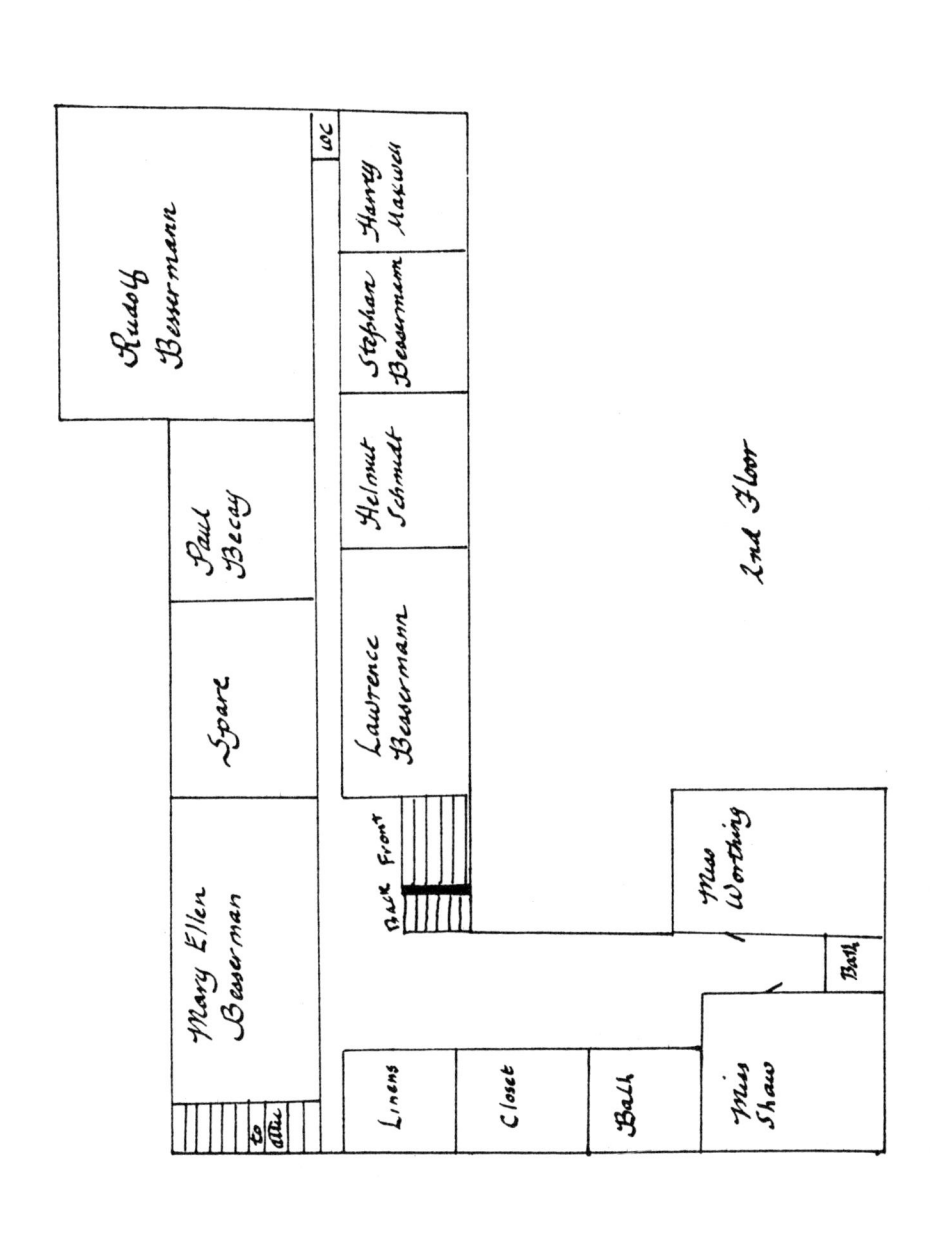

- Rudy Besserman
- Paul Becy
- Spare
- Mary Ellen Besserman
- to attic
- WC
- Harry Maxwell
- Stephan Besserman
- Helmut Schmidt
- Lawrence Besserman
- Back / Front
- Linens
- Closet
- Bath
- Miss Shaw
- Bath
- Miss Worthing

Thy Sting, Oh Death

PRELUDE

Later—much later—the thing Miss Worthing would recall most vividly about that day was the bizarre incident of the bees.

From early morning, the day had been warm and clear. Only an occasional billow of cumulus, cresting the western hills, hinted at approaching rain. Meanwhile, it was one of those glorious autumn days—fierce at noon though frigid toward evening; the kind of day on which everyone in Northern California flocks to a beach, a river bank, or pool for the last little sun before winter comes in earnest.

Everyone, that is, except Miss Matilda Worthing and Miss Martha Shaw of 875 Jasmine Avenue, Jolliston, California.

Arrayed in disreputable, mud-covered overalls, battle-weary brogans, and canvas gloves, the two elderly women had spent the morning happily pottering away at those autumnal chores that any avid gardner will discover—usually at the very last minute—have not been done. Unfortunately, one of the tasks that the two ladies had neglected was the cloching of all their most treasured garden goodies.

And so, there they were on their knees in the garden at either side of what looked like a few scrawny sticks jammed at random into the soil, but which was actually quite a rare and delicate hybrid tea rose.

Around this unlovely specimen, a narrow and rather deep trench had been troweled into which the two of them—with much hesitation and mutual admonishment—were lowering a large glass bell jar.

"Careful, dear . . ."

"*Gently*, Mattie!"

"Can you move it more your way, Martha?"

"*My* way? But there's so much . . ."

"Well, I can't *see*; there's a speck in my—"

"*Do* be careful, Mattie!"

"Martha! Are you *clear*?"

When, eventually, they got it into place, each withdrew a trowel from her pocket and began to scoop soil up around the thing until the base was completely covered.

"There!" Miss Worthing exclaimed and sat back on her heels to catch her breath. "And that's the last of 'em," she added happily, while Miss Shaw, with the back of her trowel, vigorously swatted the little pile of dirt to pack it down.

Behind them, a double row of the jars, gleaming in the sunlight, stretched neatly to the bottom of the garden where the Jolliston River flowed by, sluggish and brown.

With a small grunt of satisfaction, Miss Shaw grabbed the knob on the top of the bell and gave it a gentle wiggle. A few grains of earth skittered down the pile but the jar itself was securely seated.

The two women looked at each other, fetched enormous, happy sighs, thrust their trowels back into hip pockets, and with a great deal of audible groaning, struggled to their feet.

"Thank God that's done for another year," said Miss Shaw fervently and rolled her head to ease a crick in her neck.

"And furthermore," Miss Worthing added, retreating

to the terrace and stomping her feet to get the clinging humus off her shoes, "that's about it for the year."

Miss Shaw abruptly ceased lolling her head and frowned at Miss Worthing. "But what about the fruit trees?" she asked, gesturing toward a double row of apple and pear trees running down either side of the garden.

"Never mind the trees, dear," replied Miss Worthing somewhat absently. "I don't think we should do them this year."

"Why ever not?" demanded Miss Shaw. "There's years of good bearing left in them."

Miss Worthing did not reply immediately, however, being more concerned with the intricacies of undoing bootlaces while wearing gardening gloves.

Miss Shaw clucked and cast her eyes to the heavens. "Mattie!" she called sharply.

"Hmmm?" Miss Worthing looked up vaguely. "Oh, sorry, Martha, I wasn't paying attention."

"Do tell," Miss Shaw muttered under her breath, joining Miss Worthing on the terrace. "The fruit trees?" she repeated.

"First of all, we should have done them weeks ago if we were going to do them at all," Miss Worthing explained. "And secondly, both of us are getting too old and much, much too fat to be clambering about in the treetops with pruning shears in one hand and our lives in the other."

"But the trees!" Miss Shaw insisted.

Miss Worthing once more glanced up from her recalcitrant laces and made a face. "Never mind the trees, Martha," she repeated with some small exasperation. "If the weather holds I thought we could get Tony Vasquez over to do them for us. He does owe us a favor," she added dryly.

Miss Shaw chuckled richly. "If you can call keeping his father out of the gas chamber a favor."

Miss Worthing looked offended. "No one else was going to do it," she protested.

"Never mind, dear," said Miss Shaw with a grin. "I think it's a wonderful idea," and perching rather precariously on the edge of the wheelbarrow, began attending to her own boots.

Miss Worthing's laces yielded at last. She stood up and kicked the boots off and wriggled her toes about on the warm flags. For a moment, she watched Miss Shaw, cheerfully scraping soil from the soles of her shoes, when a look of impish mischief flitted across her face. She went to the edge of the terrace and then—after pausing a moment—began stalking back and forth, alternately humming and muttering to herself and peering along an outstretched arm as though gauging various sightlines down the length of the garden.

"What are you doing?" asked Miss Shaw, looking up.

"Nothing really," replied Miss Worthing blithely, keeping her back to her friend. "But there is going to be so much more time for things now that we won't be doing the trees each year, hmmm? It just occurred to me," she continued, "that perhaps now we could put something else into the garden. Something really nice. Some kind of orchid perhaps. . . . *Cymbidiums?* No, too delicate for the climate. *Cattleyas?* Oh, dear me, no! Much too vulgar. *Phalaenopsis?* There! Of course they'd have to go under glass in the fall, too, but then we're going to have so much more time . . ."

"Matilda Worthing!" Miss Shaw erupted, her light blue eyes bulging in horror. "What are you thinking of?"

Miss Worthing burst out laughing. "I wasn't serious, dear," she said, pulling off her gloves and stuffing them into a pocket. "We'll have quite enough to do next year without orchids."

Chuckling, she pushed Miss Shaw onto a garden chaise and settled herself into a white-painted iron lawn chair. The two of them sat quietly for a long space. The sunlight on their upturned faces felt so good, especially as they knew the fair weather would end in just a few more days. And today was so quiet, too. The silence just came seeping into your bones, sending you off for a long, slumbering nap. . . .

A klaxon reveille shattered the pleasant moment. Miss Shaw sat bolt upright and said, "Damn him," with deep feeling.

Miss Worthing closed her eyes and lay back again. "The mail, dear," she said, and then spoiled it by giggling.

"It's not funny, Mattie," grumbled Miss Shaw stoutly, lumbering to her feet. "It's enough to give a body a heart attack! I've told him time after time he does *not* have to blast that thing."

"Now, now, Martha," Miss Worthing soothed. "He just knew we'd be back here on a morning like this. I think it's sweet of him to let us know he's here. Why don't you go get the mail and I'll get some lunch ready. Hmmm?"

Miss Shaw nodded and, still muttering darkly to herself, waddled off. Miss Worthing sat up to watch her friend's retreating back and sadly shook her head. Martha certainly had let herself go lately. She had always been a big woman, several inches taller than average and large-boned. Her round, somewhat foolish face, with her eyes of a clear sky-blue, was virtually untouched by wrinkles. Indeed, in spite of her seventy-five years, she still had a lovely peaches-and-cream complexion, a happy heritage of her Irish forebears. Unfortunately, as the years had increased, so had her bulk, and a tendency to be—if not untidy—in perpetual disarray. Her hair was a nimbus of snowy lawn billowing unmanageably on every occasion, and her clothes, which she deftly constructed herself, had grown alarmingly more and more tentlike. She looked, Miss Worthing considered sadly, rather like a pear with legs, especially in those dreadful denim overalls.

"But then"—she glanced down at her own expanding bulk—"I'm none too trim anymore myself." She herself might weigh what she weighed when she had retired, but the weight was by no means in all the same places. She sighed regretfully. If only Martha weren't such a good cook. Diet—she chided herself—diet and a lot more exercise.

She let herself into the utility room and shed her overalls next to the washing machine. They really were due for a major overhaul, what with manifold grass stains, mud spots, and separated seams. She should probably just get new ones.

Oh, and there was another wrinkle in her skirt. Absently, she tried to smooth it out. And the cost of dry cleaning these days! It was really no wonder people didn't wear proper tweeds any more.

She peered into the mirror above the sink and observed little more than a blur. "Oh, fiddle!" she muttered and turned the tap on to run her glasses under the cold water. Her dark blue eyes, usually magnified by her bottle-bottom lenses, appeared vague and uncertain without them. And yet, there was something—a crinkle in the corner, a twinkle in the depths—which helped one anticipate her shrewd and lively mind.

When, shortly, she could see again, she eyed the uncertain reflection in the ancient mirror without any pleasure whatever. It was really rather vexing that, being Martha's junior, she nevertheless appeared the elder of the two. Her face was nowhere near as plump as Martha's and had, as a consequence, appreciably more wrinkles, lines, wattles, and folds. Besides which, the four-and-a-half decades of concentration required by her profession (she had been a court reporter) had left her with an expression in repose of almost puritan severity. That it was a useful expression she would never have denied.

It was, for all that, still a little irritating to have a face that would frighten a horse when once she had been pretty little Mattie Worthing. . . .

"Oh, fiddle!" she muttered again. Pretty Miss Worthing indeed, with a smear of mud running from cheek to ear and her auburn, gray-streaked hair a nest of wisps and very weary curls. Briefly, she considered wrangling with it. Instead she went into the house to wash up.

Soon, having changed into an ancient, faded brown-print house dress, and with her hair combed severely back, she backed through the swinging doors into the dining room bearing an enormous teapot and a plate of microscopically thin sandwiches.

"Martha, dear . . ." she began, but Miss Shaw was nowhere in sight. She set the things down on the sideboard and went into the front room to look out the window. Sure enough, Miss Shaw was still jawing away with the mailman. She might grouse about his unquestionably deplorable horn, but he did, after all, get one of her legendary fruitcakes every Christmas, which more than amply demonstrated how much she really liked him. And, of course, he was quite fond of them, too—especially since that ridiculous business about securities checks.

Now that one had been fun. A smile tugged at the corners of her mouth. The only time she had tangled with the FBI, too. But really! There was no way Lewis could possibly have stolen the checks. And she'd made them see it. . . .

She opened the door and called out, "Martha! Stop holding Lewis up!"

A cold wind had descended out of the clear sky. The

boughs of the live oaks across the way had begun to bend and sway fitfully.

"Hi, Miss W," Lewis Carter called out with a wave. She waved back. "Come on, Martha. Lunch!"

Miss Shaw said something to the mailman that Miss Worthing couldn't hear. He laughed, and, noisily letting out the clutch, rolled away down the drive in a cloud of dust. Miss Shaw went round the side path to the back.

Miss Worthing fetched their lunch from the dining room and rearranged it on the coffee table in the front room. She heard Miss Shaw going up the back stairs as she went to switch on the furnace. That wind would bring the temperature down quickly.

Presently, her hair a flyaway cloud of cotton wool and dressed in a vast muumuu of an unsuitable baby blue that tended to make her eyes look like headlamps, Miss Shaw came dawdling back down the front stairs, sorting through the rather large bunch of envelopes in her hand.

"Anything interesting?" Miss Worthing asked over her shoulder as she poured tea into their cups.

"Not much, dear," replied Miss Shaw vaguely, flipping slowly. "Just the usual bills and solicita—Hello! Now what's this?" She sniffed at it. "Lavender scent, too." She settled onto the sofa. "Do you know anyone in . . ." She mentioned a dull but extremely expensive retirement community outside of San Francisco.

"Not that I can recall." Miss Worthing doled out sandwiches from the platter, wiped her hands, and reached out. Miss Shaw handed her the envelope and lifted her cup.

Suddenly, Miss Worthing uttered a strange little cry and sat down heavily in a chair. Miss Shaw hastily swallowed. "What's wrong, Mattie?"

For a moment, Miss Worthing could not reply. Shaking her head, she merely glanced down at the light mauve sheets of paper in her hand and bit her lower lip. Then, turning aside, she gazed for a long, long moment into the empty grate, a faintly lost expression on her face as of someone staring into the dim, sad past.

"Bad news, Mattie?" asked Miss Shaw gently.

Miss Worthing took a quick breath as though she were about to say something and then shook her head again. "No," she finally whispered. "It's nothing—nothing . . . Oh, Martha!" Her voice trailed off as she groped for words. Shaking her head again, she laid the letter down and with a slightly trembling hand, picked up her teacup and drank deeply. As she put it down, she gave a weak chuckle. "Now I wish I hadn't quit smoking."

"Mattie?" Miss Shaw prodded delicately.

Miss Worthing sighed and smiled wanly at her friend. "Nothing's wrong exactly, Martha," she said quietly. "It's just that there's been a terrible misunderstanding. A terrible misunderstanding," she repeated in a whisper and lapsed again into silence.

Miss Shaw poured Miss Worthing another cup of tea and stirred in milk and sugar. Miss Worthing accepted it with a grateful glance and again drank it straight down. "Oh dear," she muttered, and set her cup down. "I suppose I'd better just out with it?" She said it as though asking a question. Miss Shaw merely nibbled at her sandwich.

"My aunt," Miss Worthing announced quietly, "has moved to the Bay Area."

Miss Shaw stopped chewing, swallowed loudly, and gaped at Miss Worthing. "Lady Fairgrief! Here? The battle axe?" Instantly, Miss Shaw's fat little hand covered her mouth as she turned quite pink.

A half smile twitched across Miss Worthing's face. "She is a bit of a dragon," she conceded mildly. Her glance once more went to the letter. "It all goes back to '29 or so, after father died—"

"—and you were penniless." Miss Shaw finished the all too familiar formula.

Miss Worthing nodded. "They—Uncle Arthur and she—were here, or rather in San Francisco, at the consulate. They had me over to dinner three or four times a week. Aunt Eulalia maintained I wasn't eating properly."

"You weren't," observed Miss Shaw crisply and finished her sandwich.

"I was in school," stated Miss Worthing even more crisply. "There simply wasn't much money after my tuition."

"Well, what happened?"

"Nothing *happened*, Martha," replied Miss Worthing rather shortly, and immediately put out a hand toward her friend. "I'm sorry; I really don't mean to be hasty. I've just been suddenly remembering"—she shook her head sadly at the recollection—"so much about that unhappy time." She picked up the letter. "Anyway, my clothes began to get more and more frayed, my hair was generally all anyhow and my *shoes* . . . but you remember what I was like when we met."

Miss Shaw pursed her mouth and nodded, her face carefully noncommittal.

"I was ashamed to go to dinner anymore. Everyone else was in evening things and there I was." She gestured vaguely. "My pride couldn't stand it. I stopped accepting their invitations. And then—before I really knew it—Uncle Arthur was called back to England for something and"—she shrugged—"I haven't seen them since."

"But you sent her . . ."

". . . a few trifles of money since the war." Miss Worthing waved a hand in a dismissive gesture.

"What's the difficulty?"

"I feel so horribly guilty."

"Why, Mattie?" insisted Miss Shaw.

Miss Worthing opened the letter. "You might as well

hear it." She held the pages, covered with thin scrawling, up to the light:

"'Dearest Matilda: In good conscience, I know I should have written you ere this. Such a lack of communication with one's very own flesh and blood may seem unfeeling or even reprehensible. Nevertheless, I had for many years believed that you had taken some offense at something I or my dear departed husband may have done or said to you for which you found it awkward to communicate with us. Your kindnesses over the years have persuaded me that perhaps this is not so.'"

Miss Worthing looked up. Once again there were tears in her eyes. "Do you see, Martha? All these years, she's thought I was offended."

Miss Shaw nodded solemnly. "It's bad all right. Still," she pointed out, "she wasn't without justification. Think how things must have looked to her."

Miss Worthing rose and began to pace the floor. A few wisps of hair had escaped from their pins, adding to her air of distress. "Whatever shall I do? Whatever shall I do?"

Miss Shaw leaned forward and once more poured tea into Miss Worthing's cup. "Sit down," she said simply, "drink your tea, and read the rest of the letter."

Obediently, Miss Worthing resumed her seat.

"Besides," continued Miss Shaw, "you're the one who is always telling me that nothing's any good until we have all the facts."

"You're right, of course." Miss Worthing smiled and picked up the letter:

"'As you can see from the return address,'" she read, "'I have now returned to the country of my birth. Unfortunately, this is not the agreeable community I was led to believe it was. Altogether too many people here have given up on life—a foolish thing to do even at my great age.'"

"How old is she, Mattie?" Miss Shaw interrupted.

Miss Worthing considered a moment. "Goodness! Let me see now. She was about ten years younger than Father and he was born in '78, so she must be—yes, she must be at least ninety-five or ninety-six."

"Great Heavens! That is getting on. But I'm interrupting."

"'And so,'" Miss Worthing continued reading, "'by the time you receive this letter, I shall be staying for a time quite near you. My dear friend Rudolf Bessermann has invited me to come to him indefinitely, having gone so far as to remodel his conservatory for me.'"

"That must have cost old Rudy a wrench," Miss Shaw observed in surprise. "Him and his flowers!"

"Yes, and I can't imagine why Rudolf didn't mention it to me at the Opera board meeting last week."

"There were, I gather, other subjects to discuss," remarked Miss Shaw very dryly indeed.

"Good Lord, yes. What an ugly to-do that was. 'He was the great friend of my beloved Arthur,'" Miss Worthing continued reading, "'and he will be a great comfort to me. I will arrive in Jolliston on Halloween'."

"She arrived yesterday."

"Yes," replied Miss Worthing shortly. She finished reading: "'I would consider it an honor and a privilege if I were allowed to call upon you. While I am still far sturdier than I have any right being, I cannot last all *that* much longer. I should very much like to see you and be once more what I have, in my heart ever been, your affectionate Aunt, Eulalia, Lady Fairgrief.'" Miss Worthing folded the letter. "Oh dear!"

The two ladies sat for a long moment in silence broken only by a curious buzzing in the distance.

"Well, Mattie?"

"Well, Martha?"

"May I make a suggestion?"

"Of course, dear."

"I think this afternoon you should write a note to Lady Fairgrief. We can send it round to Bessermann's by special messenger."

"That's a good idea, Martha."

"Also, let's invite her to dinner, for—let's see, today's Thursday, how about Tuesday?"

"Splendid! We'll thaw out that leg of lamb and . . ."

The buzzing had grown a good deal louder.

"What on earth is that?" Miss Worthing wondered aloud.

"It's not a plane."

"I know, it's too steady. That droning reminds me of something."

Miss Shaw stuck her head out of the window and hastily pulled it back in, slamming the window shut. "Quickly, Mattie. Close the doors. I'll get the upstairs windows." She made for the stairs.

"What is it, Martha?"

"An enormous swarm of bees is coming in this direction."

"Martha," Miss Worthing spoke sharply, "don't be ridiculous. This is November. Bees swarm in June."

"I can't help that now, Mattie," said Miss Shaw breathlessly, pounding up the stairs. "Hurry!" Her voice trailed down from the upstairs hallway.

Miss Worthing checked the lower windows and doors and rejoined Miss Shaw at the front window. It was acrawl with bees.

"They're not clumping together." Miss Worthing bent over and peered at the golden bodies.

"Huh?"

"There doesn't seem to be a queen. They're not trying to get round her and protect her. It's not really a swarm. Yes! There go a few just flying away now. They're confused—and probably angry, too. Oh, the poor dears."

Miss Shaw glanced at Miss Worthing with irritation. Not fond of insects at the best of times, the stinging varieties were entirely anathema. "What do you mean, 'poor dears'?"

"They're all going to die. It's autumn, and there's no queen. Why would they even leave the hive?" She went to the bookshelves surrounding the room, thoughtfully took down a volume, and hastily ran down the index. "Lord, I hate books like this! The most fascinating things to a layman always have one cryptic reference buried in the text. What on earth, for example, is a 'laying worker'?"

"Mattie!"

"To be sure, Martha." She flipped pages. "Here it is: 'An unusual swarming of a hive will on rare occasions be brought about, some say, when too much honey has been taken too late in the years.'" She looked up. "They panic, I expect—'or if the hive has been physically damaged.' Hmmm." Miss Worthing rejoined her friend at the window. "Now who would do such a thing?"

"Take too much honey?" asked Miss Shaw sourly. "With some of the idiots around here who think they're farmers?"

Already the mass of bees was smaller. Most were flying off haphazardly. Many others, though, were tumbling off into the flower bed below the window.

"Drat!" muttered Miss Shaw. "Now we'll have to clear their bodies away before we get every ant in Jolliston County. But"—she turned to Miss Worthing and seized her arm—"we'll do nothing of the sort today. Those little monsters are probably in no mood to be toyed with. We'll just stay indoors for the rest of the afternoon."

Miss Worthing nodded unhappily, her eyes still following the fumbling insects. "I think you're right, Martha. Pity too. Such a lovely day!"

Miss Shaw threw back the sliding door of a credenza to

reveal an imposing array of bottles. "Let's have a toddy," she suggested heartily, seizing a bottle of dark rum. "Then we'll have a nap. This evening we can write to Lady Fairgrief and maybe we can take in a movie?" she suggested diffidently.

Miss Worthing smiled affectionately at her friend. "Martha, you're so practical. That's a grand idea. I do want to see that film Larry was going on so about. You know, something about wars in space or some such."

"Science fiction, Mattie?"

"Don't be a snob, dear. I expect it will be very entertaining."

The two ladies went into the kitchen with the bottle of rum. Miss Worthing once more put the kettle on while Miss Shaw measured spirits and lemon juice into tumblers.

"And I will write," Miss Worthing sighed, pouring boiling water into the glasses, "a long, long note to my dear old aunt."

"Don't forget to ask her to dine on Tuesday," Miss Shaw reminded.

"Yes," Miss Worthing said, handing Miss Shaw a linen table napkin for her glass. "And you know," she added thoughtfully, picking up her own drink, "I'm really quite curious to see her again after all these years."

Which was just as well, because Lady Fairgrief came round to Miss Worthing's house rather earlier than Tuesday.

chapter
ONE

Earlier that morning—right after breakfast—on a hillside behind his father's house, Stephan Bessermann stalked back and forth in the rose garden.

The garden was a small, quite formal affair, surrounded on three sides by ramparts of Lombardy poplars. In spite of its real size, the elder Bessermann had yet contrived to set the various clumps of bushes and rose trees out in such a way as to make it appear rather larger than it was.

In the summer it had been a bewildering riot of multicolored blossoms and delicately suggested odors. By now, however, most of the bushes had long since been pruned back and the area resembled a disheartening thicket of naked branches, a few brown leaves here and there, and dark, plum-colored thorns. Only two elegant little rose trees, standing at either side of a long bench to one side of the path, sported a few late blooms—of a rich cream on one tree, on the other the color of flame.

The bench, supported by fat and laughing fauns, had been made of gleaming white Italian marble and anyone sitting on it beheld a sweeping view of the whole Jolliston River Valley—an ancient and mighty caldera fallen in on itself and filled with tiny villages and tidy vineyards which produced some of the finest wine in the world.

Stephan was not, however, admiring views. As he stalked back and forth in front of the bench he fumbled about with a pack of cigarettes as though trying to make up his mind whether or not to smoke one. Finally, he muttered, "The hell with it," and, ripping the pack open, thumped one out. When it was lit, he bent over from the waist and shuffled the pack away into the pocket of a shabby brown-leather jacket lying on the bench.

He was a thickly built man; his faded blue jeans and yellow polo shirt revealed solid muscles, weightlifter's muscles, of the kind that easily go to fat. His movements, though, were lithe and fluid, like an athlete or an actor.

He had very light blue eyes and long thinning blond hair, which was whippy and disheveled in the intermittent breezes. His pale eyebrows were knitted in a concentrated frown and—as sometimes happens in very fair people when under the influence of strong emotion—his face was mottled with patches of deep pink.

He took a long deep drag on the cigarette and sat down on the bench, visibly trying to get a grip of himself. Then, as the sound reached him of someone treading on gravel, he rose once more to his feet.

Through the tangle of desiccated leaves still lingering on the poplars, he watched his cousin, Mary Ellen Bessermann, strolling toward the rose garden, her hands in her pockets. She was dressed simply—a tweed skirt, a white long-sleeved man's dress shirt, bare legs, brown Oxfords, and white cotton socks. It was characteristic that, on her, such an ordinary, domestic ensemble contrived to be almost elegant.

Her hair was short. During her student days in Germany, she had decided that that was the easiest way to handle it. It was raven black and straight as a die, and a comb and blow dryer were all she ever used or needed. As far as makeup was concerned, on her it would have been a mockery, given her pink-and-white, almost Rubenesque, complexion. Her eyes, beneath a strongly defined brow, were large and limpid brown and quite remarkably beautiful.

She waved casually as she came through the trees, but her glance, searching his face as she drew near, was not at all casual. When she saw that he was only barely containing himself, she shook her head sadly, raised a long-fingered hand, and gently stroked his cheek. A wisp of smoke rose into her face and her glance flickered to the cigarette, which she took from Stephan's hand.

"Lord, it smells good," she said, inhaled deeply, and then cocked her head slightly as she eyed her cousin speculatively for a moment, a smile tugging at the corners of her mouth.

Presently, he, too, began to grin. "Well, you were right," he said as he sat down on the bench and leaned back, propped on his elbows. "It wasn't a good morning."

Mary Ellen threw the cigarette onto the gravel and carefully ground it out with her foot. "We shouldn't be smoking," she said inconsequently, and sat down next to him. "I gather then," she added dryly, "that he still won't hear of it?"

Stephan snorted. "I could barely get my mouth open. Just told me not to mention it again. You know," he added with seeming irrelevance, "I could break Helmut's neck sometimes."

"Great," she observed, "you and Uncle Rudy can plot it out together." She sighed and shook her head with a small frown. "I just can't help wondering if we wouldn't have had an easier time of it if he and Uncle Rudy could just get this thing settled once and for all."

"I know," said Stephan grimly. "All I ever seem to get out of Dad these days is 'This is not a good time to talk of such things, Stephan.'" He imitated his father's accent with ruthless fidelity and then suddenly lurched to his feet and stared angrily toward the house. "The only trouble is, damn it, that apparently there's never going to be a good time for it." Like a small boy, he kicked at the gravel on the path, scattering it in all directions, some of it pinging against the marble of the bench.

"Steve!" said Mary Ellen, rubbing her shins. "Please!"

He looked round at her in surprise and then abruptly laughed and resumed his seat. "I'm sorry." He pulled her toward him. "I guess I'm overreacting."

"Just a bit," she agreed, snuggling closer to him. After a moment, she began to chuckle quietly.

"Mmmm?" he asked.

"I just can't help thinking how very old-fashioned we're being."

He cupped her chin and raised her face toward his own. "That we are," he whispered, and kissed her. For a long moment, they stared into one another's eyes, until she turned away, began rummaging in his jacket pocket, and sat up to light another cigarette.

"You do have to admit," she said, waving the match about, "that this is a trifle Victorian. Here we are—a reasonably adult man and a reasonably adult woman quite smitten with one another and who want to get married."

"And like dutiful children—" he began.

"Mindful of the fact," she interrupted and held up an admonishing finger, "that they haven't a sou between them."

"We have asked our parents," Stephan resumed, "in this case, parent in the singular—for permission to wed . . . What's so funny?"

"To 'wed'?" Mary Ellen repeated. "Really, Steve!"

"It's no worse than 'smitten,' for chrissake," he protested and then shrugged. "Anyway, it always comes to the same tableau," he finished in a singularly flat voice. "Permission denied." He turned toward her. "You know, sometimes I wish—"

"Hush." She touched his lips. "I know what you're

thinking. And sometimes, I want it too. But we can't be that way." Unconsciously, she played with the chain of a gold crucifix round her neck.

He turned away. "Why not?" he asked leadenly and stared down at his balled fists.

"Because we agreed we would get married."

"Does it look as though that will ever happen?" he protested, turning abruptly back to face her. "It could go on like this for years."

"Then it will go on for years," she replied placidly, two spots of vivid color in her cheeks belying her calm.

"God, Mary Ellen." His voice was a hoarse whisper. "Do you know what that would do to us? To me? To you?"

"And do you have any idea," she asked quickly, "what kind of a life we'd have if we took to cheating? Especially after he was gone? The guilt! Just to mention one thing."

"Yeah." He scowled. "We were raised good Catholics."

"Are you sorry?"

"Sometimes."

She said nothing for a moment, merely looking at him as though she had expected some other answer. "Times like this?" she asked.

He nodded.

"It doesn't work that way," she said almost sternly.

"Do you think I don't know it?" he replied. For a long moment, he said nothing more. Then, frowning, he turned his head away. "Sometimes," he said, his voice almost lost it was so low, "I think that Larry did the right thing. Maybe if I'd had the courage to fight back, too . . ." He shrugged and then uttered a snort of unamused laughter. "Unfortunately, there is the simple fact that I can't stand rock 'n' roll. I suppose I could get a job as an instructor at some conservatory somewhere. The name should be good enough at least for that, but I'm not going to give up everything here to take you away to live on the salary of a college instructor. . . ."

"Steve," she reminded him with a glint of humor in her eye, "I am capable of making a living, too, you know."

He turned back. Again, neither said anything as the same thing went through their minds. Finally, Stephan articulated it. "Do you want to? Shall we just go away, get piddling little jobs at some two-bit university where they think it's hot stuff to have Rudolf Bessermann's son and cousin teaching a bunch of untalented dolts who have settled that they're going to teach music appreciation to third graders—"

"No," replied Mary Ellen simply. "No, I don't and neither do you. Although," she added again with that hint of humor, "I doubt if it would be quite as dreadful as you've outlined."

At that, he grinned. "No, but damn near."

"I suppose," she agreed vaguely and then, unexpectedly, she flushed and looked down. "Steve," she said softly, "there is something else, too, you know."

"What?" he asked, surprised.

She looked up into his face and said, "We could go back to Europe and sing."

The man's face immediately closed tight.

"We have been trained for it," she pointed out. "And you're awfully good, you know."

"Not as good as you are."

"That's ridiculous, Steve. I just have the kind of voice that matures earlier than yours will."

Nevertheless, his expression could not have been plainer.

"I'm sorry," she said and explained, "I haven't brought this up before because I know how much you dislike performing."

He shook his head. "Oh, Mary Ellen," he said almost sadly, "it's not that. I don't hate performing. I'm just not very good."

"Steve, that's crazy."

"No, it's not," he said with finality. "And I'm going to get my doctorate if it kills me."

"Okay," she said softly. She reached toward him and took his hand in her own. "So let's forget it, Steve. Okay? We've been over all the rest of it before. Time and again. We stay here. And it's really not so bad, you know," she said almost tenderly. "We have everything to gain if we just exercise a little patience and everything to lose if we don't."

He nodded and then swept her into a bear hug. "Thank God," he said, "that somebody around here's got some common sense," and, incongruously, he began to chuckle.

"What's so funny?" she demanded, pulling away in surprise.

"I have the perfect solution. We'll invent a new heresy." He grinned and reached a hand toward her.

"'Never!'" she suddenly cried out in ringing tones and sprang to her feet. "'Here I stand. Burn me though you will. I can do no more!'" She struck a pose.

"You idiot." Stephan pulled her down again. "That was Martin Luther."

She laughed and once more snuggled against him. "I could have sworn it was Joan of Arc."

After a few minutes, they gradually became aware of a heavy crushing sound on the gravel accompanied by a loud and regular squeak.

"What's that?" Stephan asked, glancing toward the surrounding trees.

"It's Lady Fairgrief." Mary Ellen snickered and ran her fingers through her hair.

"What's funny?"

"I asked her this morning if she wanted her chair oiled. But she just cackled in that evil way of hers and said that it was"—her voice took on the quavering clipped tones of an elderly Englishwoman—"'a convenient method of announcing her impending presence.'"

"She is a bit much." He smiled too. "I had really forgotten how much I liked her."

"I'm so glad to hear it, Stephan," cried the lady in question as the wheelchair, pushed by her maid, emerged through the poplars.

She looked every one of her ninety-odd years: her face was a map of folds and wrinkles, all overwritten with the myriad small lines that come to the truly old. Her eyelids drooped, her cheeks were sunken, and her mouth was thin and surrounded by a network of tiny wrinkles. An enormous beak of a nose jutted out from her face to be almost matched by her pointed, determined, witchlike chin, from which an assortment of wrinkled crepe draperies of skin hung about her scrawny neck.

Only her eyes belied her age—astonishingly alert, clear black pools. Her baby-fine snow-white hair was beautifully dressed, and she sat with a perfectly straight back in her chair clad in a stiff black-satin gown. A thick woolen blanket was tucked round her useless legs, and a woolen shawl of black hairpin lace was draped over her shoulders, covering her bare, age-spotted arms. Her hands—arthritic claws displaying alarming, scarlet-painted nails—toyed with a jeweled tortoise-shell lorgnette.

Stephan flushed to the roots of his hair. He kept forgetting that she still had the hearing of a girl. "I'm sorry, Lady Fairgrief, I was just . . ."

The ancient crone in the chair gave a malicious cackle. "Not at all, my dear boy. So much better to hear one is liked straight from the horse's mouth, as it were, than as a leftover goody for tea." She turned her bright eyes to Mary Ellen. "And now you can see how useful my squeaking wheel can be." She pulled her shawl closer around her.

"Are you cold, my lady?" the maid, a buxom hearty woman, asked anxiously.

"Don't be silly, Maude," replied Lady Fairgrief grumpily. "At my age, I'm always cold."

"Then it's straight back to the house."

"Fiddlesticks! Go back yourself."

Stephan and Mary Ellen exhanged a glance. Lady Fairgrief had only been in the house for a day and already her eternal wrangling with her maid was a continual source of sniggering delight.

"I won't have you catching your death, my lady," said Maude rather grimly.

"I won't have to catch it," replied Lady Fairgrief tartly. "It's close enough to pounce on me. Besides," she groused, "it's warmer than England." The old woman darted a look at Mary Ellen and winked. "You go back to the house," the old woman instructed her maid. "Put the kettle on. Mary Ellen can wheel me back."

"But my lady . . ."

"Maude!"

A wealth of meaning was invested in that one syllable. Maude pursed her lips and, acknowledging defeat, stalked back down the path.

"Now," Lady Fairgrief said, tucking her blanket more snugly about her legs. "What seems to be troubling you two, other than the grossly obvious fact that you're head over heels in love?"

Stephan looked uncomfortable; Mary Ellen merely arched an eyebrow. "You know," she said pleasantly, "two hundred years ago, you'd have been charred to a cinder at the stake."

"A good deal later than that in some of the places I've been to," observed the old woman cheerfully and then added crisply, "but it hardly needed necromancy to discern what's eating you two."

"We don't exactly advertise it," protested Mary Ellen. "In fact, we go out of our way to avoid doing so."

"Perhaps you think you do," said her ladyship and

24

twinkled at her. "But never mind *my* pacts with obliging demons, what are you two doing about it?"

"It's Dad," Stephan said. "Mary Ellen and I are third cousins, or second cousins, removed something or other—I never could keep the thing straight."

"You're second cousins, once removed," Lady Fairgrief explained. "And your father is a devout Catholic, right?"

"In a nutshell," Mary Ellen replied. "He says we're within the canonical degrees of . . ." She looked at Stephan.

"Consanguinity?" supplied the old lady.

The two nodded. Lady Fairgrief pursed her mouth into a volcano of wrinkles and glanced from one to the other. "You are, you know," she said gently. "Wanting to change it isn't going to change it."

Mary Ellen and Stephan's hands found each other. For a moment, they looked very much like lost children.

"Still," continued the old woman musingly, "I should have thought that these days you could get a dispensation easily enough. In the Middle Ages if you were rich enough and suitably obliging to the local bishop you could all but marry your sister. I know people who've been marrying *first* cousins halfway back to the flood and not a bit of harm done at all—unless, of course, you object to your children looking like amiable ponies—"

"That's just it," Stephan interrupted, cutting off this remarkable exposition of genetics. "I talked to Monsignor O'Halloran about it and that's more or less what he said. He was flabbergasted that Dad was fussing."

"I see," Lady Fairgrief said. "And what did Rudolf say when you told him that?"

Mary Ellen sighed. "He keeps on saying that the Church may change but he's too old for it."

The old woman laughed. "I would have expected something like that." Thoughtfully, she rubbed the bridge of her nose for a moment and stared out over the valley. "Wonderful view," she said absently and then turned back to them. "How long ago was this?"

"Six months ago," Stephan said and added, with disgust in his voice once more, "and again this morning."

Lady Fairgrief turned back to considering the Jolliston Valley.

Lord, Mary Ellen thought to herself, *she must be nearly a hundred and she can still see all that way.*

As though in answer, Lady Fairgrief glanced at her and grinned. "I am grateful that my years haven't diminished my sight too much. But then, I was always long-sighted." She chortled and groped about in the blankets for her lorgnette. "Of course, I can't see anything within ten feet of me." She peered at them through the lenses. "Hmmm," she muttered and folded the thing up. "Do you think it would do any good if I talked to Rudolf?"

They spoke almost simultaneously.

"Would you?" asked Mary Ellen.

"That would be *great,* Lady F!" Stephan exclaimed.

"Very well," she said, frowning ferociously at Stephan. "I will do it, but under one condition."

"What's that?"

"Do *not* call me Lady F. It sounds like the title of a film about someone's doxie. Call me Eulalia, or Lady Fairgrief or even—God save us—Lally."

The young man nodded solemnly.

"I don't know why but it's always annoyed the very devil out of me," she finished. "And I assure you that's an accomplishment." She pulled her shawl about her. "It is getting a bit windy up here, Mary Ellen. Would you take me down?"

Mary Ellen stood up. As she did so, Lady Fairgrief pointed toward her legs. "You have such lovely long legs, dear. You should have been a dancer."

"I'd rather sing," the younger woman replied, taking the handles of the chair.

"Oh, and one more thing," said her ladyship, holding up an arresting claw. "I can only talk to your father, Stephan. I can't make him change his mind. I can only try."

"Of course," Stephan agreed. "It's good of you even to do that."

Lady Fairgrief signaled to Mary Ellen to drive on. "You know," she cautioned as they strolled down the path, "I really meant that about horsiness in one's children. There are some teddibly aristocratic families in England that always looked to me like the models for Gulliver's Houyhnhnms, although now that I think of it, they weren't nearly as articulate as the Houyhnhnms. Still, if you're willing to tackle the pope, I suppose I can take on Rudy. And what is that extraordinary man doing?"

They had rounded the poplars and were descending by degrees to the lawn behind the house. A small silver-haired man in a three-piece gray-plaid business suit was hopping about from tree to tree picking up branches and scattered leaves.

Mary Ellen snorted contemptuously. "That, my dear, is our own Helmut Schmidt and the immediate cause of Uncle Rudolf's temperament this morning."

"I wondered about that. Who is he?"

"He's the general director of the Jolliston Opera Company, our modest local effort. Some people think it gets more modest the more he makes an effort. And he is, believe it or not, pricking about the greensward because he 'wanted to gather some autumn leaves.'"

"How perfectly inane," commented her ladyship, but the object of their conversation had seen them.

"Ah-hah!" he exclaimed theatrically. He pranced mincingly toward them and bowed from the waist with a flourish as Lady Fairgrief clutched her shawl in a none too covert gesture of irritation.

"Und you must be the great English lady of vich I am

hearing so much. Vill you present me, Mary Ellen?" he enquired, clasping an enormous bouquet of oak leaves and beech branches to his chest. "Haff you seen Stephan?" he asked when introductions had been effected. "I am haffing vonderful idea for afternoon."

"Yes," replied Mary Ellen with a wink at the old woman. "We left him smoking in the rose garden, Herr Schmidt."

"Luffly, luffly," the little man twittered and flung himself away toward the poplars.

Lady Fairgrief stared blankly at his retreating back and then enquired, "Where on earth did you ever find such a specimen?"

Mary Ellen merely laughed in reply and opened the French doors at the back of the house. "I suppose he is rather a drip, but he is surprisingly good at what he does. Do you want to go in right away?"

"No," replied Lady Fairgrief. "Wheel me over into the sun."

She gestured toward a patch of sunlight shining on the stones of the terrace. Obediently, Mary Ellen closed the door and pushed the chair to the indicated spot.

"You're a biddable child," the old woman said with a wicked grin.

"That," observed Mary Ellen, "is what a number of men have thought, too."

"I didn't mean that!" Lady Fairgrief snapped. "What I did mean was that you—and Stephan—are rather considerate people."

"Lady Fairgrief," said Mary Ellen with a smile, "are you trying to say something?"

"I am indeed, my dear. I want to know what you're doing here? Here I've been hearing progress reports on the two of you for years now and when I come to visit your cousin, what do I find but that the two of your are here being unofficial housekeeper and butler to your cousin? What's the matter, dear?" she asked, her voice all sweet acid, "the vagabond life of a performer too antipathetic for you?"

A slight frown flickered across the younger woman's face, but other than that she refused to be goaded. "Something like that," she agreed mildly. "But Steve is working on his dissertation, you know. As for me . . ." She gazed out across the lawn toward the rose garden. "I want to be where Steve is."

"And Rudy?"

"I love my uncle—my cousin—very much," she answered. "And for someone like me, this"—and she gestured with her hand to include the whole estate—"suits me right down to the ground."

"Does it, dear?" asked Lady Fairgrief dubiously.

Mary Ellen cocked her head. "Don't you think so?"

The old lady again pursed her lips into a maze of wrinkles and looked thoughtful. "Well, now," she said diffidently, "I hardly know you two."

"My dear aunt," Mary Ellen laughed, "you've known Steve and me since we were babies."

"And I haven't seen much of you since then either," replied her ladyship tightly. "Adults, even ones as young as you and Stephan, are rather different from infants. Nevertheless"—she shrugged her shoulders to settle her shawl more evenly—"you're right. I do have an opinion."

"I thought you might," said Mary Ellen dryly.

"Yes, I do. Something's not right here."

Whatever Mary Ellen had been expecting, it had not been that. "I'm sorry," she said, giving her head a little shake, her expression quizzical.

"Can't you feel it, child?" the old woman asked, and then immediately answered her own question. "No, I don't suppose you do. You've been living with it."

Mary Ellen gave a little laugh and, again shaking her

head, said, "I still don't know what you're talking about."

"Tensions, girl!" Lady Fairgrief barked, making a sharp gesture with the fingers of one hand. "Tensions you can feel the minute you come into this house."

"Oh! That!" Mary Ellen said in a small voice, her face gone perfectly blank.

"Yes, that! It's not healthy."

"There've been . . ." Mary Ellen hesitated on the word. ". . . disagreements," she finally said. "It's only been lately, you know. And then . . ." Her voice trailed off.

"And then there's you," Lady Fairgrief finished it for her. "You and Stephan being a pretty pair of fools."

Mary Ellen raised an eyebrow. "You know, Lady Fairgrief, somehow I thought that's what you'd say."

"Well, my dear," the old woman continued in tones of the utmost rationality, "you are both remarkably talented and furthermore one day you'll be rich. If neither of you has the guts for a fight now"—she didn't even pause when Mary Ellen flushed furiously—"then your fortunes perhaps might help. That combined with the fact that you're such an unusually placid person and Stephan so extraordinarily sensitive—"

"You're trying to imply that I'm lazy and weak and that Steve is merely touchy," Mary Ellen interrupted angrily, her eyes narrowed and her color gone suddenly high. "Well, I beg to differ with you."

"If so, I'm glad to hear it," replied Lady Fairgrief tranquilly. "But I want to see you two fight for what is rightfully yours. This marriage business and the way you've taken it lying down is damnably symptomatic of the way you both seem to be living your lives."

"Oh?"

"Don't 'oh' me. You know I'm right. And do calm down, you're puffing like a beached whale. All I'm trying to say is that you've both been blessed with extraordinary good looks, voices, you will have wealth, and you both have had splendid, even unique, educations. All of that without even mentioning the Bessermann name."

Mary Ellen said nothing, visibly trying to regain control.

"I'm a very old woman, Mary Ellen," continued Lady Fairgrief more gently. "It offends me to see youth and ability wasted. Look at Lawrence. He may be making the most horrible noises imaginable with that rock and roll band—the silly thing actually sent me a copy of their most recent album—but at least he's out there, involved in music, and making a go of it."

"Yes, and the very mention of his name sends Uncle Rudy off into a tizzy."

"Does it?" asked her ladyship. "Is that such a bad thing that dear old Rudy hasn't got his way with Larry?"

"He keeps threatening to disown him."

Her ladyship very nearly snorted. "So what? He's making excellent money of his own, isn't he?"

"I don't know."

"And even if he isn't, what has that to do with you? Or is it money? Is that what's keeping you here? To live off the bounty of the land?"

"That's not fair."

"No, I don't suppose it is, but I can only repeat, what are you and Stephan going to make of your life?"

Angrily, Mary Ellen turned her whole body toward the garden and said nothing more. Then, gradually, the set of her shoulders relaxed as she wrestled her anger under control. Finally, she laughed. "You may be good for me after all," she said. "That's the first time in months I've been really angry." She regarded the old woman quietly for a moment. "The funny thing is that Uncle Rudolf has rather broadly hinted at more or less the same thing—that we're wasting time."

"I'm not surprised, you know. He had to fight."

Mary Ellen stood silently.

"I'm getting chilly, Mary Ellen. Please take me in."

They went indoors.

"Park me there beside the fire," Lady Fairgrief instructed, "and then get back to the rose garden."

"Am I that transparent?" Mary Ellen laughed.

Lady Fairgrief gazed out the window at the younger woman darting back across the lawn. "Nevertheless," she whispered to herself, "I think I'll wait until after luncheon to speak to Rudolf.

"Maude!" she yelled out shrilly. "Come get me! I want some tea."

chapter
TWO

"Thank you, my dear," said her ladyship as Mary Ellen parked her in front of the closed library doors. "Now, before I go in, I want to know something."

"Yes?"

"Before lunch you told me that your cousin was having some kind of altercation with that fellow Schmidt. Do you know the details?"

Mary Ellen made a wry face. "Anyone in Jolliston who has anything to do with the opera company knows."

"Well?"

"Helmut has the idea that we should try to grow into a large regional company, like the Ashland Festival or Seattle."

Lady Fairgrief blinked. "And Rudy disapproves of this?" she asked, somewhat taken aback.

"Of course not." Mary Ellen smiled. "But Uncle Rudy wants to use local singers and American talent generally."

"And Schmidt?"

"He wants to import a big name or two for each production from Europe or New York."

"Wouldn't that be rather expensive?"

"It's more than just the expense of it that Uncle Rudy

objects to. But to answer your question, yes it would. So much so that it would probably cut our season in half."

"I see."

"Unfortunately," Mary Ellen continued, "there are a lot of people here in the Valley who agree with Helmut."

"And what does Rudy have to say about them?"

Mary Ellen grinned impishly. "Well, he called them a bunch of provincial cloth heads at the last meeting. It had a very interesting effect on everyone's temper."

"I would imagine so," murmured her ladyship.

"But from what I have been able to gather," the younger woman went on soberly, "Uncle Rudy has threatened Helmut privately with quitting his own seat on the board and"—she paused briefly— "withholding his own contribution."

Lady Fairgrief eyed Mary Ellen and said evenly, "And what would be the probable result of that?"

"I don't know if the opera company could survive without Uncle Rudy's personal and financial help, but I'm pretty certain that Helmut's position would become . . ." She hesitated.

"Threatened?" asked Lady Fairgrief.

Mary Ellen nodded.

"I see," said her ladyship grimly. "Thank you, dear," she dismissed the younger woman. "That will be all."

"Would you like me to see if Uncle Rudy's in there?"

"No," replied her ladyship, "he said he'd be in there after luncheon and I think this is a splendid opportunity to talk to him."

Mary Ellen leaned down and lightly brushed the old woman's cheek with her lips. "Thank you for doing this, Tante Lally," she whispered. "Good luck."

When she had vanished in the direction of the kitchen, Lady Fairgrief paused a moment. Good luck indeed. Rudolf Bessermann was about to get the rough edge of her tongue and she hated being angry with her friend.

On the other hand it had to be done. Friendship demanded it and she held firm, if perhaps old-fashioned, ideas about the obligations of friendship. Nevertheless, considering the other two subjects on her agenda, this sordid little tale about a power struggle in the local opera company did not bode well at all.

She breathed a brief prayer for guidance, patience, and, above all, intelligence, and lifting a hand, rapped on the door of the library. In a moment the door opened, framing Rudolf Bessermann. "Yes, Lally?"

"Rudy," she said, "I've come to beard the lion in its den. Wheel me in." It was an appropriate simile, she thought as she looked at him.

Rudolf Bessermann was a big man, at seventy-two still hale and vital. His hair, formerly the rich gold of ripened wheat, was a mane of white contrasting with his florid complexion. His large wide-nostriled nose was a veritable road map of minute blue-and-red veins, the result of a lifetime of enthusiastic beer drinking, and his eyes were of so intense a blue that they used to almost startle his audiences. He was dressed in a pair of simple black trousers and a white dress shirt open at the collar.

He sighed and shook his head as he smiled at her. "I have to admit I have been expecting this."

"Were you, my dear?" asked her ladyship as Bessermann stepped behind her and, taking the handles of her chair, wheeled her through the doors of the library and along its appreciable length to an alcove, which sheltered a couch and a small coffee table.

He parked her and then sat facing her on the very edge of the cushion, his hands clasped, fingers interwoven, around his knees. "Yes, Lally, I have. I know you too well not to know that you must think that some things are . . ." He hesitated.

"Askew?" suggested her ladyship.

"Just so," said Bessermann.

"Well, you're right," said Lady Fairgrief. "I am in no position to lecture you, Rudy, but I could not help but notice that there was an awful lot of tension round that luncheon table."

"Nor could I," he conceded. "Helmut was not at his best."

"I do gather," said her ladyship dryly, "that you and he are not exactly seeing eye to eye."

He raised and lowered a shoulder. "We are having a disagreement over the opera company."

"So I've heard. Would I be out of place asking for an explanation?"

"Lally." He smiled at her. "This is your place."

"I know you keep saying that, Rudy, and really it's most kind. I even have to admit," she added with some diffidence, allowing the subject of Schmidt momentarily to drop, "that when you invited me here I was to a great degree relieved. I feel safe when I'm here with you."

"*Ja*, it is as I would wish." The man's voice was carefully noncommittal. "But?" he prompted.

Lady Fairgrief took a deep breath and looked at the man levelly for a moment. "Well, to begin," she said, "I had no idea when you did suggest that I come to you that so much of the burden would fall on Mary Ellen and Stephan."

Bessermann frowned but, before he could say anything, she plunged on. "See here, Rudy, it was lovely of you to have me and I'm delighted to be here. But when you suggested having a house party to welcome me, I . . ." She smiled and added wryly, "I have to admit that I was thinking of the old days of good shooting, good bridge, good food, and good friends."

"But Lally, we have all that here."

"Yes, my dear, but in the old days there were also thundering herds of well-trained servants to take care of everything. Here all there is my poor old Maude, Stephan, and Mary Ellen."

"There is Harvey, Lally," said Bessermann.

"Rudy, don't be simple," her ladyship snapped. "That man's nearly as old as I am, if not older. How on earth do you expect him to help out with a houseful of people? And I'm sure I fail to see what's so funny, Rudy."

For Bessermann had begun to chuckle richly. "I'm sorry, Lally, but the thought of you, Helmut, and Paul constituting a houseful of people is rather funny."

"Rudolf Bessermann, I'm a houseful all by myself," she rejoined and then frowned severely. "But I refuse to be put off. Things aren't right around here and I want to get to the bottom of it."

"Why?" he asked.

"Because I'm afraid of what you're doing to your friends and children."

"I see," he said rather coldly. "You've been talking to Stephan and Mary Ellen, then."

"Would you have expected me not to?"

"No," he said after a moment, his full lips tight.

"Rudy," she said and leaned toward him in her chair, "I have to admit I fail utterly to see your reasoning."

"Lally, what they want isn't right."

"Is it wrong?" she challenged.

"To my mind, it is the same thing."

"Rudy, I've known cousins a great deal closer than Stephan and Mary Ellen marry to no harm whatever."

"Lally, I speak not only as a Catholic but as a scientist. It is not right." There was a clear note of finality in the man's voice.

For a moment, she said nothing. *All right,* she was thinking rapidly, *there are other routes to the desired end, you know.*

"Very well!" she said aloud, "but you should know that I think you do take a lot on yourself, old friend."

Bessermann nodded briefly. "I do," he conceded. "If no one else will, I have to." He began to rise. "And now, Lally, if—"

"Oh my dear Rudy"—she shook her head at him—"you're not getting off the hook quite all that easily."

"Oh?"

"Yes. I will, for the moment, concede your point about those two children. They are young, they live in your house, and eat your bread and salt. So be it. Although," she added very dryly indeed, "if you are really as adamant about it as all that I don't think it's a good idea to keep them here together."

"But this is their home," he protested.

"And they're in daily proximity one to the other, too. Do you think *that's* wise under the circumstances?"

"I will not drive my children away," he said with a flash of angry stubbornness. "One of mine has already gone from me."

"I know," she said. "You see, I had a letter from Larry."

At the mention of his elder son's name, Bessermann's face suddenly lit up. He sat down and looked at her with almost a greedy expression. But the light was just as quickly extinguished as he observed bitterly, "Begging you to intercede for him, no doubt."

"Hardly that," she replied, "but I do gather there was quite a falling out."

"He left me, Lally," the man whispered, a look of bewildered hurt in his eyes. "He just walked out of here and left me."

"Rudy, my dear," she said gently, "he wanted his own career."

"As a rock musician?" he asked and then added with a sneer, "Musician!"

"Rudy, my dear, as much as I might deplore the idiom of rock, the playing of it is, for all that, an honorable trade."

"But he could have been the greatest basso since Kipnis," Bessermann said, a whole world of regret in his voice. "However," he went on, his voice now like steel, "if he doesn't want it, very well. He gets nothing more from me."

"Going to be another Mr. Pontifex, Rudy?" she asked sarcastically.

"Who?"

She clicked her tongue. "A character in a novel called *The Way of All Flesh* who threatened to cut his son off completely if he didn't become a clergyman. Clergyman. Operatic basso. What's the difference? Is that what you're going to do? Cut Larry off?"

"I have drafted a codicil to my will, Lally, yes," replied Bessermann very quietly.

"Rudolf!" she exclaimed, really deeply shocked.

A look of pain flickered across the man's face. "Lally, are you going to be angry with me, too?"

"Rudy, I'm already angry with you. Can't you see what you're doing to yourself? You're successfully managing to alienate every single person who loves you. Schmidt, Mary Ellen, Stephan, Larry. Why are you doing these things?"

"Because I am right," said the inflexible Teutonic paterfamilias.

"Rudolf Bessermann"—she waggled a finger at him—"even if you are right and everyone else is wrong, do you suppose you can prove your point with blackmail?"

"Blackmail?" the man exploded.

"Yes, blackmail, Rudy, and don't look so righteously offended. There'll be no fuzzy thinking on this point, thank you. Don't you realize how dangerous it is for people of our age to get like this? It's too easy to get all solid and crabbed and refuse to see the world as it really is and instead demand that it be the way we want it. Believe me, I know. It's an awful thing to see people seizing up mentally and presently all you hear from them is 'Don't confuse me with facts, please; my mind's quite made up.'

Well, from where I sit, that's, in effect, what you're telling your children, your colleagues . . ."

"Lally," his color was definitely up now, "I have to do what I think is right."

"And what if you're not right and all you've succeeded in doing is bringing them to their knees with sheer muscle power?"

"Blackmail?" the man repeated angrily.

"That's right, Rudy, blackmail. Emotional—with your children; and financial, too. Certainly, financial with your friend Herr Schmidt."

And to her great relief, instead of waxing even more wroth, Bessermann took a deep breath and frowned. "I'm sorry," he said more calmly after a moment. "I had not thought of it that way."

"I thought not, Rudy," she said. "I hoped not. You're too young to get senile on me."

At that, Bessermann actually laughed. "Lally, Lally, I'm seventy-two."

"So what. You're still a marvelous specimen of a man."

"You won't get round me that way, old woman."

"I didn't suppose I would," she replied with a grin. "I expect you've had too many compliments to be particularly responsive to the blandishments of an old girl like me."

"You're pretty terrific when you get going, though," he observed with a rueful smile.

"You will think about what I've said?" she asked, almost anxiously.

"I will," he said. "I will. You have made good sense to me." He stood up. "But now I definitely do have to get back to work. I have paper work to do no matter how I decide."

"Very well, Rudy," she said. Suddenly she felt herself almost sag in her chair. The experience had utterly exhausted her.

Perceiving it, Bessermann looked deeply chagrined. "And I am more sorry than I can tell you," he said gently, "that you had to exhaust yourself like this for me."

"Rudy, you're my very dear friend."

"Come," he said, "I will take you to Maude."

"Thank you," she said. "I really think I must have a nap."

"But not too long," he said, kicking off the brake on her chair. "Helmut and I have cooked up something nice for you this afternoon."

"Oh?"

"Now, now, Lally. If I told you, it wouldn't be a surprise."

chapter
THREE

She dreamed. Part of her knew it was only a dream, but it really did not matter very much because it was not the kind of dream one readily relinquishes when one has lived such a very long time.

It was before the war. The first one. Somehow she knew that, though in her dream no one had yet begun to think of war. She and Arthur were still young, still very bright, very gay, and oh so very much in love.

They were in a concert room . . . or was it London after all? No. It wasn't a room, but a hall rather. An opera house? Munich? Milano? No, it was a hall. Berlin, then?

The place was fully lit, the way they did it then, and at one end of the hall a piano and two men in evening clothes, making music. And such music, she thought, and tears crept from beneath her closed lids, because there was no way back, nothing to bring again the joy that had been then, before the war, before the end of everything.

Gradually, she began to waken, unwillingly, trying to hold onto that fugitive vision of another, happier era, when the world was younger—more naive perhaps—but somehow so very much more alive . . .

. . . and still she heard the music. Only now the words began to make sense to her, meaning drifting into the twilit world between sleeping and waking. *"Ich such' in Schnee vergeben nach ihrer tritte Spur . . ."* She heard the words, and before she could restrain herself, their meaning swept relentlessly through her mind: ". . . I seek her footprint in forgotten snows." And she woke.

"Arthur?" she called. But it was only a whisper unheard in the darkened room. Beside her bed, Maude nodded as she dozed fitfully.

Then she distinguished the music drifting down the corridor and through her door. Stephan was singing *Die Winterreise*—"The Winter Journey."

With a well-practiced inward gesture, she shut off the wave of nostalgia for the dim lost past and nudged Maude, who woke noisily.

"Yes, my lady?"

"Stephan is singing. One of the Schubert song cycles. Hurry! Get my chair."

The maid stood and swung the chair around to the side of the bed. "Upsidaisy, my lady," she said annoyingly, putting her arms round the shriveled body and hoisting it into the chair.

Lady Fairgrief frowned, as she always did, at the ritual phrase, but was much too pleased at the moment to remain irritated. "Oh, Maude," she exclaimed with a fiery twinkle in her eye. "This is why I was so glad to come. Music! The great songs and arias. And only us to hear them."

Maude nodded sleepily and yawned. "Yes, my lady."

"Don't stand there gaping like a cow. Fetch my glass. Now," said Lady Fairgrief when the lorgnette was produced, "wheel me out gently. Try not to make any sound, although," she listened for a moment, "they're taking a long time between the songs."

Disappointment swept across her face. "Oh, I do hope they haven't stopped."

Just then the piano started to play the staccato chords

of the next song. When the voice came in, however, it was a more mature voice than had sung before, richer and fuller, with an indescribable shimmer and tempered-steel focus that penetrated the door as though it were not there.

"Oh, glory!" exclaimed her ladyship. "Rudy is singing."

Maude opened the door and quickly wheeled Lady Fairgrief down the corridor to the enormous living room, and as unobtrusively as possible, parked her in a space between the divan and an overstuffed easy chair.

Mary Ellen sat to one side of her and on the other sat Helmut Schmidt. She nodded briefly to both of them, but her attention was already fixed on the singer.

Harvey Maxwell, Bessermann's sometime dresser and valet, stood in the door of the breakfast room, an expression of frank adoration on his wizened features. On the opposite side of the divan, Rudolf's doctor, the last member of the party to join them, was staring at the ensemble with self-conscious rapture.

Rudolf Bessermann still possessed a great tenor voice. He stood at the bow of the piano radiating the vitality and energy of the great vocal artist in the performing mode: relaxed yet concentrated to almost a burning intensity. His eyes were closed and he was completely absorbed by the songs as, one by one, they poured from his mouth, a constant stream of sound, each word of Müller's indifferent verse transmogrified with meaning and feeling.

His son was accompanying him and doing it extremely well, his eyes—like those of everyone else in the room—glued to his father to catch and run with every shifting nuance of color and rhythm. Together they exhibited a perfect example of the kind of teamwork that can lift the art song out of its inherent banality to the very fullness of glory.

They were going straight through the cycle without stopping, the way it should be done. Absently, Lady Fairgrief noticed a cocktail on the table next to her and had no idea how it had gotten there. She found herself almost stiff with concentration.

The musicians, their faces glistening with effort, approached the final songs of the cycle. *Der Wegwieser*—"The Signpost." Simple broken chords in the piano; in the voice, notes repeated on the same pitch, pointing up the despair in the words, ". . . I must travel down a path from which no one returns . . ." And the final coda—soft, ethereal. In the dimming, almost eerie, light of the last autumn afternoon, Bessermann softened to a bare core tone, plangent, almost breathy. He opened his eyes, and his glance, for some reason, caught that of Lady Fairgrief, who experienced a surge of abstract romantic pity. Tears welled inexplicably in her eyes as her mind repeated the phrase, over and over again, *"die noch keiner ging zurück . . . die noch keiner ging zurück . . ."* until she felt she could not bear it another moment. The pedal went down soundlessly and the low G minor chord seemed to vibrate into nothingness and silence.

Presently, it was time for the next song.

For years Bessermann had enjoyed telling stories of the incredibly rude ways by which most singers indicate to their accompanist they are ready to go on: they nod imperiously; they swivel their bodies like a grotesque athlete; they raise an arrogant brow. . . . He was much more subtle than that. He alternated between lifting his head from a bowed position, if there had been applause, or, if there had not, by lifting his hand to the piano. This time, of course, he chose the latter.

What no one, it seems, had observed was a bee—a large bee—which had crawled out of the enormous heap of foliage Herr Schmidt had piled up on the piano. The insect was excessively confused. The evening chill was already descending on the motionless group around the piano. For the bee's part, the chill was fatal; it would die of the cold.

But now, groggy and dimly angry, it walked about on the piano seeking light and warmth. The tenor, in the bow of the piano, stood between it and the light, his sweating body exuding heat. The bee's wings moved uncertainly, trying to gather the strength to fly into the light, into the warmth.

It was spared the effort.

Bessermann's palm, descending for the signal to Stephan, landed on the already confused insect. It stung him. "*Mein Gott!*" Bessermann yelled.

He looked down. The bee was still buzzing angrily. The heat of his hand had, in fact, warmed it somewhat. It flew toward the light. Bessermann's face happened to be in the way. It stung him again and then flew out the window.

"A bee! Oh God, save me!" the big tenor yelled, and immediately all hell broke loose. Bessermann was violently allergic to bee venom.

Lady Fairgrief watched in a horrified trance as the doctor rushed to the tenor, who stood swaying at the piano. Stephan leapt to his feet to help the doctor, and Mary Ellen was already on the telephone to what sounded like a nurse's exchange.

Maude tried to wheel her away but Lady Fairgrief made a savage gesture indicating that she be left alone. Maude stood back and wrung her hands. Stephan and the doctor lowered Bessermann into a chair. Already the man's face was suffused, his breathing labored.

"Quick, Steve!" the doctor ordered. "Get my bag; it's in my car." He bent over the man again as Stephan ran out the front door.

Mary Ellen turned away from the telephone. "Miss Martinez is on her way."

"Good," said the doctor, taking the tenor's tie off and ineffectually trying to give him artificial respiration. "Mary Ellen, for God's sake, help me get him on the floor."

Somehow, in spite of the frantic running about, Lady Fairgrief sustained the impression that it was all a well-rehearsed routine.

"And, of course, it would have to be," she muttered to herself. "He dotes on roses and is allergic to bee venom—Larry is, too, I seem to recall. It must be vital that they all know what to do."

Stephan came rushing in with the doctor's bag. He had already removed a syringe and a small bottle. He filled the syringe and handed it to the doctor, who gave the injection. Presently, Bessermann appeared to be able to breathe again. "A bee," he whispered hoarsely. "A bee!"

The doctor bent over him. "Try to stay calm, Rudy," he ordered. "It must have been a yellow jacket or something; you've been stung twice."

"K-k-keh . . ." The man tried to say something, choked, and could not speak.

"Steve, quick! We've got to get him to bed."

Stephan and the doctor picked the massive man up in a bosun's hold and disappeared with him up the stairs, Mary Ellen running ahead. Where only a few moments before music had evoked the essence of high Romantic tranquility, now there was a silence, a heavy silence broken only by a curious whimpering. Lady Fairgrief looked about to find Helmut Schmidt standing rigid against a wall, his handsome features contorted with sorrow, his knuckles stuck in his mouth.

"Well, Herr Schmidt." Her voice was scathing. "You did a wonderful job of picking those leaves. Any more pretty decorating schemes?"

"Don't say it, lady, please don't say it," the little man begged her. "My old, old friend."

"Oh come, come," Lady Fairgrief chided in annoyance. "At least the doctor was here. He'll pull through."

"*Ja, ja.*" He nodded eagerly, as though trying to convince himself. "Und a bee sting!" He ran a hand through his thick white hair. "Is such a small thing."

Which was altogether going too far.

"Herr Schmidt," enquired Lady Fairgrief coldly, "have you ever been stung by a bee?"

The little man gave her a crazy look and laughed wildly. "Have I ever been stung? Oh *ja*, lady, I have been stung in my time." He shrugged. "But it was a long time ago." He appeared to think for a moment. "I had forgotten," he said, and walked out the back door.

A few moments later, she heard a car engine start and tires squeal away down the drive. "What a tiresome little man," she said to Maude, who was standing at the foot of the stairs looking up.

"Do you think there's something I could do up there?" the maid asked.

"Probably not," Lady Fairgrief sighed. "I think they all know what their part in the thing should be. Come on, Maude," she said in an effort to be cheerful. "Take me to the kitchen and make me a cup of tea and we'll sing sad songs of the death of kings."

chapter
FOUR

Miss Worthing woke annoyed that the sun was already leeching out of the sky. There were several things she wanted to get finished and done with after all, not the least of which was to clean up the dead bees in the front of the house. Martha had been quite right; they would attract ants if they were not cleared away immediately.

She could hear vague noises down below; Miss Shaw was already up and about. Miss Worthing put on a simple ecrue silk blouse, a navy wool skirt, and a pair of solid short-heeled black shoes, and started downstairs to throw cold water into her face.

"Martha?" she called as she descended.

Miss Shaw emerged from the door of the kitchen in a generous black suit, a frilly white-cotton blouse, and a pair of enormous black spike heels.

"Yes, dear?"

"There are a few things I want to do before supper. Do I have time?"

"Oh sure," Miss Shaw replied cheerfully. "I'm just making some soup and sandwiches. You know, something light before we go."

"Go?"

"We are still going to the movies, aren't we?"

"Oh, right!" Miss Worthing exclaimed. "Still want to go yourself?" She looked dubiously at her friend's feet.

Miss Shaw nodded. "But the only theater around here showing that film is in Santa Rosa."

Miss Worthing shrugged. "Then we'll just have to clean the little beasties up tomorrow."

"Okay. What's up now?"

"I have to write to my aunt and you have to change your shoes if you're going to drive."

Miss Shaw chortled massively and retreated to the kitchen. Miss Worthing sat herself down at the dining-room table. Taking notepaper and her immense antique fountain pen, she set herself to the disagreeable chore of eating fifty-year-old crow. It took just about an hour and when it was done, she felt it struck just the right note, as it were, between full-scale horror (which she quite honestly felt) and a dignified and sorrowful apology (which was even more sincerely felt). It had quite exhausted her.

She was sealing the envelope as the doorbell rang. "Come in," she called, and looked up to see one of the scruffy teen-aged runners for Jolliston's only local messenger service. He had a very strange expression on his face and held himself rigid in the doorway.

"What happened in your front yard?" he asked. "There's a million dead bees out there."

"I know," she replied, smiling a little at his discomfort. "Just be glad you don't have to clean them up."

He took the envelope and stared at the address. "You want this delivered tonight?"

"Do you have any more pickups to do?"

He shook his woolly head.

"Well then, if you wouldn't mind."

"Naw," he said, "it's just a bit out of the way."

Miss Worthing acknowledged the hint with the appropriate tip and opened the door for the boy to leave.

"Sure is funny," the boy observed as he gingerly

stepped over the little bodies on the porch. "I heard there's a few angry beekeepers in town, too. Wonder if it has something to do with them."
Miss Worthing stared after the boy. "It always comes," she mused aloud. "I don't know why, but you always find out when you have to." She made a beeline herself for the telephone.
The telephone at the opposite end rang for a long time. Finally, it was picked up and a gruff voice snapped, "Beekeepers' Association."
"May I speak to Arlen Lloyd," she asked politely.
"Speaking," the voice growled.
"Arly? Matilda Worthing."
The voice merely grunted acknowledgment.
"You sound unhappy."
"Have good reasons today."
"Oh?"
"Yup! Lost two hives."
"In November?" protested Miss Worthing. At the same time a small spark of satisfaction glowed into life within her.
Mr. Lloyd merely grunted again.
"Well I thought I had better call," she began cautiously. "We had a small swarm descend on us today. I'm afraid the cold got most of them. I wondered if they were yours."
"Prob'ly."
"What happened?" she asked, rather wishing her neighbor were not such a laconic man.
"Someone tore two hives to shreds."
"What?" she gasped.
"'Struth! Boards scattered. Honeycomb jist thrown everywhere. That's whatcha seen, 'twern't no proper swarm, jist some confused and angry bees. Damn hippies!" the man finished with a mutter.
Privately, Miss Worthing considered it extremely un-

51

likely that hippies would be messing about with beehives.

"Mattie?"

"Yes," she replied.

The man's voice was quietly hopeful. "Didja see the queen?"

"Arly," she said slowly. "There wasn't a queen."

The man made a disgusted noise. "Hadda be. Neither of 'em was anywhere on the pieces of the hives left over there."

"They didn't clump, Arly. They either flew off—back toward your orchard now that I think of it—or they died. We have to go out tomorrow and pick them up."

There was a long silence at the other end of the wire.

"Arly?"

"Yup, still here. Tell ya what, Mattie. I'll send someone round to pick 'em up. I wanna take a look at 'em."

Well, Miss Worthing thought to herself, *that's one chore removed.* "Okay, Arly," she said aloud. "Sorry." She hung up and shook her head feeling uncomfortably baffled. Why would anyone vandalize a beehive? Where were the queens? Would anyone want a queen all by herself? They were the most notoriously stupid creatures in the hive. Why would anyone risk a potentially fatal stinging doing such a thing?

"Mattie!" Miss Shaw called from the dining room. "Soup's on!"

"All right, Martha," she called back and went into supper, dismissing it from her mind.

Later, after eating, they set out for Santa Rosa.

"Santa Rosa!" Miss Worthing protested mildly.

"It's the closest place that movie's showing."

"At least"—Miss Worthing settled in for the hour's ride—"we don't have to get up early in the morning."

"Oh yes we do," grunted Miss Shaw, aggressively slamming into gear. "We have a jillion little corpses to dispose of."

Miss Worthing explained that it was no longer necessary.

"Poor Arly," Miss Shaw clucked. "That's a nasty loss." Which, considering the fits she had had when Mr. Lloyd had moved his numerous hives into the lot next door, was very generous indeed of Miss Shaw.

"Especially, when it's someone who has the first penny he ever made," observed Miss Worthing astringently. "Now why on earth would someone do such a thing?"

Miss Shaw, however, merely shook her head and, negotiating the entrance to the freeway, muttered, "I don't suppose we'll ever know, either."

chapter
FIVE

Mary Ellen stood at the foot of the bed. Her face was drawn and white, setting off her black hair and dark eyes. The last seven hours had been a nightmare. It always was whenever Bessermann got stung. Each time she wondered how much even his massive physique could take the punishment of it. Not that he looked so massive at the moment.

He lay on his back, his breathing stertorous and labored, his face still suffused and puffy. He appeared to be sleeping quietly enough though, the bedclothes tucked round his neck beneath his chin.

"He suddenly looks so fragile," she whispered to Harvey, who stood next to her.

"He'll be just fine, Miss Mary Ellen," replied the old man, also in a whisper. "Don't you worry."

The nurse was a middle-aged Chicana with a dark Indian complexion and black hair streaked with white. She sat in a chair at the head of the bed, stiff and starched. She gave them a severe look to indicate that they should be quiet.

Harvey returned to his seat on the opposite side of the bed from the nurse, to keep watch over his old friend. He was a very old man indeed, bent with rheumatism, scarecrow thin. His hair was little more than a stray gray lock or two scattered on a skull covered with age spots. His eyes were rheumy and his hands constantly trembled, but he kept to his duties with a slow and fixed determination always—almost perversely—dressed in the cutaway coat and pin-striped trousers of a long-vanished generation of servants.

Mary Ellen indicated to the nurse that she wanted to speak to her. They tiptoed into the hall.

"Yes, Miss Bessermann?" asked the nurse softly.

"Is there any reason why you have the covers round his neck like that?"

"Doctor's orders, miss."

"It's just he hates it so," Mary Ellen explained.

"You mustn't trouble yourself, Miss Bessermann," Miss Martinez soothed. "He's not really conscious right now, you know, and I'm sure the doctor knows best."

"Yes," the younger woman nodded, "yes, I know. Paul is a wonderful doctor."

A door next to the sick room opened suddenly and the doctor looked out. In his mid-thirties and quite good-looking in a conventional way, like most members of his profession he was expensively, if not particularly well, dressed: an ill-fitting sports coat, a white shirt, no tie, baggy gray-wool trousers, and a pair of unfortunate oxblood Italian loafers on his feet. His hair, lank and brown, was, as always, immaculately trimmed and groomed. His face was lined with fatigue and, perhaps, too much good living—his lips were too red and there were dark bags beneath his eyes. The red in his eyes, however, was unquestionably, at the moment, from weariness.

"Good to hear that from you, Mary Ellen," he said with a smile and then turned to the nurse. "I thought I told you not to leave him. What are you doing out here?"

"It's all right, Paul." Mary Ellen put a hand on the doctor's arm. "It's my fault. I called Miss Martinez out here to ask her to pull the bedclothes down from Uncle Rudolf's throat." He smiled and seemed about to say something else, then turned again to the nurse. "That will be all, Nurse."

"Yes, Doctor." The starch went back into the sickroom.

"I know he probably wouldn't like it," Dr. Becay explained when the door was shut again, "but he's got to keep his chest warm. You're a singer. You know what hystamine shock does to the respiratory tract."

Mary Ellen sighed and nodded. He took her by the shoulders and gently shook her. "Now who's the doctor here?"

Suddenly, she started helplessly to cry. With a curious grunt, he pulled her toward him. For a long moment, she hid her face against his chest. Gently, he stroked her hair. "Mary Ellen!" he whispered after a moment, his voice gone hoarse and intense.

She raised her head up and looked at him, abruptly stiffened, and deliberately stood back from the circle of his arms.

"Paul!" she said quietly. "I . . . I didn't know! I'm sorry." She turned and fled down the corridor, her white shirt receding into the gloom. He stared after her a minute and then started to go back into his room. Stephan was standing in the door of his own room across the corridor, glaring at him.

"Hello, Steve," said Becay rather casually.

"Leave her alone, Paul!"

"Now, Steve . . ."

"Don't give me that," the younger man whispered savagely, his body tensed. "I've known for months you were in love with her. But she's mine and she's going to stay mine."

"Your father doesn't seem to think so," the doctor replied pointedly, a disdainful expression on his dissipated features. "He's set on my marrying her."

"Has he said so?"

"Well, not in so many words perhaps..."

"She never will."

"Don't be too sure."

Stephan's eyes flashed with hostility, but when he replied it was evenly enough: "I'm not worried about you, Paul." He turned away, and shutting his bedroom door, followed in Mary Ellen's path down the corridor.

Becay stared after him a moment, his face an expressionless mask. Before he could return to his own room, the nurse stuck her head out of Bessermann's room.

"Doctor! Quickly! Something's wrong."

He pushed past her into the room. It was immediately obvious that Bessermann was going through some kind of crisis. Becay pulled back the bedclothes and palpated the chest.

"Oh Christ, I was afraid of this. Nurse, get an intubation unit. Harvey, run downstairs and tell Mary Ellen." He pulled himself up quickly. "No, better safe! Tell her to get a priest here."

"No," Harvey gasped. "You can't mean it."

"I mean it, now move it!"

The old man staggered out of the bedroom and down the hall, yelling at the top of his lungs, "Miss Mary Ellen, Miss Mary Ellen."

The nurse sorted through his bag while Becay made a cursory examination of the patient. Suddenly, Harvey was back at the foot of the bed.

"What are you doing here?" Becay barked at him, annoyed that his attempt to get the old man out of the room had failed.

"I already told Miss Mary Ellen," the old man answered and then pulled a very stubborn face. "My place is here."

"Oh, never mind!" he snapped. "Nurse! Where is that unit?"

She looked up from rummaging in his bag, and held up a cellophane envelope within which a length of rubber tubing lay curled. "I have it right here, Doctor, but I can't find any lubricant."

"Nonsense! There's a brand-new jar of petroleum jelly in there."

"Doctor?"

"Woman!" yelled Harvey unexpectedly and lunged at the bag, snatching up the jar. Quickly the nurse brought the other impedimenta to the bedside, her lips pursed angrily.

"Now," ordered the doctor, "Nurse, hold his shoulders. He's a very strong man. Harvey, damn it all, make yourself useful. Hold his legs down."

The doctor took a large dollop of the petroleum jelly and smeared it over the length of the tube. Then, gesturing to his two assistants to give him room, he began forcing it down the gulping esophagus of the supine man. Loud retching sounds accompanied the effort. The man's body writhed.

"Singers!" Becay muttered almost viciously, continuing to force the tube down Bessermann's throat. "Now *hold* him," he ordered and straightened. "Steve!"

The younger man entered immediately.

"Drive down to the hospital and get a couple of tanks of oxygen. You still have that tent we used last summer?"

Stephan jerked his head toward the door. "It's in the closet at the end of the corridor," he said.

"Okay. Get Mary Ellen to bring it in, then get down to the hospital. Don't let them screw you up. Tell 'em to call me if there's any problem. But here." He tossed some keys. "Take my car. It's faster."

Stephan fielded the keys and cut out the door. Becay continued to labor over the man's body. "Breathe, Rudy," he whispered urgently. Grotesque sucking noises resounded through the otherwise silent room. Becay looked up to find Mary Ellen standing by the bed. Behind her at the door was a small mover's dolly on which was a cardboard carton emblazoned with the logo of a well-known medical supply house.

"The priest is here," she said softly.

"Send him in, but," the doctor's face lit up, "I think we've beaten it again. The tube's gone past the worst swelling. Thank God his lower lungs were clearer." He looked down at his patient. "Singers," he muttered again, this time with something akin to affection.

Bessermann's breathing was considerably easier by the time the priest had finished his anointing. As he finished, Bessermann's eyes opened. He moved his lips as though to say thank you to the priest, closed his eyes again, and presently was asleep.

Mary Ellen and Becay had just managed to rig up the oxygen tent when Stephan wheeled a tank in on a trolley. He tossed the keys back to the doctor. "Thanks, Paul," he said quietly and turned to Mary Ellen. "I just saw Monsignor leave . . ." His eyes asked the unspoken question.

"Paul?" she asked.

The doctor looked up from thumping Bessermann's chest and smiled at them. "He's going to be all right." Becay sat down on the chair at the head of the bed and breathed very deeply. At that moment, he looked incredibly young; his hair hung down into his face and his cheeks were flushed with effort.

"Look at 'im," Harvey whispered to the nurse. "He's such a fine doctor."

The nurse sniffed and continued to check the fittings of the tent. Harvey made a disgusted noise and went over to put a hand on Becay's shoulder. "Thank you, Doctor Paul." He glanced down at the bed. "I don't know what I'd do with myself if . . ." He broke off and, opening the tent, gently nestled a blanket closer around his old friend's throat.

"Nurse." Becay stood up. "I'll be next door if I'm needed again." He gestured that she come a little closer. "And try," he said into her ear, "not to let Harvey fuss Mr. Bessermann too much."

"Very well, Doctor," replied the nurse shortly and turned away.

"She's a formal one." He grinned at Stephan and Mary Ellen when they had followed him into the hall. "I'm hungry," he said in a surprised voice.

Mary Ellen uttered a weak giggle. "I'm not surprised. You didn't eat a thing at dinner."

"No one did," said Steve quietly.

"I hardly remember dinner," the doctor said and then yawned. "Well, I'm going to go down and raid the fridge and then I'm going to get some sleep, but before I forget, do you think you ought to call Larry?"

"I thought you said he would be okay," said Mary Ellen rather nervously.

"I'm almost positive he will be," Becay reassured her, "but I just thought maybe you would like to be together now."

Mary Ellen and Stephan looked at each other.

"You don't think it'll upset him?" asked Mary Ellen.

"Of course, it will." Becay grinned. "But I can't think of a better time to try to effect a reconciliation."

"I think Paul's right," Stephan agreed, taking her arm. He nodded to the doctor, who nodded back.

"I'll just go down the back stairs to the kitchen, if you don't mind?" said Becay to Mary Ellen.

"Of course I don't mind, Paul. Would you like me to fix you an omelette or something?"

"No, I'll manage," he said. Still, however, he did not move.

"Okay. And thanks, Paul," Mary Ellen said.

Stephan was leading her down the hall toward the main staircase when she turned to say something further. Instead, she caught an expression on the doctor's face that he probably had not meant her to see.

"Good night, Paul," she said quickly and followed Stephan down the hall to the stairs. By the time she reached the bottom, Stephan was already on the telephone.

"Yes. He's at Harrah's. You may have to keep trying. Yes, thank you. Call us back." He hung up and took her into his arms. "He'll be fine, Mary Ellen. Don't fret."

"It's just everything, Steve. Sometimes I find myself wishing—"

"Hush," he said gently. "That's not the kind of thing we can allow ourselves to think." He turned and pulled back the draperies, looking out through the windows of the French doors. "Want some air?" he asked, opening the door briefly. From somewhere in the Valley came the sound of a rooster crowing. "Listen, it's morning."

The grandfather clock at the foot of the stairs softly bonged four times.

"Steve," Mary Ellen protested, "it's cold out there."

"I know," he said and took a few deep breaths before closing the door and once more pulling the draperies to cover it. He pulled her to him and held her closely. "I really think we should try to get some sleep. First student at one."

She groaned and kissed his cheek. "I won't even think about students—"

She was interrupted by the telephone ringing, shrill and insistent in the still morning silence. Stephan grabbed it.

"Stevie," his brother's voice crackled over the long-distance connection. "What's wrong?"

"It's Dad, Larry. He was stung again last night."

"Christ!" Lawrence Bessermann exclaimed. "Is he—"

"He's out of danger now," Stephan interrupted. "Paul Becay was here when it happened."

"Thank God for that."

"Yes," Stephan added dryly, winking at Mary Ellen, who colored and aimed a kick at his leg. "Thank God for that. Anyway, Paul said, and I agree with him, that if you could get here, this might be a good time—"

"I'll catch the first plane out of here," his brother said. "I'll be home tomorrow."

"It's okay?"

"Yeah, no problem. I know what it's like for him and you could probably use an extra pair of hands. Besides, the pianist's got a cousin who wants a few days out here and he's supposed to be pretty good."

"Great, Larry. It'll be good to see you again. Do you want someone to meet you in San Francisco?"

"Forget it. You'll have your hands full there. I'll catch an air taxi to Jolliston Field. I'll call for someone to come get me there. You and the kid haven't been to bed yet, right?"

"Right!"

"So sack out. I'll be there when you see me."

"Thanks, Larry. See ya!"

"See ya!"

Stephan hung up. "He's on his way home."

Mary Ellen nodded. "I'm glad," she said and then surprised him by suddenly muttering fiercely, "Damn it all!"

"Huh?"

"It was such a great afternoon."

Stephan put an arm round her shoulder. "There will be others, you know," he said gently. "Go on. It's way past bed time. I'll see to the windows and lamps and set the coffee maker. Okay?"

"Thanks, Steve," she said gratefully.

Halfway up the stairs, however, she turned back and looked down at him. "Steve." She smiled. "I almost forgot. You were really playing beautifully this afternoon."

"Yeah? Thanks. I felt pretty good about it, too." Even in the dim light, she could see that his eyes were dark with fatigue. "But, under the circumstances," he spoke very softly, "I'm just as glad we never got to the next song."

"Oh?"

"Yeah," he repeated absently. "*Der Totenaker*—'The Graveyard.'"

"Steve!"

"Go to bed, Mary Ellen," he said shortly, shaking his head. "Stupid fancies."

"G'night, Steve."

"G'night, my love."

chapter
SIX

Mary Ellen, however, did not go to bed. Once in her room, she sat down and put her head into her hands and stayed that way for a long, long time. Finally, she heaved a sigh and, placing her hands on the arms of her chair, pushed herself to her feet. Her skin felt tight against her face and fatigue had given it an almost ivory sheen.

A sharp pang of longing went through her as she looked at her bed, still unruffled since the previous morning. But there was coffee and breakfast to be made and Harvey would be next to useless this morning.

Maybe I can borrow Maude for awhile, she thought to herself as she changed into a bathrobe. Later, after a long shower and shampoo, she was at least awake, if not alert and rested. She changed into a dark blue shirtwaist dress and, on an impulse, added a white-lace collar that had belonged to her mother. She slipped her feet into a pair of penny loafers. It was going to be a long day; she might as well be comfortable.

But she did look like a housemaid, she decided, checking the ensemble in the mirror on her door. She shrugged. Sometimes—she reflected bitterly—that's exactly what she was. It didn't matter anyway.

As she descended the stairs, light was already pouring

through the back windows. Outside, birds were chirping and from somewhere in the valley the distant sound of a chain saw penetrated the morning calm. Someone had left the back doors open and absently she closed them.

"Maude! *Maude!*" She suddenly heard Lady Fairgrief calling. "Where is that woman? Maude!"

Lightly, she ran to the doorway of the conservatory, which had been converted to a suite for the old woman.

"What is it?" she asked.

"Oh, Mary Ellen! Thank God!" Lady Fairgrief, encased in a voluminous flannel nightgown, lay propped up in bed on mounds of pillows. "I can't raise Maude. Where could she be?"

"Do you need anything?"

"I suppose I mustn't make a fuss after all everyone's been through, dear," the old lady grumbled, "but really, I would rather like to get up."

Mary Ellen grinned and entered the room. "No problem!" She pulled the wheelchair to. "Let's get you up and then we'll search Maude out."

"Thank you, dear." Lady Fairgrief pushed herself upright and indicated a closet. "There's a particularly heavy dressing gown in there. Would you get it, please?"

Mary Ellen opened the closet. A quilted robe of lavendar silk with gray trim hung on the door. She took it out and helped her ladyship into it. And then, against the old woman's protests, brushed her hair out and carefully arranged it.

"Thank you, dear" Lady Fairgrief said happily, and glared at her reflection in the hand mirror Mary Ellen held for her. "That was duty above and beyond. And wait until I see Maude," she added grimly. "Now swing the chair round to the side of the bed. That's it. Now all you have to do is to put your arm round my waist, you've got it. Let me put my arm round your neck. Now, put your other arm under my legs, poor shriveled things that they are. And to think men once thought I had pretty legs. When they got to see 'em, of course. Now, swing me over into the seat. That's got it! Now, put the arm up and lock it back there. Thank you, my dear."

"You're light as a feather." Mary Ellen smiled, locking the chair arm into place. "Do you want to go into the breakfast room?"

"No, dear. I think not this morning. I'd just be in the way." She put a hand on Mary Ellen's sleeve. "Would you mind taking me out onto the terrace? That's why I asked for my quilted gown. There's sun out and it looks to be a fine day. Then," she added malevolently, "when you find Maude, by all means tell her where she can find me."

Mary Ellen agreed with a small chuckle, taking the handles of the chair.

"How is my poor Rudy?" the old lady asked as they crossed the enormous living room.

"He's going to be just fine," replied the young woman happily. "Paul said last night, or rather this morning," she corrected herself dryly, "that he was pretty much out of danger."

"That's splendid."

On the terrace, Mary Ellen parked the chair next to a wrought-iron table. "Are you going to be all right here?" she asked.

"Right as rain." Lady Fairgrief smiled. "Now you go do whatever you need do and if you see Maude . . ."

Early morning newness surrounding her, she sank back into her chair. This was the best time of day, when the world was still awash with the clarity after sleep, when you didn't feel the weight of years so heavily as in the evening. And the simple pleasures—watching birds zip in and out of the branches of the trees or a fat ungainly lizard drag itself into the sun to warm up to a nice torpor (just like you)—they all added zest to the victory of just getting through another night.

A late robin was arguing with a worm in the lawn when the doors behind her opened and shut. The robin flipped away and the lizard disappeared from sight as though it had never been there.

Paul Becay was crossing the lawn. He was dressed this morning in a good green-plaid wool shirt, a pair of brown-wool trousers, and white shoes that gleamed as though they were made of vinyl.

She grinned happily to herself and remembered a comment her husband had once made—in all uncharitableness—about Americans' wonderful teeth and their really terrible shoes. . . .

The doctor sat down next to her. "Good morning, Lady Fairgrief." He took her hand in both of his. "I'm afraid we didn't get to meet very formally yesterday. I'm Paul Becay."

"We certainly were glad of your being here," she replied graciously. "Rudolf gave us quite a turn."

"Yes," the young man sighed. "He did that. I wish he'd be more careful."

"It was hardly his fault this time, Doctor," she observed tartly.

"True enough," he said and sank back into his chair.

He's exhausted, she observed to herself. And little wonder. "Doctor," she asked him. "Do you think I should leave?"

He waved a dismissing hand. "I wouldn't bother if I were you. Rudy will be up and about before afternoon, if I know him." He snorted. "The man's got the lungs of an ox."

"I know." Lady Fairgrief laughed. "I remember when he was younger he used to make my poor husband measure his chest expansion with my maid's tape measure. He was incredibly vain about it." She shook her head and thought a minute. "I suppose, though, we should all be grateful for it today."

"Indeed," Becay concurred rather vaguely, looking toward the house. "You know, I could really go for a cup of coffee," he said, changing the subject.

"So could I," her ladyship agreed, twisting about in her chair and looking toward the blank expanse of the breakfast-room windows. "Mary Ellen went in to make some . . ." Her voice drifted off as Maude emerged from the door carrying a tray.

"I've brought you coffee, my lady," she said rather breathlessly.

"Where have you been?" snapped the old woman. "Mary Ellen had to get me out of bed."

Becay raised an amused eyebrow and stood up. "If coffee's on, I'll go in and get some."

"Oh, don't move," Maude urged him. "I'll get it for you." She turned to go.

"Maude!" commanded Lady Fairgrief.

The doctor chuckled and made a slight bow to Lady Fairgrief. "I'll get it," he said and went in, leaving Maude wringing her hands.

She was a tall, strongly built woman with the ruddy complexion of indefatigable health and a bust like the prow of a liner. She had, however, sharp and somewhat inquisitive facial features, which gave her the rather furtive expression of a weasel or—as now, being chastized—the defeated expression of a mouse. Nor did she mitigate this unfortunate resemblance by invariably dressing in the mousiest browns or the very dullest grays.

"Well?" demanded Lady Fairgrief.

Maude offered her excuse, "I'm sorry, your ladyship, but it was the nurse."

"What nurse?"

"The nurse for poor Mr. Bessermann."

"Oh? And what about the nurse?"

"Well, you see it's like this." Maude clasped her hands together and sat down on the edge of the chair Becay had vacated. "I got up fairly early, as I do. When I went into the kitchen to get a cup of tea, there she was, bold as brass, looking around the cupboards."

"What was she doing?" enquired Lady Fairgrief sarcastically. "Stealing the spoons?"

"That's just it," replied Maude inconsequently. "I asks her what she's doing, I does. And it turns out that it's only the poor dear was hungry. No one in the whole house had thought to provide her with a meal."

"They were busy," observed Lady Fairgrief in a quiet murmur.

"And the poor thing," Maude went on without even a breath. "She was that tuckered out! Well, naturally, I puts her down at the kitchen table and brews up tea as quick as ever I can and then fixed a good breakfast for her. It was only my Christian duty," she concluded, virtuous and triumphant.

"You still haven't explained why you didn't come get me when you'd finished your act of charity of the day."

"Well." Maude clenched a hand and leaned forward conspiratorily. "We did get to talking." The weasel began to dominate. "And do you know what she said?"

"No, but I think I'm about to find out," Lady Fairgrief commented to the air.

Maude proceeded to go into elaborate and rather disgusting detail about the sickroom procedures the night before while Lady Fairgrief observed with sour recognition the intense irritation growing within her she always felt when she allowed herself to listen to servants' gossip.

". . . and Harvey! Why, he was that bossy and rude," continued Maude quite relentlessly, ignoring the clear signs of her ladyship's annoyance. "She told me everything that went on in that room, and poor Mr. Bessermann, why—"

"He's alive!" A rough voice spoke behind the two women making them jump in surprise. Harvey Maxwell came around the table and shook a very angry finger at Maude. "Maude Bennett, you was ever the nastiest-minded old gossip I ever knowed. That old nurse last night didn't 'alf try to 'elp. Mr. Rudy's alive and well this morning because of Dr. Paul and I won't 'ave none of your vicious claver in this 'ouse. Mr. Rudy, 'e swears by Dr. Paul!"

"Harvey!" Lady Fairgrief commanded. "Keep your voice down! Remember yourself!"

"I'm sure I'm sorry, your ladyship," Harvey said to her. "But this 'ere woman's been nattering on for the thirty years I've known 'er."

Maude was practically incoherent with rage and in an effort to stop the ensuing din, Lady Fairgrief suddenly banged an open hand on the table top. "Both of you! Stop this instant! Do you hear?"

"Your ladyship," Maude protested. "I have never in me life been a *vicious gossip!* Why, I'm sure—"

"All right, Maude, knock it off!" enjoined Lady Fairgrief tersely.

Immediately, Maude clamped her mouth shut. When Lady Fairgrief reverted to American slang, it invariably indicated that her patience had really reached its end.

"Harvey, why don't you go do something in the garden," the old woman suggested. "Gather ferns if you can't find any flowers. But both of you," she scowled at each of them in turn, "get ahold of yourselves. Rudy is recovering nicely and it just won't do to have two of his friends squabbling like this."

She turned to Maude. "And really, Maude! What business does that nurse have talking about a patient anyway?"

"She's been a nurse a long time."

"That is hardly an excuse," retorted her ladyship. "I think I'll have a little chat with the doctor."

"Now that's a good idea." Harvey nodded shortly.

"Oh no, my lady." Maude suddenly was pleading. "You mustn't do that. She's not a young person and she's on a very tiny pension. Please, don't say anything."

Lady Fairgrief was brought up short. If there was one thing in the world for which she had the deepest sympathy, it was for anyone in today's world trying to make a go of it on a pension.

She sighed. "Very well, Maude. We'll discuss it later." Harvey still hovered, looking belligerent.

"What do you say, Harvey?" she asked.

"Mr. Rudy will be needing quiet . . ." he began doubtfully.

"All the more reason we shouldn't bicker."

"Just the same," he continued, "when it's all over, I'm going to tell Miss Bessermann she shouldn't have that gabby nurse back next time."

"Next time?"

"Of course. This happens two, three times a year," he replied and then noticed the astonishment on the two women's faces. "It's never been as bad as this before, I 'ave to admit, but it's 'is roses."

"I thought as much," Lady Fairgrief said almost to herself. "Maude," she asked the maid, "would that suit you? A quiet arrangement not to have her back?"

Maude looked daggers at Harvey. "Yes, my lady," she conceded eventually.

"Good! Now take me in. I want my bath and breakfast."

chapter SEVEN

Later, after luncheon, Lady Fairgrief instructed Maude to park her in the enormous living room next to the piano. Earlier, she had noted the book of Schubert's songs lying where Stephan had left it the day before. Dismissing Maude to her own devices, she turned the pages of the book back to the beginning of the interrupted song cycle and began to read the songs to herself, weakly humming the tunes and mentally translating the texts.

She was there when Bessermann discovered her at it. For all that he was such a big man, he moved gracefully and lightly upon his feet, the carpeting of the stairs absorbing the sound of his tread. Then too, he descended more slowly than he would have ordinarily done. The stinging had definitely taken its toll, though he would cheerfully have died before admitting it.

He was halfway down the stairs when he heard the soft cracked-voice humming in the pervasive silence of the cavernous living room. He peered over the balustrade and smiled, a look of boundless affection flitting across his strongly featured face.

As old as the mountains, he thought, *and crippled besides*. But her back was still ramrod straight and her mind as keen as a razor.

She had got herself up in a thick navy-wool suit. And though the blanket that covered her useless legs was securely tucked in place, he knew perfectly well that she would have on the pair of shoes to match that suit precisely. Beneath her jacket was a simple silk blouse of a dazzling whiteness upon which reposed a truly fabulous choker of matched blue-gray pearls.

She sat in her chair regally erect, the book held up to catch the light from the French doors at the back. She did not notice him as he slowly walked toward her until he rounded her chair and his shadow cut off her light. She glanced around irritably and immediately broke into a happy smile. "Rudolf! You're up!"

The large, ruddy-faced man smiled in turn and bent down to kiss her lavender-scented cheek. "I couldn't stay in bed forever, my dear." He took a chair and pulled it next to hers. "Now, Lally." He took her hands in his. "Paul told me you had asked him about going. I won't hear any more of it, understood?"

"Rudolf." She held up her lorgnette and peered through it at him. He looked like a farmer in his faded bluejeans and a worn blue cambric workshirt unbuttoned sufficiently at the top to reveal the bristling white thatch on his chest. "You know very well that had you been really ill," she said quietly, "it would have been unthinkable to stay and be a burden to Mary Ellen."

"Nonsense," he said quickly. "Mary Ellen tells me that both you and Maude have been wonderful to have around. And when I invited you here," he said, the slight tendency to the North German w sound where a v ought to be slipping through, "it was to stay with me. I want this to be your home now, my dearest Lally."

Lady Fairgrief squeezed his hand with her own and said nothing, not knowing what on earth she could say.

Bessermann relieved the awkward moment. He gestured toward the music in her hand. "What are you reading?"

"*Die Winterreise*," she answered shyly. "I'm sorry."

"But why apologize?" he asked. "I'm only sorry we didn't get to finish it before that insect . . ." A frown crossed his face.

"Yes?"

"It doesn't matter." He shook his head briefly. "It's gone now." Gently, he took the book from her. He glanced at the page to which it was opened and softly hummed a bar and then cleared his throat violently. "Sorry, Lally," he apologized for the raucous noise. "It's that damned tube. My throat is still irritated." He appeared to be intensely peeved and, with a few blunt fingers, prodded the tender flesh beneath his chin.

"Oh, Rudy." She suddenly burst out laughing. "Sometimes you are so very typically a singer."

"Well"—he shrugged his massive shoulders—"why shouldn't I be?" He gestured about the room. "I've done all this by singing. You don't make fortunes in Austria being an apiculture laboratory assistant." He laughed, too, as he handed the book back to her. "You will hear the whole thing yet," he said. "I promise. Just as soon as my throat is well again."

She leaned forward in her chair and touched his arm. "Rudy," she said urgently, looking into the younger man's eyes. "I don't care if I never hear you sing again. I admit that it would be a loss to me, but just being with you is enough. You and my dear, dear Arthur were such good friends. To be with you, to talk to you. Somehow it helps to bring my wonderful man back to me."

His hand covered hers on his arm. "I know. And he was the best friend a man could have," he acknowledged softly.

He stood up suddenly. "But come! I show you my garden."

The first stop was an enormous growth of late chrysanthemums, all in vigorous bloom.

"Fancy," she shook her head. "November blossoms."

"That, my dear, is California for you." He bent to examine a flower with brown edges. "Nothing serious," he murmured and straightened, looking relieved.

"You really do have a green thumb," she said with admiration. "I did too, once upon a time." She sighed quietly as once more he took the handles of her chair. "Tell me"— she attempted to twist about and ask over her shoulder— "do you do all this by yourself?"

"What do you think I am, Lally?" He laughed. "Superman? I have two full-time men." He wheeled her into the rose garden and parked her beside the marble bench and looked out over the valley. "It is so pleasant here," he said happily.

"Rudolf?" began her ladyship rather tentatively. "Do you really think it's a good idea to do so much yourself? Harvey told us this morning that you get stung several times each year."

"*Ja,*" was the noncommittal response.

"Well then, why do you do it?"

He turned toward her, an expression of surprise giving way almost immediately to amusement. "You ask me that?"

"What do you mean?"

"Do you take care of yourself?" he asked, with considerable enjoyment. "Hmmm? You can no longer take exercise, yet you still go out in all weathers. You eat virtually what you want to eat and you still have this incredible zest for life. How old *are* you, Lally?"

Lady Fairgrief sniffed and sat up in her chair. "Really, Rudolf, I am a lady." Then she caught his glance. "I only admit to ninety-five," she cackled. "I'll add onto it when I reach a hundred." She raised her glass to peer at him. "And it's not all that far off, so don't look smug.

"Besides," she added, wrapping a blanket round her hands, "just because a part of you doesn't work anymore is hardly a good reason to stop living."

"So?" he asked. "Since I was a child I have loved to garden. But till they develop these wonderful antihistamines, I have not done it since before Vienna. Much, much too dangerous! Now, of course, is risk, but things worth doing sometimes need risk to be taken."

"Of course," Lady Fairgrief agreed. "Still . . ."

"Und so," he continued, "you don't want me to garden my roses because one day I may die of a bee. And then I, in my turn, wish you would not have breakfast on the terrace when it is nearly winter."

"I don't want to lose you," she said gently.

He took her hand. "And I don't want to lose you, Lally. So you see, we worry because we are selfish."

"You disgusting cynic," she said tartly, snatching her hand away from him.

They laughed together.

"Look, Lally." He pointed across the valley toward the eaves of a large house jutting above a grove of live oaks on the banks of the Jolliston River. "That is the house of your so famous niece, Miss Worthing."

Lady Fairgrief stared in the direction Bessermann was pointing. "Why it *is* the old family house!" she exclaimed. "I thought it would have been torn down ages ago and the site rebuilt. Goodness, Matilda must have done herself *very*—" She caught herself in mid-flow. "What do you mean, 'so famous niece'?"

"You mean you don't know? She was instrumental in finding a most horrible murderer—a mass murderer—last year. It was in all the papers. Poor woman was shot in the knee."

"Matilda?"

"*Ja*, Lally." He smiled at her astonishment. "She has one of the finest minds in our valley, if not in California."

"I don't know what that has to do with getting herself riddled with bullets, but I do remember her as a sharp lass.

"Which reminds me." She lifted her glass once more and peered at Bessermann, who had spread himself out on the marble bench. "Matilda has written me a note. I'm to go there for dinner on Tuesday. If you can lend us a car, Maude can drive us over."

"Of course," he replied and stood up. "Und now I have to get back to the house. There is a meeting of the Board of the Opera Company tomorrow and my illness has kept me from some very important business."

"Oh?" said her ladyship, eyeing Bessermann intently.

He laughed. "No. Don't worry, Lally; I haven't forgotten what you said. I will behave better in the future. But I do plan," he added with a touch of grimness, "to put some teeth into my legacy so that when I'm gone I can still be a watch dog."

Lady Fairgrief shook her head and chuckled. "Well, since that won't happen for years and years, I don't want you fussing yourself unnecessarily. You have been very ill."

Bessermann agreed with a smile. "Years and years," he said. "But I won't be fussed. It is nothing that will take very long, an hour maybe with my lawyer. But," he added, "this is also my afternoon to teach."

"Teach!" exclaimed her ladyship. "Rudolf Bessermann you are simply not well enough to teach voice lessons today."

"Don't worry, Lally." He smiled at her outburst. "Today Steve and Mary Ellen take lessons. I just sit in an easy chair with coffee and good brandy and make oracular observations. It's easy."

"This," she snickered, "I have got to see, you old ham."

He nodded. "It's true," he said seriously. "Today only,

though. Usually I really teach." He went round behind her to take the handles of her chair.

"I'll bet you do," she said dryly and then chuckled. "Do you remember that silly man in Salzburg who just wouldn't play your accompaniments the way you wanted them? He kept saying he was a great teacher and knew how they should be done. I thought you were going to horsewhip the man."

"Bah," he frowned as he kicked off the brake of her chair and began pushing it back down the garden toward the house. "It's too easy to be a bad voice teacher. Empty theory-mongering with no roots in praxis. I taught my sons and Mary Ellen. From them, I thought I might as well take on a few others, a very few others. I'm afraid my standards are rather high and then, of course," he concluded modestly, "I'm very expensive."

"Good." She nodded with evident approval. "With you it's good value for money."

"It is. I studied *bel canto* in Italy before it vanished from even that country. My dear, if I could tell you of some of the people I have taken on, some from the purest pity . . . I think they study voice with trained dogs before they come to me." He launched into what was clearly a set speech.

"I have one girl—she comes today, as a matter of fact. I begin working with her a year ago and she tell me her teacher tell her expand the throat. The throat," he repeated in a scandalized tone. "Not *la gola*, that is correct, but the throat!"

"The words are the same in Italian, Rudy," her ladyship pointed out mildly. "You used to tell me all the time, *apri bene la gola*, open your throat up."

The tenor waved this aside as but a quibble. "But she expand her neck! Like a bull frog! That poor woman could get her neck so large you could put a pickle jar in it, but for all that, this tiny wheezing sound emerge, like a dog whining. And people charge money to impart such nonsense. What is it, Miss Martinez?"

The nurse was on the terrace, looking toward them with a worried expression on her face. Her whites, as could only be expected after her all-night vigil, looked limp and dingy in the bright afternoon sun.

"I'm sorry, Mr. Bessermann," she said hesitantly. "But I thought I ought to keep an eye on you."

Lady Fairgrief and Bessermann exchanged a glance. "Dr. Becay says I am fine now," the tenor said.

"I know, but I thought I should stay around, perhaps, and . . . you know . . ."

"Keep an eye on me." He smiled as he repeated her words.

"Nurse?" said Lady Fairgrief sharply.

"Yes?" Miss Martinez turned her worried glance toward the old lady.

"I think you are fussing unnecessarily. Did the doctor say you should remain?"

"No," the nurse admitted. "But—"

"No buts," Lady Fairgrief interrupted firmly.

"*Ja*," Bessermann concurred more mildly. "I appreciate very much your concern, but you had better go. Registry will have something for you."

"It's not that, Mr. Bessermann," she pleaded rather vaguely.

"Well then, what is it?" asked Lady Fairgrief, and then gestured toward Bessermann. "Rudolf, would you mind?"

"Of course, my dear." He answered her unspoken question and went into the house.

"Miss Martinez," the old woman began coldly. "I believe that is your name?"

The nurse nodded.

"What business, may I ask," demanded her ladyship, "do you have discussing your patient with the servants?"

"Do you really want to know?"

"No, I don't. I think you've said quite enough already."

The younger woman suddenly put a hand to her head and made a small moan. "I just don't know what to do."

The nurse was quite obviously in distress, and, almost in spite of herself, Lady Fairgrief found herself warming to her. "What is it, my dear?" she asked more gently. "Money?"

"No, it's not money. It's . . . it's . . . well!" Miss Martinez shook her head as though trying to clear it. "I do suppose you're right. I'm probably just being silly."

"What do you mean?"

"I'm not even certain I should . . ."

"But what is troubling you?" her ladyship insisted.

The nurse took hold of herself and inhaled deeply. "I *don't* know," she said presently. "*That's* the trouble. But I do know I'm going to refuse anything for the next few weeks. There are still bugs flying around," she added rather mysteriously.

"You really do care about Mr. Bessermann, don't you?" Lady Fairgrief suddenly asked.

Miss Martinez was quickly transformed by a surprisingly winning smile. "I remember him, from the old days." She looked off toward the rose garden. "I wanted to be a singer, too, but it was the Depression and I was a Mexican and in California that meant . . ." She shrugged and didn't finish the sentence.

"I am sorry," her ladyship murmured.

"I remember him best as Siegfried," the nurse said absently. "That voice! Those lungs!" She sighed happily and then, as though the mention of lungs had drawn a shadow over her reminiscence, she frowned. "Anyway, he was magnificent."

"I remember too, dear," said Lady Fairgrief quietly, her mind already whirling with plans to talk Harvey out of

80

his unseemly vendetta against this earnest and agreeable woman, who was equally devoted to Bessermann.

"And so," the nurse abruptly returned to the present, "I want to keep him healthy."

"Well, my dear," Lady Fairgrief reassured her, "you can be certain that we will all keep our eyes on him. Now, why don't you wheel me inside and then get on home. I'm going to see to it, incidentally, that you're paid for your two weeks' waiting in reserve."

"But that's not necessary," Miss Martinez protested.

"I think it is." Her ladyship wagged a finger. "It's really most kind of you to be concerned."

The nurse took the handles of the chair and pushed the old lady into the living room, where Stephan and Mary Ellen and an intense young woman dressed in singular garb (it had the appearance of being manufactured from patchwork quilts) had all joined Bessermann.

"I am sorry," Lady Fairgrief apologized. "I quite forgot you were going to be teaching. Miss Martinez, would you please take me to my room?" She smiled at Bessermann. "I'll take a nap while you're busy."

He held out an open palm toward her and smiled. "Then you're going to need these." He put two small marble-sized pink balls covered with cotton wool into her hand. "They're ear plugs made of beeswax and cotton; the sine qua non of life in a singer's household."

He looked questioningly at the nurse.

"I'll be leaving as soon as I've put Lady Fairgrief to bed," Miss Martinez replied with a smile.

"That will be wonderful, and thank you again for your help." He smiled in return and turned his attention back to his student.

The ear plugs did indeed cut off noises for which, considering the truly awesome cataracts of sound erupting from the living room, Lady Fairgrief confessed herself grateful. Almost immediately, she began nodding and pulled her blankets round her into a snug cocoon of warmth. A faint thought, lingering in the background of her mind, tried briefly to obtrude and rouse her.

"Later!" she thought, and fell directly into a sound sleep.

chapter EIGHT

Someone was shaking her violently.

"Wake up, my lady!" She heard it as from a great distance. "Please! Wake up!"

She opened her eyes. Maude was standing over her and calling to her, but it was faint, so very faint, as though she were hearing through the wrong end of a telephone.

"What nonsense," she muttered and was astonished at how loud she sounded to herself. "Speak up, Maude," she commanded. "What's wrong?"

To her surprise, Maude stood up and stuck her fingers into her ears.

"I must be still asleep and dreaming," she decided. "The woman is acting like someone in Wonderland."

Then she remembered. "Oh, the ear plugs!" and she promptly pulled them out. Immediately, sound flooded back upon her. "Well, what is it?" she snapped.

"It's Mr. Bessermann, ma'am," Maude replied, her face gone white as a sheet.

"What's wrong with him?" She tried to sit up, a quick dart of apprehension going through the pit of her stomach. "Get my heavy gown," she instructed.

"He's had to go back to bed," the maid said breathlessly as she helped Lady Fairgrief into her chair.

"Why?" she asked nervously. "Did he get stung again?"

"No, he's taken a cold."

"A cold!" She discovered herself to be furious. "Maude Bennett! A cold! What do you mean, frightening the life out of me like that? A cold! A cold!" she repeated even louder. "When I think of what I have to put up with from you—"

"No more than I put up with from you, my lady," Maude rejoined tartly and swung the chair about.

Her ladyship made what sounded suspiciously like a snort. "Too true, my dear," she said, calming down. "You've definitely a point there." She chortled quietly for a moment and then asked, "But why on earth did you get me up?"

"He said he wants to see you."

"Oh! Well, then, let's get up there."

Stephan was waiting for them at the foot of the stairs, his face pale and distracted in the gloom. Perhaps for the first time she noticed how remarkably well developed his physique was, especially dressed as he was now in a body-hugging T-shirt and jeans. Without a word, he took the handles of the chair while Maude held the foot platforms. His casual strength impressed her.

Was it all that surprising that—after eight years of separation while Mary Ellen had been in Germany and he in Los Angeles—when the two of them had met again, it was with the electric responsiveness of a pair of splendid animals?

Really, Eulalia! She clicked her tongue and shook her head to clear her thoughts. "Stephan?" She extended a hand around to touch his when they reached the landing. "What's wrong?"

"He started coughing during the last lesson," replied the young man cheerfully enough. "Mary Ellen felt his forehead and he was burning up. He was waiting for Mr.

Quinn, his lawyer, but we shooed him up to bed right away." He frowned. "He can't seem to shake it."

"And the fever?"

"That's what's got us worried. It's quite high and he's gone vague."

"Do you think it has something to do with yesterday?" she asked anxiously.

"It probably weakened him, but," he paused to consider a moment, "I don't think so. His throat's sore, but you'd expect that."

She sighed and wished she felt more relief than she did. "Why does he want to see me?"

"I don't know." He shrugged and knocked on his father's door.

Mary Ellen quickly opened it. She was still dressed in the gray-wool skirt and white shirt she had worn to teach in that afternoon. "I don't understand it, Steve," she whispered, her expression puzzled. "It's not like any cold I've ever seen before. He keeps hacking."

"Paul?"

"He's on his way."

Lady Fairgrief cleared her throat.

"I'm sorry." Mary Ellen recollected herself with a start. "Come on in."

Stephan wheeled Lady Fairgrief to the edge of the bed.

Bessermann waved a hand at his son and his cousin. "You two," he rasped. "Wait in the hall."

For a long time after they withdrew, Bessermann lay on his back, breathing heavily, his face pinched and drawn. "Lally?" he finally whispered.

"I'm right here, Rudy," she said soothingly, taking his hand in hers.

"This is a visitation."

Startled, she uttered a weak giggle. "What nonsense is this, Rudolf Bessermann?"

"No nonsense, Lally. Yesterday; the bee. Today this."

He lay still and breathed deeply and harshly for a moment. "I will let them get married."

"I think that's much the wisest decision, my dear." She squeezed his hand.

He turned his head on its side to look at her. "Please, Lally," he whispered urgently. "Take care of them."

She leaned forward with an urgency of her own. "Rudolf, you will stop this folderol immediately. You have a cold, a rather nasty one probably, but a cold. You're acting like doom itself."

"I'm a singer," he said simply and coughed again. "When something happens to the throat or the chest, it's . . ." He waved a hand knowing she understood.

Apparently she did understand for she nodded placidly. "I remember once, it was either in Munich or Berlin—that lovely little room on Unter den Linden." Once more she squeezed his hand, limp and fiery in her own. "I think I dreamed of it just the other day. Do you remember? You had a cold and were so worried because you thought"—she mentioned a certain royal personage—"was going to be there, and you didn't find out until afterward that she was deaf as a post."

He smiled weakly at her, as she chuckled at the memory. "*Ja*, I remember," he said after a moment.

"I thought Arthur was going to wire the Royal College of Surgeons for advice." She leaned over and gently touched his cheek. "And you know, dearest Rudy, you still sang so very beautifully."

The door opened behind them and Mary Ellen came in. "Uncle Rudolf, Paul's here." She took the handles of Lady Fairgrief's chair as the doctor bustled in.

"Now what's troubling you this time, you old faker," she heard him say briskly before the door closed behind them.

"No!" she commanded when she realized that Stephan and Mary Ellen were going to take her downstairs again. "I'm waiting right here till the doctor comes out."

Just then, Harvey appeared up the back stairs carrying an enormous tray of mugs and a coffee pot. He set it down on the hall table and started pouring the coffee. He looked unbearably wretched.

"I thought we could all use some," he said thickly as he handed round the thick clay mugs.

"That was very thoughtful, Harvey," said Mary Ellen gently as she followed him with troubled eyes. "But please, try not to worry. He's just been weakened by yesterday's accident."

"I'm sure you're right, Miss Mary Ellen," said the old man and started to pick up the tray again. The door to Bessermann's room opened and, suddenly, everyone stiffened to attention.

"Now try to get some sleep, Rudy," the doctor said back into the room. "I'll leave something with Mary Ellen if you have any problems dozing off."

He came out and shut the door behind him. He must have been called in the middle of a tennis match. He was still dressed in tennis whites rather the worse for wear. He eyed the expectant faces. "Is there another cup of coffee?"

Harvey immediately handed him a cup, and reached to take the doctor's bag, but the old man's hands trembled so much, liquid slopped over the rim and ran down the sides.

"You know, I'm not sure I believe this is happening," Becay muttered almost to himself as he wiped the mug with his hand.

"What is it?" Mary Ellen asked in a sharp voice.

"Pneumonia," the doctor replied shortly and sipped his coffee. Almost everyone immediately relaxed.

"Why are you all so relieved?" Lady Fairgrief asked in disbelief. "It's still a very serious disease, especially for people Rudolf's age."

"She's right, gang," Becay concurred, looking rather

grim. "And I'm not sure we should move him to a hospital at this point."

"He wouldn't 'ave gone anyway," Harvey muttered. "He'd rather fight here at 'ome."

A small murmur of agreement came from Stephan and Mary Ellen. "Should we get a nurse?" Stephan asked.

"I don't think it will be necessary, Steve." Becay shook his head and then looked consideringly at Harvey. "I'll stick around and, besides, Harvey here can probably take care of him as well as any nurse."

"Thank you, Dr. Paul," the old man muttered.

"Well, what can *we* do?" Mary Ellen asked.

"Nothing," Becay replied. "I'm going to go over to the hospital and get an antibiotic I.V. But he's strong as an ox, you know, and I just gave him a good dose of v-cyclin. We can always rig up the tent again. . . ." His voice trailed off. Looking down, he seemed suddenly very interested in Lady Fairgrief. "Now you I'm worried about."

"Don't be silly, young man," she snapped at him. "Other than a pair of useless limbs, I'm as strong as that ox in there."

"It's all the excitement," Becay pursued.

"Don't fuss me, boy," she warned him and then smiled at his grin. "Mary Ellen and Maude here are going to take me down and give me my supper and then I'm going to bed."

"Are you sure you're okay?" asked Stephan solicitously.

"Listen, all of you," she said imperiously. "Rudolf Bessermann is one of my oldest and certainly one of my dearest friends. I'm not going to leave him."

She glared round the circle of faces. Suddenly, Mary Ellen smiled and nodded her head. "He wants you here, Tante Lally," she said quietly.

"Thank you, my dear," acknowledged Lady Fairgrief regally. "Maude," she summoned. "Take me down."

Later, in the darkness of the night, Lady Fairgrief stared for a long, long time out of the window. She was not really very sleepy, but it had been a kindness to be taken to her room and thus to be no source of difficulty. Another indignity of being old and infirm, which she tolerated in the unhappily certain knowledge that it was the only decent or charitable thing to do. She had, however, resolutely refused to be put to bed. Instead, Maude had parked her next to the window and wrapped her snugly in blankets.

Presently, she had dozed off. A thought, however, awakened her and kept her awake listening to the rising wind whispering through the trees outside her window.

"It all seems so very unlikely," she addressed the chilly quiet aloud. Somewhere, in the recesses of the house, she thought she dimly heard folks stirring.

"I do hope Maude's getting a good night's sleep. Mary Ellen will need a lot of help tomorrow."

She frowned for a few moments longer. "Very unlikely, Eulalia, old thing," she murmured and tried to put it from her mind.

Soon, she slept again.

chapter
NINE

Outside, the world turned bitter. The last few glimmerings of summer were over. It was winter and the wind howled round the house like some ancient dispossessed ghost searching for a way in.

Late in the afternoon, Mr. Larry arrived. Harvey heard him in the hall outside the door talking with Miss Mary Ellen and Mr. Steve. But he didn't pay much attention. He just sat there, not paying much attention to anything—other than seeing that the slow drip, drip of the intravenous injection never went too fast or too slow, just the way young Dr. Paul had instructed him.

He looked up and nodded his head when Miss Mary Ellen or that old Maude brought him a tray, or when they came to take it away again, untouched. He was firm when Bessermann thrashed about and tried to throw off the blankets, getting up to tuck them back underneath his chin and trying to soothe his flaming body. He tried not to listen when Bessermann's eyes opened and he muttered almost crossly, "*Es war eine Biene . . . eine Biene . . . ich kenne Bienen gut . . . sehr gut . . .*" He was delirious and what did it mean anyway? "It was a bee, I know bees, it was a bee . . ."

Later, in a lucid moment, Bessermann asked for his rosary. Harvey took his own and put it into the clutching fingers of the half-conscious man, who quieted as soon as he felt the beads beneath his fingers. After a time, he slept once more.

Harvey gave appropriate thanks, and continued his indefatigable vigil, watching the drip, drip, drip, and praying without ceasing to every heavenly power who might imaginably be listening that they all might wake from this nightmare soon.

And he remembered the day, the afternoon, nearly fifty years gone by, when he knew that his voice—never very good—was gone, that he could no longer sing, not even well enough for the small insignificant houses that dotted the German and Austrian landscape then, houses in which he had already eked out a hand-to-mouth existence for twenty-odd years. Bessermann was so young then, working his way to the very top, vibrant and strong, with a voice that brought shouts and bravos from the burghers and their wives, usually as stolid as cattle in their stalls. He remembered his own despair that night at the booing; the intendant shaking his head regretfully; the sure knowledge that nothing remained . . .

And this youngster asking him if he wanted to be a dresser. A dresser! That time-honored tradition of the also-ran . . . Cocky kid! Knew he was on his way to the stellar heights . . .

I'm an old man these two decades since, he thought to himself. *And he's old now, too.* He found himself suddenly aware of it. He moistened the cloth on Bessermann's forehead, and smiled. "I'm glad I never became a burden," he whispered gently, thinking he wouldn't be heard.

But the eyes opened, and through tears of pain, smiled back. "You were never but a friend," Bessermann whispered. "I'm so thirsty."

Harvey held a glass to Bessermann's lips. He was asleep again before it was drained.

Later, he opened his eyes again. "The window," he croaked. "Open!"

But Harvey had to shake his head. "It's cold outside, Rudy. Lie still and sleep."

"At least the covers?" The blue eyes were pleading.

"Dr. Paul says not, Rudy." He dripped more cold water onto the cloth. Weakly, Bessermann nodded and then, once more, was unconscious.

"*Ja*," Harvey muttered. "*Schlaff! Schlaff gut, mein kleiner Rudi.*" And then, quietly, he began to sing, muttering the words beneath his breath, his aged and cracked throat barely carrying the tune: "*Guten Abend, gut Nacht, mit Rosen bedacht*" (Good night, good night: to sleep bedecked with roses) until he had to stop and stare once more at the drip, drip, drip of the I.V., lest he lose control and start to cry like a babe.

The doctor came in. He bent over his patient and gently palpated his chest.

"How is he, Dr. Paul?"

"It's hard to say, Harvey." Becay looked exhausted.

Harvey smiled at him. "Don't you think you should get some rest?"

Becay managed a lopsided grin. "I was going to suggest the same thing to you. You've been here all night and all day."

"I won't leave him, sir," the old man said quietly and with dignity. "This is my duty, and I'm to do it."

But later, when the doctor left, the drip, drip, drip of the fluid became too much. First, he nodded and righted himself with a violent jerk. Then, gradually, he drifted off into a deep, dreamless—but emotion-filled—sleep.

And all the emotion was profound loss.

Downstairs, Becay was on the telephone. The others sat stunned around the piano. "I need that X-ray unit out here as soon as possible," he was saying firmly into the phone. "No, I don't give a damn if they want double time," he snarled into the phone. "Just get the bastards out here pronto." He slammed the phone down.

"Paul?" It was Lawrence Bessermann. "How is he?"

Lawrence was a tall man, quite remarkably lean, dressed in a pair of worn black-leather pants and a wholly inadequately ironed blue cambric shirt. His hair, ash blond and untrimmed, was a flyaway bush of ringlets. His red beard, too, was full and untidy.

"It's bad," Becay said. He looked at Lawrence for a long moment and then glanced around at Mary Ellen and Stephan. "His lungs keep getting fuller and fuller no matter how much antibiotic I pour into him."

"Can't something be done?" asked Mary Ellen.

"I don't know what," admitted the doctor woefully. "I'm afraid to move him to a hospital at this point."

Suddenly, overhead, there was a loud thump. Almost before the sound had stopped, Stephan bounded up the stairs three by three with Paul Becay in close pursuit. Lawrence grabbed Mary Ellen's arm and they too dashed up the stairs.

They found Stephan helping Harvey to his feet and Becay feeling Bessermann's pulse. Harvey's face was beet red as he dusted off his hands and the knees of his trousers.

"I fell asleep, Miss Mary Ellen," he explained, tears of embarrassment in his eyes. A faint, throaty rasp came from the bed. ". . . and he fell off the chair." Bessermann tried vainly to laugh; it only set him coughing again.

Lawrence pulled the blankets up around his father's throat. "Take it easy, Dad," he murmured gently. He sat down on the edge of the bed and, after replacing the headcloth, dripped some water onto it.

Becay nodded absently and turned his attention to Harvey. "I'm sorry, Harvey," he said as gently as possible, "but it's high time you got some rest. I don't want two patients in the one house."

"Yes, Harvey," agreed Mary Ellen quickly, putting a hand to the old man's cheek. "Steve and I can stay with him while you get some rest."

"Go on, Harvey," Stephan too urged, going to the door. "I'll go and fix you a hot toddy. It'll help you sleep."

The old man nodded mutely and stumbled out of the room.

Lawrence stood up. "He's asleep again, I think," he whispered. He glanced at his cousin. "If you need anything, just call."

"Go to bed, Larry." Mary Ellen smiled at him. "You've had a long trip."

"I'm not really sleepy," he said simply. "I'll be awake for at least a few more hours."

She nodded gratefully. "Okay. Thanks. If I need anything, I'll call."

Becay put a hand on Lawrence's shoulder. "Come on, Larry," he said, and they left the room together.

Mary Ellen sat down in the chair, taking Harvey's place, watching the slow drip, drip of the intravenous injection, listening to the slow tortured breathing of her cousin and, outside, the clamor of the wind, howling round the house.

chapter
TEN

Stephan rinsed out the tumbler and put it on the drainboard. He leaned his head over the sink and shook it slightly but quickly, as though a sudden cold shiver had rushed over him. Then, abruptly, he turned the cold-water tap on full and plunged his neck beneath the flow.

After a few minutes of that, he straightened, blowing water. He dried his face as well as he could on an inadequate hand towel and went back into the living room. At the foot of the stairs, swaddled in blankets and shawls, sat Lady Fairgrief.

"Stephan," she asked softly. "How is he?"

He sighed and sat down on the stairs. "Not good, Tante Lally," he said, reverting—as had Mary Ellen earlier—to the childhood name.

He fished a crumpled pack of cigarettes out of his jeans pocket, stared at them impatiently for a moment as though wondering from where they had come, and then put them back.

"I thought I heard a crash," she said, half as a statement, half as a question.

The young man snorted. "Harvey fell asleep and then fell off his chair."

"Did you send him to bed?"

Stephan nodded.

"Who's with him now?"

"Mary Ellen. I was on my way back to join her."

"Please," she suddenly implored in a small voice, "take me up there. I want to be with him too."

"Won't Maude kick up a fuss?" He smiled at her.

"She's asleep. I wouldn't get out of my chair last night. It's difficult, but I can still roll myself some."

She leaned forward and tapped him on the knee. "I pinned a note to my pillow," she whispered conspiratorily, and then glared at him malevolently. "Besides which, I do wish you children would remember that Maude is my maid, not my wardress."

"Come on, Tante Lally." He laughed, taking the handles of her chair. "Let's go on up," and, as gently as possible, he thumped the chair up the stairs. When they got to the top, both were mildly surprised to hear the doorbell ring.

"Lord of all the angels," muttered her ladyship venemously. "Who on earth would be calling at this hour?"

Absently, Stephan glanced at his watch. "Not so late after all," he said wryly. "It's only nine-thirty."

"You're joking!"

"Nope!" he replied, kicking on the brake. "That's all. I'll be right back."

Presently voices were heard quietly talking below.

"It was Schmidt," Stephan explained, trotting back up the stairs. "I sent him into the library. Larry and Paul are in there bitching at each other about Larry's hypochondria, which"—he chuckled and once more took the handles of her chair—"naturally enough, Larry does not quite see as hypochondria. Schmidt will mediate between them in his best broken English while oozing diplomatic unction."

"Distressing little man," observed Lady Fairgrief sourly.

"I suppose," agreed Stephan vaguely. He leaned over her to open the door to his father's room. "But he came by just to enquire after Dad. That was nice." He parked the chair at the foot of Bessermann's bed and bending down, kissed Mary Ellen's cheek.

"So was that." She smiled at him and leaned her head against the hand on her shoulder.

Outside the wind had ceased. Whatever storm had threatened had been unraveled by the wind and now the full All Hallows moon shone through the window, an occasional rag of black cloud drifting briefly across its face.

On the bed, Bessermann took a long, rasping breath and slowly opened his eyes. "So," he whispered and weakly attempted to smile. "You, my children, and you, my dearest friend, have come to sit beside me." His glance fell lovingly on Mary Ellen. "I want you to marry Stephan if you still want to."

Mary Ellen gasped in surprise and Stephan moved along the bed to take hold of his father's outstretched hand.

"I have been a fool," the old man continued. He pulled his son's hand so that he perforce had to sit on the mattress. "Help me, Stephan," said Bessermmann simply, his eyes beseeching.

"What do you want, Dad?"

"Help me to *breathe!*" He plucked helplessly at the cocoon of bedclothes as the two young people exchanged a questioning glace.

"I really think you should," said Lady Fairgrief placidly in a normal speaking voice, startlingly loud in the sickroom hush.

They turned to look at her.

"His lungs," she answered their unspoken question. "They are the strongest part of him."

She smiled at Bessermann who was hoarsely muttering, "*Ja! Ja!*"

"Dr. Becay may be a good doctor," she said with a shrewd inflection that immediately cast doubt on the man, "but sometimes, you know, the patient does know best."

Mary Ellen frowned and turned toward Stephan. Her cousin jerked his head toward the far corner of the room, to which they retired for a brief but intense conversation just out of earshot of Bessermann or Lady Fairgrief. Their faces were drawn and all color had gone, leaving them both looking grim and unhappy. Finally, Stephan sighed so hugely that Lady Fairgrief could hear it even from where she sat. He turned back to the bed and nodded to her ladyship while Mary Ellen left the room.

"I think—well, it doesn't matter what I think. If he wants it . . . he wants it," he ended lamely as Mary Ellen returned holding a porcelain basin. Stephan leaned over and hoisted his father into a sitting position. The man's powerful torso was naked. In spite of the thatch of hair on his chest, the obtruding singer's diaphragm—a solid ridge of muscle—was plainly visible beneath the ribs.

"The window." Bessermann gestured. "Air. Fresh air. Too stuffy!" He waved his hand in front of his face.

Mary Ellen glanced at Lady Fairgrief, who nodded fiercely. The wind had died down somewhat, but outdoors it was still very cold indeed. In no time, the room was like an icebox.

Absently, Lady Fairgrief pulled her blankets tighter and tighter about her, but for once, she did not even notice the cold, fascinated and appalled by the herculean struggle on the bed. In spite of the cold, Stephan and Mary Ellen soon had a sheen of perspiration on their faces, and Bessermann was pouring with sweat.

"Cough, Dad! Cough!" Stephan encouraged as he lent his strength to his father's heaving body. Mary Ellen held the basin with one hand and with the other also tried to to help support Bessermann while those mighty lungs fought for air and spewed it out again in harsh, profound, and ragged coughing.

For a moment, Bessermann lay back to rest and tried to catch his breath. Presently, he whispered, a triumphant gleam in his eye, "It's working, Stephan. Already I can feel the breath going lower." Immediately he began to cough again, and again.

Then, suddenly, the door was flung open. Becay, Lawrence, and Schmidt rushed into the room. "What the hell's going on in here?" roared Becay furiously, as he took in the scene, his face ugly with rage.

Startled, Stephan jumped up from the bed while—just as surprised—Mary Ellen whirled about, dropping the basin. Hastily, Lady Fairgrief threw her chair into reverse.

"Larry, Schmidt, see to Rudy," the doctor commanded.

Bessermann protested hoarsely as Schmidt and Lawrence stood at either side of the bed and pulled the pillows supporting him from behind his back. He collapsed back onto the mattress.

"Now, Dad." Lawrence tried to quiet his father's thrashings. He held him down while Schmidt pulled the blankets up round his friend's neck and began to make soothing German noises.

Meanwhile Becay had rounded on Mary Ellen and Stephan, who shrank back from his blazing wrath. "Who the hell do you two think you are?" demanded Becay loudly. "You goddamn singers! You all think you know more than anyone else about the mechanics, don't you? Do you know what pneumonia is? Fever? He's got a goddamn fever, his lungs are filled up, and you open the goddamn window?" He stopped, choked with his outrage. "I'm taking him to the hospital right now. I want my patient away from your goddamn interfering—"

Suddenly, Lady Fairgrief cried out in a frightened

voice, "Dr. Becay!" With a trembling hand she pointed toward her old friend on the bed.

Bessermann's face was purple and congested. His eyes opened briefly in a spasm of terror until a convulsion arched his back and lifted his body off the mattress. When it was over, he half sat up. His eyes went wildly round the room from one person to the other and tried to rasp out something to Stephan. Instead, he collapsed once more and this time lay very still.

There was a long moment of profound silence filled only by the ticking of the clock on the bureau. Then Mary Ellen screamed, "Uncle Rudolf!"

Paul Becay flung himself at the bed to begin the vain labor of trying to force some life back into the clay that had been Rudolf Bessermann while the wind blew through the open window and chased and howled about the room.

chapter ELEVEN

Maude awoke and found the note. Promptly and with immense determination, she set off to find her ladyship to put her in bed where she belonged, thus walking into the general pandemonium.

Schmidt and Becay both knelt on the mattress on either side of the tenor's body as Becay tried to force breath back into lungs that would never breathe again. After only a few minutes, Becay bowed before the inevitable. Getting up from the bed, he shut the window without a word. Mary Ellen and Stephan stood together at the foot of the bed.

"They killed him," Lawrence Bessermann was saying, shaking his woolly head, his eyes on his father's face. He spoke softly, almost to himself, yet in the suddenly still air, his sad voice sounded loud and accusatory. "I came back to be with him and now he's dead."

Becay put a hand on Lawrence's shoulder. "I'm sorry. He's definitely gone."

Mary Ellen buried her face against Stephan's shoulder.

"He asked us to help him," Stephan pleaded with his brother. "We were only doing what he asked us to do."

Lawrence raised his head to look at his brother. He opened his mouth but was forestalled by Becay. "It was still wrong," said the doctor curtly.

"Just a moment!" said Lady Fairgrief commandingly. "I was here. Rudolf tried to empty his lungs out—"

"Do you know what they were risking?" Becay snapped at her.

"No I don't, but I could hear him. He even said it was working before you idiots interfered," she shot back at Becay.

"He's still dead," said Lawrence, his face suddenly flushing.

"Yes, young man," she replied with spirit, "and you may realize someday that to die fighting is a lot better than to lie there and take it."

"I don't think you've got any right—" began Lawrence angrily.

"Gentlemen! Ladies!" It was Schmidt. "This is grotesque. Unseemly. Ve argue in the presence of the dead."

Lady Fairgrief sputtered at the utter fatuity of the remark but, surprisingly, Becay agreed with the little Austrian. "Helmut's right," he said suddenly weary. "There's no one to blame really."

"What?" demanded Lady Fairgrief.

"I don't think there was much hope for poor Rudy anyway," the doctor replied, shaking his head. "Maybe what he wanted didn't hurt him all that much."

"Paul," Mary Ellen asked in a small voice, "why is his face so congested?"

"Probably a heart attack. The effort . . ." He waved a hand and left the sentence unfinished.

"They killed him," Lawrence said to Schmidt and Becay, again in that almost wondering tone. But he was interrupted.

"Go 'way! All of you!"

They all looked round in surprise. Harvey was standing in the doorway, his face a wreck of horror and grief. "Go 'way!" he repeated. "You all stand here trying to blame each other. Go 'way and squabble like the mean things you are.

"I served him all his life," he whispered to no one in particular. "He'll be wanting a bath and laying out. There's someone to sit beside him. And I'm the only one to do it."

Mary Ellen reached a hand out to the old man, but he shrugged her off. "Go 'way!" he repeated more shrilly and flung the door open.

Maude took the handles of the wheelchair; Stephan helped her to take it down the stairs. As they entered the corridor off the living room, which led to her room, Lady Fairgrief heard Lawrence loudly demanding an autopsy.

"Don't be stupid," rejoined Becay with sudden savagery. "I was here and in attendance. It's all absolutely straightforward." Then the bedroom door shut behind her and she heard no more.

"Whew," Maude exclaimed as she turned back the bedclothes. "I never saw such carryings on in my whole life. That old fool Harvey was right for once." She turned to fetch her lady from her chair and instantly stilled her twittering. Lady Fairgrief was weeping as though all the sorrow in the world had been abruptly visited upon her.

"Come on, my lady," she urged with unwonted gentleness. "Let me put you into bed. He was a close friend, an old friend, I know." Carefully and tenderly she picked up the old woman and put her in the bed, pulling the blankets over her.

"I'm not weeping for myself, dearest Maude," her ladyship said after a minute or two had passed. "It's for those poor simple children. All their lives they'll spend wondering now if they didn't perhaps kill their father by inadvertence." She turned a beseeching glance to her maid. "But it was I who told them to do it. Me! I'm such a meddlesome old fool." She turned her head away again and wept.

Maude sat down on the side of the bed and, with a rough kindness, buoyed Lady Fairgrief on her bosom, patting her gently on the back as though she were a child.

For a few minutes, her ladyship did, in fact, seem calmer. Presently, however, her breathing began to grow heavy, deep and more ragged. "My breath, Maude!" she panted. "I can't seem to get my breath."

Alarmed, Maude laid her back upon her pillows. For a moment, it seemed to help.

"I still can't breathe properly. And my pulse!" Indeed, her ladyship felt her blood pounding loudly in her inner ear. "Oh dear, Maude! Get the doctor! Hurry!"

"Try to keep breathing, my lady," Maude pleaded. "Please try!" She turned and plunged out of the room and down the corridor.

In the living room she found Mary Ellen talking quietly into the telephone. "Miss Bessermann! Miss Bessermann!" she called urgently, her shrill voice echoing in the huge room. "Where's Dr. Becay? Quickly!"

Before Mary Ellen had a chance to say anything, however, the doors of the library were thrown open. Becay stood, silhouetted against the fully lit room behind him, his hands clutching each of the doors. "What is it?" he asked sharply.

"My lady! Please! Heart attack, I think."

"Oh Christ, I should have know that this could happen. Mary Ellen, please!" he called. "Get my bag."

"Where is it?" she asked.

"Upstairs," he replied vaguely, grabbing Maude by the arm and hustling her back down the corridor to Lady Fairgrief's suite.

Maude stood back to allow the doctor to enter first. He threw the door open and was bending over her ladyship before the maid could even shut the door behind her.

The minutes crept slowly as he quietly and urgently questioned the old woman, feeling her pulse the while. She did, in fact, seem somewhat less distressed. When

Mary Ellen brought his bag, Becay took out his stethoscope and then turned to Maude and Mary Ellen. "Okay, you two." He smiled at them. "Out! No audiences."

"Come on, Maude," Mary Ellen whispered, taking her elbow.

"My lady?" Maude asked anxiously.

Her ladyship waved a weakly dismissing hand at her maid, who, obviously reluctant, followed Mary Ellen out of the room.

"She'll be all right." Mary Ellen patted Maude on the shoulder. Whatever else she might have been going to say was cut off by an enormous yawn.

Unexpectedly, Maude frowned severely. "Really, Miss Bessermann, you should get to bed. You're quite right, I'm sure. She's had these spells before, after all, and I expect with all—" She cut herself off and ducked her head shyly. "I am sorry about Mr. Bessermann, ma'am."

Mary Ellen tried to smile and failed rather miserably. "Thank you, Maude," she said quietly and again the yawn threatened to erupt. "I have just got to get some sleep." She gestured at Lady Fairgrief's door. "You'll let me know if you need anything?"

"I will, ma'am."

"Good night, Maude." The young woman turned and disappeared down the long, dark corridor.

For a while, Maude stood sentry outside the door, listening to the occasional murmur of voices from within. It became increasingly clear that, at least for the moment, her services would not be needed. "I need a cup of tea," she muttered half aloud to herself and started down the corridor for the kitchen.

All the lamps but one were out in the living room. Faintly through the library door masculine voices buzzed in conversation. Suddenly one voice was raised angrily—she thought it was Lawrence's.

"I'm going to get a goddamn drink and when I come back you better have something better to say." The library door was jerked open.

She slipped quickly into the kitchen. Deciding not to turn on the overhead light, she leaned over the rough deal table to turn on a small lamp, and gasped in surprise. Harvey was seated at the far end of the table. A tall bottle of whisky and a water tumbler half full of neat spirits were in front of him. His face was white and drawn; every now and then a tear leaked out from an eye and trickled down his ravaged cheek.

"Hullo, Maude," he whispered, taking an enormous slug of drink.

"Harvey," she said quietly and took the kettle off the stove. "I felt I needed a cup of tea; my lady was in an awful way."

Harvey snickered drunkenly. "So's my gentleman," he muttered.

She turned her head sharply to look at him but he only took another swallow of booze. She turned the tap on and filled the kettle. By the time she turned around again, his glass had been completely replenished.

"You don't want to drink too much, Harvey," she adominished gently. "Not at your age."

"Aye," he sighed. "At my age." Suddenly his face screwed up into a caricature of an injured child's. "What's to become of me, Maude?" he wailed. "What's to become of me?" He put his head into his hands.

She went round the table and awkwardly tried to comfort him. "Now, Harvey," she soothed. "Harvey! Do you think that after forty years—"

He swung his head up abruptly. "Forty-nine come January," he corrected indistinctly.

"All right then, forty-nine," she agreed, putting the kettle on the burner. "Do you think that after all that time they'll turn you out now?" she asked incredulously.

"G'wan!" She opened a cabinet and took out a cup and saucer.

"They may have no choice," said the old man darkly and swilled yet another mouthful of Scotch.

Maude clucked and rinsed out the teapot.

"No," Harvey insisted. "'Strue. Considering what I *know*." He raised a finger and wagged it at her.

She sat down across from him. "What do you know?" she humored him.

"I know it weren't no 'eart attack wot killed 'im."

"Oh?" she said, raising an eyebrow.

The kettle began to boil. She brewed the tea and brought the pot to the table.

"Harvey," she said, "I do think you should have a cup of tea now. You've had enough of that."

"Leave me alone, woman," he hissed at her and shakily emptied the bottle into his glass. "No, it weren't no 'eart attack."

Maude put her cup down. "Course it weren't, Harvey. It was pneumonia."

He merely belched at her.

"Hmph," she sniffed and poured herself another cup of tea.

"It weren't pneumonia, either," he said offensively.

She made no reply.

"You know what it were, Maude, old girl," he leaned forward and whispered conspiratorily. "He were stung again."

Maude snorted into her cup and put it down. "Harvey Maxwell, you're a drunken fool."

"Struth," he said, wagging his head back and forth and staring at the surface of the table. "It was his face wot tells me. It's just like all the other times he got stung. And Mr. Bessermann, he knowed; didn't he just tell me he knowed a bee when he sees one."

He suddenly looked up, his expression puzzled and

lost. "He always lived before though." Tears began leaking out of his eyes again. "It's not right, I tell you, it's not right."

Maude stood up and swept away the tea things. "What's not right?" she asked disgustedly.

"He wasn't supposed to die before me. I'm too old."

"Oh is that all?" She stood beside the table before taking her departure, arms akimbo. "Well you listen to me, Harvey. You try to learn something from my lady. She's been alone a long, long time now." She opened the kitchen door.

"Put out the light, Maude, there's a good girl," he muttered to her.

She switched off the lamp. The kitchen was once more plunged into darkness, only the moonlight from the window illuminating the vague outlines of things.

"And don't say nothin'," he whispered loudly, setting the echoes to rustling. "It were a sting, I tell you, another sting."

"Stuff and nonsense, Harvey," she said back into the kitchen. "Go to bed." She pulled the door to and began walking down the darkened corridor to the living room. Then, just loud enough to startle her, there was a slight noise behind her. She whirled round, eyes peering into the gloomy corners.

"I thought something moved," she muttered and unaccountably shivered. "Probably just a mouse," she said and hurried back to see her lady and the doctor.

* * *

It was easier to handle now, numb with drink. Easier still to pretend it wasn't so. But the bottle was empty and he could not make up his mind whether to go back and sit with him or to try to negotiate the steps, those wicked steps, to the cellar for more booze.

And had he really seen what he thought he had seen? He didn't know. He didn't want to know.

"But I do," he said aloud rather peevishly, "want another drink."

"Then why don't you get one?" The voice spoke out of the darkness, startling the old man into a loud belch.

The overhead light flicked on.

"No, turn it off," Harvey yelled in a cracked and ragged voice. "It 'urts," he explained more quietly.

"Sorry," the other one said and turned the switch again. He came over to the table and hefted the empty bottle. "Do you want me to get you another bottle, Harvey?"

The old man looked up and saw the expression on the man's face. He tried to sit up straight. "I know I do not need one," he said carefully in a painful attempt at dignity, "but I would, for all that, be most grateful."

The other one smiled and said, "I'll be right back," and, opening the cellar door, he vanished. A soft diffuse radiance welled from the cellar door as the light at the foot of the stairs was switched on. For a brief moment, the sound of glass against glass rose faintly from below. Then the beam of light from the door blinked off and there were footfalls on the wooden steps.

"I couldn't find any more Johnny Walker," he said, and put a quart of gin down on the table.

"I can't mix whisky and gin," Harvey protested indistinctly. "I'll 'ave the greatest 'ead of me life in the morning."

"Mind if I do?"

Without answering, the old man suddenly folded his arms on the table and laid his head down upon them. "'Sfunny," he murmured. "I coulda sworn there was another bottle down there."

For quite an unnecessarily long time, the other busied himself at the refrigerator with ice cubes and bitters. "My, that tastes good," he said loudly, watching the muttering old man, who abruptly sat up, his eyes trying boozily to focus on the younger one.

"Whyn't you fix *me* one?" he asked, querulously contradicting his prior refusal.

"Right." The other smiled and handed him the drink.

He drained it in a few swallows and handed it back. "More," he demanded.

"Are you sure it's wise?"

"Bugger wise!" the old man growled. "That bloody old Maude was in 'ere just now saying the same bloody thing."

"I know," the other said softly. "I heard her."

"But you're right," Harvey suddenly agreed. "I should get back up there. I got to. Poor old Rudy." He rose unsteadily to his feet, legs atremble, hands clutching at the ends of the table.

"Come along," the other said and came around to help. "Let's put you to bed."

"No, no," the old man protested feebly. "I gotta sit up with poor Rudy. It's . . . it's the thing . . . I got to . . ."

"Not tonight, Harvey. You'll fall asleep."

"Oh God, I'm sorry," he suddenly whimpered. "Poor Rudy. Whatever am I going to do?"

"Right now, you're going to bed." Gently, but firmly, the man hoisted Harvey to his feet, guided him unsteadily to the back stairs and slowly on up. Presently, he stood back as the old man stumbled toward his bed and, quickly, he left the room. When, after a few minutes, he returned, Harvey had already passed out.

"Harvey," he said urgently, shaking him by the shoulder. "Wake up."

"Whatsa matter?" the old man muttered and tried to pull the covers up tighter round his head. His eyes remained shut.

"Sit up and drink this."

Blearily, he opened his eyes. The man was holding a glass of milk. "I don' wanna drink no milk. Wanna sleep." He turned over again.

"Come on, Harvey," the man said, shaking him some more. "Come on, sit up. It'll make you feel better in the morning."

"Oh all right." Harvey reluctantly struggled to a sitting position. "Give it 'ere." He took the glass. "God, that's bitter." He made a disgusted face.

"It's the Angostura you had," the other said.

The old man blinked owlishly. "Don' remember no bitters," he said into the glass and finished the milk.

"Go to sleep now, Harvey." The man stood up. "You'll feel a lot better in the morning."

"Morning," the old man sighed heavily. "I shoulda gone back up to 'im. Poor old Rudy . . ." He fell back and soon was snoring lustily.

The younger man sat on the chair at the foot of the bed and crossed his legs. After about ten minutes, the old man's breathing became deeper and more labored, harsh expulsions of air following gasping swallows.

The man continued to watch patiently for another ten minutes. Then, having made quite certain that the old man had stopped breathing altogether, he tiptoed out of the room and shut the door behind him.

chapter
TWELVE

Becay was seated on the edge of Lady Fairgrief's bed, chatting idly and fiddling with his stethoscope. He looked completely worn out. When Maude came in, he dropped the instrument into his bag, snapped the bag shut, and stood up with obvious relief.

"Here she is now," he said, trying to be hearty but clearly only waiting to be gone. "Now, I want you to take it easy for a day or two. Try not to get excited."

"Poor Rudy," her ladyship sighed from the depths of her pillows and blankets.

The doctor merely looked grim. He turned to Maude. "I'll leave you to it. There're some pills over there," he said, pointing toward the bureau.

"Should I stay with her tonight?" asked Maude anxiously.

"It might not be such a bad idea," replied Becay absently, yawning hugely.

"I can make up the sofa." The maid turned to Lady Fairgrief. "If you don't mind, ma'am." She smiled.

Lady Fairgrief waved a hand. "Whatever," she murmured.

"I just gotta get some sleep," Becay muttered, yawning again. He bowed toward Lady Fairgrief, and left the room.

"I am sorry, my lady," said Maude, shutting the door behind the doctor. "I went to the kitchen for a cup of tea."

"It's perfectly all right, Maude," said her ladyship with a slight wave of the hand. "I'm fine now. I've just been thinking."

"What about, my lady?" asked Maude, flinging a blanket over the sofa.

"That it's really very strange about Rudy," the old woman replied, frowning as once more she peered into the darkness gathered in the corners of the room.

Maude straightened up and bent over backwards and then from side to side as she tried to relieve the numerous kinks she was feeling. "Many's thought that tonight," she said vaguely as she continued her arcane calisthenics.

"Oh?"

The maid nodded. "Harvey's down in the kitchen, drunk as can be." She clucked sympathetically. "Though there's no one to blame the poor man this night."

Lady Fairgrief muttered her agreement.

"Aye," Maude went on, sitting down to take off her shoes. "He's put away a whole bottle of Johnny Walker and muttering all kinds of dark things."

"Maude," asked Lady Fairgrief casually. "What happened?"

As she recounted the conversation in the kitchen, Maude moved about the room preparing herself for bed. She did not see, therefore, the sparkling gleam of interest in the old woman's black eyes.

"But, of course, if you ask me, ma'am," Maude concluded, lying down on the couch and flinging another blanket over herself. "Of course, it weren't naught but the spirits speaking." She lay back and put her hands behind her head.

"Quite," agreed her ladyship tersely and said no more.

Silence descended upon them until soon, still lying awake and worrying the darkness to deliver up its meaning, she could hear Maude's regular breathing. There was something there, lying in her mind. But what? And how annoying it was to have something tugging at the ends of your mind like that and not be able to get at it. Perhaps . . . No! Then: that's it! Of course . . .

"Maude!" she cried sharply.

"Yes, my lady." The long-suffering maid sat up almost immediately.

"Bring me the telephone."

"But my lady, it's quite gone four in the morning."

"All the better," replied the redoubtable old woman.

* * *

Across the Jolliston Valley, the telephone beside Miss Worthing's bed rang shrilly. More amused than annoyed, she regarded the offending thing for a longish moment before picking it up.

"Hello," she said dully.

"Matilda!" The reply was peremptory to the point of rudeness.

"Aunt Eulalia," Miss Worthing observed astringently, "your voice hasn't changed in forty years."

"I'm so glad," replied her ladyship dryly. "Did I wake you?"

Her niece chuckled. "My dear aunt," she said, peering nearsightedly at the radium dial beside the bed. "Only you could even think to ask such a question at this hour of the morning. But," she added with another small chuckle, "as it happens, I usually get up around this time."

"Splendid!" exclaimed her ladyship. "Come and get me."

In the background, Miss Worthing heard another voice suddenly raised in expostulation.

"Shut up, Maude!" commanded Lady Fairgrief. "Well, Matilda?"

"Of course," Miss Worthing answered, rather bewildered. "I expect I can be there in about an hour."

"Good," her ladyship muttered and without further ado, hung up.

Miss Worthing stared blankly at the telephone for a moment as though not quite believing the conversation. Finally, with a shrug, a groan, and an immense reluctance, she leaned over and turned on her lamp. The light flooded the immediate surroundings with vague and blurry images as she groped about on the night table for her glasses. Then, with the world once more in focus, she swung her feet out from under the blankets and stood up.

"Oh, Lord!" she exclaimed, dancing from one foot to another, "it's like ice in here this morning."

Hastily, she donned her bedroom slippers and put a heavy dressing gown over her white flannel night dress. In the corridor she paused only to turn the thermostat up to a decent temperature and hurriedly opened the door next to her own.

"Martha!" she called sharply. "Wake up! The most extraordinary thing."

Miss Shaw sat up in bed and flicked on her own bedside lamp. Miss Worthing flinched at the vision of color greeting her still sleep-dulled eyes, for Miss Shaw's sleep attire ran to both the frilly and irridescent.

"I heard the telephone ring," her friend said, trying to smooth the cloud of her white hair into place. "What's wrong?"

"My aunt just called me to come over there and get her."

"No!"

Miss Worthing nodded. "Yes, indeed. No explanations, no waiting. Just come and get her."

"Do you suppose something's happened?" Miss Shaw was struggling into an enormous cerise and gentian dressing gown, during which operation Miss Worthing regarded her friend for a brief moment with almost transcendent despair.

"Martha," she asked, "do you suppose anyone telephones people at four-thirty in the morning if something hasn't happened?"

"There is that," agreed Miss Shaw comfortably as she padded out into the hall. "Get ready, Mattie," she called over her shoulder as she began to waddle rather stiffly down the stairs. "I'll get some coffee on."

Within a scant half hour, the two ladies were in their car, wrapped to the ears in tweed and fur.

"What on earth could have happened?" Miss Shaw mused aloud.

"I do hope she hasn't had a quarrel with Rudolf," said Miss Worthing fervently.

"Nonsense!" Miss Shaw immediately rejoined. "They've been friends for years. Besides which, have you ever known anyone to have a fight with Rudy?"

"Aren't you forgetting," asked Miss Worthing thoughtfully, "that fearful row with Schmidt?"

"Oh well," Miss Shaw observed in acid dismissal, "the opera company!"

"Yes," Miss Worthing sighed her agreement. "Such disagreeable people."

Around them, the roadside fields were beginning to lighten. The patterned rime of the frost dusted the turned soil and covered the leaves of the live oaks with delicate light-refracting lace. A flock of crows rose scolding from the road as they came around a bend and their headlights caught the serene and empty eye of a doe on the shoulder, placidly chewing her cud. She disappeared with a flick of a white tail and the automobile sped on across the valley. Lights came on in farm houses and dogs barked loudly in the pale, clear, crisp fall dawn.

At the entrance of the Bessermann property, they swung through heavy, ornate iron gates and then drove for what seemed like a mile along a beautifully landscaped private road until, rounding a plantation of spruce, they beheld the house, a large and welcoming antebellum-type mansion with a pillared portico all in dazzling white. A large suspended lantern hung in the center of the portico, its light looking bleak and washed out in the new daylight. They pulled up as close to the stairs as possible.

"You wait here, Martha," Miss Worthing said, opening her door. "I shall only be a minute. Maude will probably be coming along, too."

Miss Shaw watched as Miss Worthing used the large antique knocker, and within seconds she had vanished within the house. Presently, the door opened and someone came running toward the car. It took a moment for her to recognize Mary Ellen Bessermann. The poor woman looked exhausted and was inadequately clad for the cold in jeans and a Berkeley sweat shirt. "Please, Miss Shaw," she said through the quickly opened window, her teeth chattering, "Lady Fairgrief asked if you could come in a moment." Puzzled, Miss Shaw followed the girl into the house.

Lady Fairgrief, erect in her wheelchair, was swathed in an enormous chinchilla cape with a large hat of the same fur covering most of her head. "Wonderful." The old woman smiled after Martha had been introduced. "Matilda and I need your help. Maude won't be coming with me.

"Now, Mary Ellen"—she turned to the young woman—"we'll be back as quickly as we can. You can ask Maude to help you with things when she gets up but the poor creature has had rather a long night. Not," she finished sourly as she pulled her cape around her, "that you haven't either."

"All right, Tante Lally." The girl bent over and kissed

the old woman's cheek. "Hurry back. Thank you very much for coming over," Mary Ellen continued to Miss Worthing as she opened the door for them.

"Martha," Miss Worthing instructed, stooping to grasp the foot platforms, "you take the handles. I can get these."

"You'll have to," Miss Shaw observed with a chuckle. "I can't bend like that."

"I can do it, Miss Worthing," Mary Ellen volunteered.

"No problem, dear." Miss Worthing smiled up at her and then grunted as she lifted the chair down the three steps to the walkway. "We've got to get used to doing it."

Lady Fairgrief was placed safely into the back seat of the automobile. Mary Ellen, hugging herself, stood looking at her indecisively, her pale skin mottled with the cold.

"Go back in," commanded her ladyship through the window. "I promise you we won't be long."

Mary Ellen nodded dumbly and, turning about, trotted back up the stairs and into the house. Miss Shaw started the engine.

"Now." Miss Worthing twisted around in the front seat to face her ancient relative, her blue eyes enormous and severe. "What is this all about?"

Lady Fairgrief began to talk.

* * *

Sometime later, in the living room of Miss Worthing and Miss Shaw's home, Lady Fairgrief lay back on the sofa to which she had been moved, looking shrunken and uncomfortable in a heavy brown-tweed suit, ecrue silk clasped at the throat with a fabulous baroque. The chinchilla was thrown casually at the end of the sofa. She picked up a cup from the end table and took a long sip.

Miss Worthing, looking much as she had in earlier

years—severely tailored in heather tweed and Cuban heels—stood silently at the window, her face blank of expression. Miss Shaw, in turn, gazed at her friend with a speculative gleam in her eye.

Her ladyship grimaced and, with a small clatter, put the cup back down. "Tepid," she muttered, half to herself.

Miss Shaw grinned. "Sorry. I should have made some tea before this," she said and hoisted herself to her feet, the sudden sharpness of the electric-blue rayon blouse she wore so incongruously with her swaths of gray wool causing her ladyship to blink and look away.

"Lovely," commented Lady Fairgrief ambiguously and then gestured toward her niece. "Does she often go off like that?"

"Often," replied Miss Shaw calmly, stacking dirty breakfast plates and coffee cups onto a tray. "It's a result of her profession."

Her ladyship raised an inquiring eyebrow.

"We were both court reporters. You knew that?" Miss Shaw asked. The old woman nodded. "Well, to do the job properly, you have to concentrate very, very intently."

"Why?"

"Because you have to listen for sounds that make up the words being blathered, rather than the words themselves. It's all basic shorthand technique, but I do remember once, oh years ago, some silly nit of a lawyer was winding up a particularly enthusiastic peroration when he suddenly noticed poor Mattie's rather blank expression. He remarked that she looked like a total idiot."

"Such impertinence!" her ladyship exclaimed.

"To be sure," Miss Shaw agreed and then chuckled. "Nevertheless, Mattie stoutly maintains she never noticed the remark until she was transcribing her notes."

"I had no idea."

"I never used it myself except for reporting," Miss Shaw said, waddling off toward the kitchen. "But she always says it's made all the difference to what she modestly refers to as her intellectual life."

"She was a formidable youngster," Lady Fairgrief observed, mostly to herself, for Miss Shaw had already vanished through the dining room into the kitchen, where she could be heard rattling about.

After a few minutes, Miss Worthing turned back from contemplating the view from the window. "Where's Martha?" she asked.

"In the kitchen making tea," her aunt replied. "Well?"

Miss Worthing took a deep breath and let it all out in a long, slow sigh. "I'm very much afraid you may be right. Horrible! And no autopsy?"

"No. I might have hoped for one but I heard Lawrence request one and Dr. Becay said there wasn't any need for it."

"I see. Could you suggest it to Mary Ellen?"

"I expect I could. But it would have to be Stephan and Lawrence's decision. They are his sons, you know. And if they were consulted, it might, well, warn whoever it is that someone is suspicious."

"Nevertheless, something might be found."

"Or nothing, Matilda. I think we must tread very carefully."

Miss Worthing sighed and nodded. "You're quite right, of course. But without that autopsy, I think it's going to be the very dickens to prove."

"There are also," her ladyship added, "quite a distressing number of loose ends."

"Precisely," Miss Worthing said and, sitting down, winked solemnly at her aunt. "Do you suppose, dearest Aunt Eulalia," she said in a voice carefully bland, "that Miss Bessermann could use some help with the . . ." She hesitated briefly. ". . . with the arrangements."

"I did mention to Mary Ellen," Lady Fairgrief replied, her voice as carefully controlled as that of her niece, "that you'd want to do your Christian duty."

Miss Worthing's glance met that of her aunt and for a moment they both chuckled silently. Miss Worthing, however, sobered quickly. "Yes, there it is. Duty," she observed in a quiet voice. "But in more than one sense."

At this juncture, Miss Shaw surged forth from the dining room, a truly enormous brown earthenware teapot in hand. "I thought we could use lots of tea," she said cheerily. "Especially if we've got planning to do."

Miss Worthing fetched clean cups from the dining room. "We can and we do," she called back into the living room. "And Aunt Eulalia and I had better put you into the picture."

"What picture?" Miss Shaw asked.

"Pour us a cup of tea, Martha," said Lady Fairgrief querulously, "and we'll tell you."

"Very well." Miss Shaw chuckled ponderously and handed filled cups round. "Nice and hot, too."

Lady Fairgrief sipped the steaming tea noisily and happily.

"Aunt Eulalia," Miss Worthing began, after taking a good swallow of her own tea, "has kindly volunteered us to Mary Ellen to 'help out'."

"Meanwhile"—Miss Shaw grinned broadly—"getting us on the premises to snoop."

"Exactly," concurred her ladyship. "Poor Mary Ellen has had virtually no sleep in forty-eight hours. Harvey is going to be practically useless—judging," she added in a dry aside, "from what Maude told me. Maude herself is probably out like a light for the next sixteen hours, and I just had to talk to someone. So naturally," she concluded, "I suggested you and Matilda would want to be good neighbors."

"I think we would want to be so in any case." Miss

Worthing suddenly laughed. "But knowing what we know now, we can get on the scene with a perfectly justifiable excuse."

"Besides," Lady Fairgrief concluded, "whoever would suspect a trio of old ladies?"

"Oh, I don't know about that," Miss Shaw demurred. "Mattie's become quite famous around Jolliston."

"Rudolf did mention something about you being shot," remarked Lady Fairgrief indignantly. "Do you mean you go in for this kind of thing often?"

"Not what you'd call often, Aunt Eulalia. Do be fair." Miss Worthing blushed slightly. "But, you know, even here in our valley, some rather awful things have happened. Besides," she concluded irrelevantly, "I was only grazed by a pistol shot."

"Mattie's definitely got a way with a crook," Miss Shaw suddenly interjected with cheerful vulgarity.

"Well, I never," her ladyship muttered and slurped tea.

Abruptly, Miss Worthing got to her feet. "Now you try to get some rest, Aunt Eulalia." She moved the teapot within reach of the sofa. "We have to clean up and pack a few things. If you need anything, holler. We'll be ready to go in half an hour. Try to rest." She arranged the chinchilla over the old woman's recumbent body.

"Come, Martha." She took the arm of her friend. "There's work to be done."

chapter
THIRTEEN

The three ladies were silent as they drove back to Bessermann's house, partly because there was so little left to say and partly because the balmy weather had returned. Like a relationship in music of minor key to major was the way Lady Fairgrief found herself thinking about it. For the moment she was content to imagine that the world never changed, that the warm darts of breeze moving the naked branches of the trees along the way were zephyrs that had blown yesterday and would blow again tomorrow.

The mood, however, was not destined to last.

"That's Sam Marshall's car," Miss Worthing exclaimed as they came to a halt before the house.

"Who is Sam Marshall?" her ladyship enquired.

"He's the sheriff," Miss Shaw explained. "Do you suppose," she asked Miss Worthing, "that someone else has figured out what's going on?"

Miss Worthing and Miss Shaw helped Lady Fairgrief out of the back seat and into her chair. As they approached the house, the front door opened and Mary Ellen and Sam Marshall, hat in hand, emerged.

"Well now, you be sure to call us if there's anything we can do, ma'am," Marshall, a large man gone to belly and dewlap, was saying, shrugging himself into a voluminous sheepskin coat. "Sure am sorry."

He stuck his hand out. Mary Ellen shook it awkwardly and caught sight of the returning women. "Oh God, I'm glad you're back," she called out.

The sheriff put his hat on and turned to see to whom she was speaking. He frowned ever so slightly and pushed his hat up as he scratched his forehead. "Why hello there, Miss Worthing," he said, half in greeting, half in question. "How are you doing?"

"I'm just fine, Sam," replied Miss Worthing quietly, "though it is a sad day."

The man gazed at her speculatively for a long moment. "What you doin' here, ma'am?" he finally asked, shoving his hands into the pockets of his jacket.

"Why, Sam," she protested mildly, and gathered the fur collar of her coat closer round her throat, "doing my Christian duty to a neighbor."

Marshall turned a quizzical look on Miss Shaw, who opened her blue eyes with a look of surprised innocence and nodded agreement, a captious feather on her hat bobbing back and forth wildly as she did so.

Finally, he frowned and glanced at Lady Fairgrief, beside whose chair Mary Ellen was crouched, whispering intently. "You must be that Lady Fairgrief," he said almost accusingly.

"I am," she replied calmly, placing a hand on Mary Ellen's arm where it rested on her knee. "I am very sorry you have had to come out here."

The sheriff shrugged. "Got to with a suicide."

Miss Worthing and Miss Shaw gasped. "Suicide!" Miss Worthing exclaimed after catching her breath. Her eyes slewed round to meet Lady Fairgrief's intense glare.

"Yup," Marshall continued, considering her coldly. "The old servant did hisself in this morning. 'Sokay though."

Miss Worthing and Lady Fairgrief continued to regard each other as though trying to make some important telepathic exchange.

"Anything you want to talk to me about, Miss Worthing?" the sheriff interrupted, glancing from one to the other.

Miss Worthing quickly turned her attention back to Marshall and switched on a smile. "No," she said, shaking her head, "thank you, though, Sam."

The man drew breath as though he were going to say something, thought better of it, and shrugged. "Well then, good day to you all." He tipped his hat. "Sorry about your uncle, Miss Bessermann," he said gently, and, after one more frown in Miss Worthing's direction, he drove off in the official blue-and-tan car.

"Now what's this about a suicide?" Miss Worthing immediately demanded of Mary Ellen.

"It's true," the younger woman replied, her voice trembling with cold—she still wore only the jeans and tattered sweatshirt she had worn earlier. "I went into his bedroom this morning and found his . . ." Her voice rose. ". . . found his . . ."

"Mary Ellen!" Lady Fairgrief suddenly took charge. "It's cold out here."

"I'm sorry, Tante Lally." Mary Ellen sobered instantly. "Let's go in."

In the monstrous living room, a log fire was burning cheerfully if ineffectually on the grate, in front of which Lady Fairgrief indicated she should be parked.

"Where's the kitchen, dear?" Miss Shaw asked, removing her hat, overcoat, and gloves and tossing them on a chair. "I'll rustle up something warming."

Mary Ellen showed her and then returned and all but fell into a large chair.

"Now tell us what happened," Miss Worthing instructed gently, shedding her own overcoat and helping Lady Fairgrief out of her cape.

Mary Ellen made a vague gesture with her hands and then clenched her fists tightly. "I went to get him this morning. I heard he had got really plastered last night and I thought I would just tell him to stay in bed." She paused a moment, her face a rigid mask. "He was lying on his side with all the blankets pulled up around him like—like a child who doesn't want to get up. I was just going to go back out when I realized he wasn't snoring. He always snored so loud. . . ."

Again, she took a moment to get a grip on herself.

"I—I reached out a hand to shake him by the shoulder and he just rolled over, staring at the ceiling." She glanced up and looked back and forth from Lady Fairgrief to Miss Worthing.

"I screamed. A lot. Everyone came running from all over the house. Paul examined him quickly . . ."

"That's Paul Becay," Lady Fairgrief murmured to Miss Worthing.

". . . and he confirmed that he was dead," Mary Ellen concluded.

"Did he say how?" Miss Worthing asked, still holding her coat and the chinchilla.

Mary Ellen nodded and then seemed to notice the coats for the first time. She got up, swept Miss Shaw's wraps from the chair, took Miss Worthing and Lady Fairgrief's wraps, and opened a closet beneath the stairs.

"There was a glass of milk next to the bed. There was still something left in it. Paul tasted it and . . . and . . . Oh God, poor old Harvey." Tears began to shimmer in her eyes as she hung the coats on hangers and disappeared within.

"Did he ever take drugs, my dear?" Miss Worthing again asked quietly.

"We all did on occasion." Mary Ellen's reply was somewhat muffled. "We were never very careful about them, either."

"Why is that?"

"Well, we're all 'artistic,'" she replied from the depths. "We get worked up over a lesson, a rehearsal, a performance. All of us took pills sometimes, to sleep or just to level out."

"Do you know what Harvey took last night?" Mary Ellen emerged shaking her head.

"Really?" Miss Worthing's eyebrows shot up.

"Why should I?" Mary Ellen frowned.

"No real reason," Miss Worthing replied with a casual wave. "It just seems odd that you would keep that sort of thing about without some kinds of precaution."

"Why?" Mary Ellen reiterated more sharply. "We are all adults in this house."

"Was what you all took a barbiturate or a calmative, like Valium?"

"I took, take Valium," the younger woman said shortly. "What is all this?"

Fortunately, Miss Shaw chose this moment to waddle into view pushing a tea trolley. Miss Worthing stood up. "Why here's Martha with tea!" she said loudly, rather obviously changing the subject.

"I'm sorry, Miss Worthing." Mary Ellen also stood up and laid a hand on Miss Worthing's arm. "It really is awfully nice of you to come over and try to help."

"Why don't you take a nice long nap," Lady Fairgrief suddenly suggested without taking her eyes from the fire, which she had watched continuously throughout the discussion. "You've been up and about for the lion's share of two and a half days."

Mary Ellen's shoulders slumped. "I know." Again tears were troubling her voice. "But I couldn't sleep. I kept remembering poor Uncle Rudolf and now . . ."

"Now, now, dear." Miss Shaw patted her shoulder and said comfortingly, "Go get yourself a good stiff drink and then have a solid nap. There's plenty out there for me to fix a lovely supper for later on and we're here to help as much as we can."

"You know." Mary Ellen suddenly smiled at them.

"Until today, I thought neighbors like you were a thing out of someone's romantic imagination. I'm glad I was wrong."

She went toward the stairs. "I don't really need a drink, I think," she added. "I'll just go to bed."

"Nonsense," Miss Worthing said firmly. "Martha will bring a toddy up to your room directly."

Miss Shaw nodded massively.

"You're both very kind, and thank you, Tante Lally, for bringing them." Again, she turned to go.

"One more thing, Mary Ellen?" said Miss Worthing.

"Yes?"

"I gather that Dr. Becay is staying with you."

Mary Ellen nodded. "He used to—that is, Uncle Rudy used to ask him to stay quite often."

"Doesn't he have his own establishment?" asked Lady Fairgrief.

"Of course," Mary Ellen said and then flushed slightly. "But he was over here a lot, what with"—she hesitated only slightly—"one thing and another and he and Helmut are kind of buddies, too. But you knew that, Miss Worthing, didn't you?"

"I suppose now that you mention it, they have been pretty thick lately," Miss Worthing replied and then asked, "Is Herr Schmidt staying with you, too?"

"I think Larry asked him to come over, too. And I guess I'm glad. They've both been a real help with," she took a breath and finished, "the arrangements."

"Go on to bed, Mary Ellen," commanded her ladyship. "I've good reason to be grateful for Dr. Becay's presence here myself."

For a long moment, after Mary Ellen had vanished, Miss Worthing and Miss Shaw sat staring at one another while Lady Fairgrief returned to brooding into the fireplace, saying nothing. Finally, Miss Worthing pursed her mouth and shook her head decisively. "Aunt Eulalia," she said crisply, "you've got to send Maude away."

Lady Fairgrief sighed. "I know." She told them where her maid was likely to be found and Miss Worthing set off to get her.

"I'll be seeing to dinner," Miss Shaw muttered vaguely and headed back toward the kitchen.

"Don't forget Mary Ellen's toddy," her ladyship called after her.

"No fear." Miss Shaw chuckled as she too vanished down the hall.

Soon, from the opposite corridor, Miss Worthing appeared with Maude, the latter wrapped in a dressing gown that looked like a relic of World War II, still rubbing the sleep from her eyes, her grizzled gray hair all anyhow.

"Yes, your ladyship." She yawned mightily.

"Maude, wake up!" the old woman snapped.

Maude's eyebrows came together in a frown and she peered blearily at her employer. "Mmmph?" she enquired.

"You're going to San Francisco for a few days."

"Are we leaving Mr. Bessermann's before the funeral?" Maude asked in surprise. "Why I would've thought that we—"

"Not we," her ladyship interrupted. "You. I'm staying here."

"Then I'll do no such thing," Maude retorted, instantly more alert. "My place is here with you—unless you're giving me the sack?" she asked in sudden alarm.

"Of course not." Lady Fairgrief scowled.

"Well then, I ain't going." She folded her arms and tried, with uncommon success, to look like Gibraltar.

"Maude," the old woman said in an unexpectedly quiet voice and patted the broad arm of the chair beside which she sat. "Sit down here, beside me. I have to tell you something."

Blinking in surprise, Maude did as she was told, sitting on the very edge of the cushions.

"My niece here and I," her ladyship began, sitting forward in her chair and speaking very quietly, "we are very concerned about your well-being."

"What's my well-being got to do with leaving you?"

"Will you shut up and listen," Lady Fairgrief groused loudly. "We can't tell you right away, but you have got to get out of this house." She slapped the arm of Maude's chair briskly. "Now."

Maude's mouth began to tighten. Hastily, Miss Worthing sat down next to the maid on the other arm of her chair. "Please, Maude, do it," she urged. "Miss Shaw will drive you to a very nice hotel where we stay ourselves when we're in San Francisco. Please, my dear! There's no telling what the danger might be."

"Danger?" Maude's head shot up, her face suddenly pale.

"Matilda, must you put your foot in it?" Lady Fairgrief snapped. She returned her attentions to her maid. "There is, of course, the possibility that there's no such thing."

"And you know," Miss Worthing interrupted, struggling to keep a grin off her face, "if you're worried about Lady Fairgrief, I can be a lady's maid for a few days. I'm rather used to impossible chores."

Lady Fairgrief glared furiously at Miss Worthing before continuing with Maude. "Anyway, Maude, my dear," she said after harrumphing once or twice, "we've been together these thirty-five years. I don't want anything to happen to you."

"Why, my lady," Maude said, touched, "that's the nicest thing you ever said to me."

"Well, it's true," her ladyship grumbled. "Now go to San Francisco!" she commanded and relaxed back into her chair.

"Very well, ma'am," Maude acquiesced suddenly.

Miss Shaw emerged from the direction of the kitchen with a steaming tumbler on a tray. "I'm going up to Mary

Ellen's room now," she said by way of explanation and then nodded in Maude's direction.

"Yes," Miss Worthing said, "she's going."

"Thank the Lord," Miss Shaw rejoined. "I'll take her to town when I come down."

Presently, she lumbered back down the stairs and vanished into the closet. "There's a pot roast on, and everything's more or less ready," she said as she emerged, shuffling back into her furs. "You'll have to peel the veggies, though, and do remember not to add them until an hour before serving. And please, remember wines should be uncorked—"

"Martha," said Miss Worthing shortly, "I do know how to cook too, you know."

"Pies and cookies and puff pastry do not make a good cook," replied Miss Shaw crushingly as she and Maude departed.

"You don't suppose, my dear Matilda," Lady Fairgrief said after they had gone, "that we are being silly?" The question was put rather diffidently.

"You know, Aunt Eulalia," Miss Worthing said after a long moment's consideration, "we may very well be. Nevertheless, I doubt it."

They sat in silence, the ancient crone in her wheelchair, the younger (though by no means young) woman in the chair Maude had vacated. They sat side by side staring at the dull-red gray-ash-covered embers that were all that remained now of the fire.

"No," Miss Worthing continued in a sorrowful tone, "there's so much anger, so much hate, so much potential for violence in the world that I'm only surprised it doesn't erupt more often than it does."

A brief smile flickered across Lady Fairgrief's wise old features. "There, there, Matilda," she said with almost Olympian serenity. "You and I've been around quite long enough to know that one must simply learn to deal with wickedness and then get on it with it. Which is what we have to do here."

"I know, Aunt Eulalia, I know." Her niece sighed and stood up. "But sometimes I do rather wish that Adam and Eve had had a little more consideration for their offspring."

Lady Fairgrief laughed. "Well, they didn't, you know. And now we've got to pick up the pieces."

"Yes, well . . ." Miss Worthing suddenly drew in an enormous breath and sighed again. "In regard to this particular jigsaw puzzle, here's what I want you to do this afternoon."

chapter

FOURTEEN

Some hours later, the rich aroma of simmering pot roast was billowing beautifully and, very softly, Miss Worthing was muttering balefully to herself as she worked at the kitchen table, more or less peeling vegetables. She looked up to see Mary Ellen coming down the back stairs dressed in khaki culottes and another of the seemingly innumerable white Oxford cloth men's dress shirts she possessed. She appeared rested, but her face was still taut and drawn from fatigue and grief.

"Hello, dear," Miss Worthing said gently. "Feeling better?"

"Somewhat." Mary Ellen yawned. "Is there any coffee?"

Miss Worthing gestured toward the stove with her paring knife. "I thought you'd probably want some."

Mary Ellen smiled at the older woman gratefully as she poured herself coffee. She drank it slowly, staring out the window of the back door. When she was through, she poured herself another and glanced toward Miss Worthing wrestling (if the truth be known) less than adequately with the pile of carrots, turnips, and potatoes. The older woman—her hair afrizzle and a scowl of irritation on her expressive face—was the picture of frustration.

After a moment, Mary Ellen's shoulders began to shake with soundless mirth. Finally she clucked, "You are really too much. Here." She put the coffee cup down and took the knife from Miss Worthing. "Let me."

"I don't mind," Miss Worthing protested.

"I'm sure you don't," Mary Ellen rejoined with a grin, "but you're driving me wild with that knife and besides"—a frown flickered across her face—"it's better to be doing something."

Miss Worthing relinquished the pile of vegetables and stood up. Cautiously, she lifted the top of the soup kettle on the stove and sniffed appreciatively. "My, that smells good," she murmured.

"It certainly does," Mary Ellen agreed, closing her eyes and inhaling. "What is it?"

"Pot roast. Martha is talented," Miss Worthing responded vaguely as she peered into the cloudy depth of the pot.

Mary Ellen arched an eyebrow. "But she was only here a matter of minutes," she protested.

"Oh?" Miss Worthing turned round and looked at her companion. "And how do you know?"

"I saw her and Maude drive away."

Miss Worthing gave a thoughtful stir to the *mirepoix*, added a few drops of wine, and stirred some more. "Well, my dear," she finally said, "I don't think . . . I mean, would you mind not saying anything about it right away, hmmm?"

"Why, is something wrong?"

Miss Worthing hesitated again before replying. "No, not exactly . . ." she began, covering the pot. Suddenly, she heard the knife bounce off the wall. Startled, she whirled around to see Mary Ellen hugging her breasts with one arm and the other covering her face.

"I'm sorry," Mary Ellen finally blurted out when the spasm of anger or grief had passed. "It just . . . It *all* just hit me." She took a few deep breaths and let them out in long, shuddering sighs. "I'll be all right now, thank you," she said eventually as Miss Worthing handed her a paper towel.

The older woman picked up the knife and washed it off in the sink.

"Thank you," Mary Ellen repeated, taking the knife and another deep breath. "I'm sorry," she said after a moment and with a ring in her voice, "there is something wrong." It was a statement and there would be no fudging the issue.

Miss Worthing sat across the table from the younger woman and tried to think very rapidly. It was simply a question of whom to trust. Could she trust this woman? It seemed so very unlikely that she could be involved in such a calculated and wicked thing. But many people seem unlikely to be involved in wickedness, and look at them all.

But—and how very heavily this weighed—they just had to have an ally in this house. Lady Fairgrief was long past this kind of adventure and neither she nor Miss Shaw were exactly chipper young things, either.

All in all, wishing that she had more data, and even more desirous of the time to work that data out when she got it, she took a long breath and got herself a cup of coffee. "Mary Ellen," she said quietly, "my aunt thinks, and I'm afraid I rather have to agree with her, that your father, your uncle, rather—"

"He was my cousin, but he was like a father to me."

"To be sure. Well, your cousin's death was, I'm afraid, distinctly . . ." She paused reflectively for a long moment as though searching intently for precisely the right word. She gave up the struggle. "Distinctly odd."

Mary Ellen's hand fell with a thump to the table in front of her. "So even Tante Lally," she said in a hoarse whisper, her eyes avoiding contact with Miss Worthing's, "thinks that Steve and I . . ."

Miss Worthing could think of absolutely nothing to say because there *was* nothing to say. The possibility unquestionably existed. . . .

Mary Ellen raised a bewildered and appalled countenance to Miss Worthing. "No," she began on a rising note. "No!" she fairly shouted and stood up wildly.

"Mary Ellen," Miss Worthing commanded in a grave voice. "Sit down."

Mary Ellen did not reply. She just stood there, staring at the older woman, her head moving in little jerks from side to side, an expression almost of loathing on her face.

"Do *you?*" she challenged in a suddenly ringing voice. "Do *you* think it's true?"

At which point, Miss Worthing made an abrupt and wholly irrational decision. "No," she replied, glancing down at her hands folded around the coffee mug and wondering what on earth she was doing. "No, my dear, I do not."

"Then why didn't you say so?"

"You and Steve were quite miraculously stupid," replied Miss Worthing bluntly.

"He had pneumonia," Mary Ellen countered.

"I know, and can't you see that that is precisely what makes the whole thing stink to high heaven?"

"But Steve and I didn't do anything he didn't want done!" Mary Ellen continued to protest, and in the process followed, to Miss Worthing's intense relief, an irrelevant tangent.

"I know that perfectly well, Mary Ellen," replied Miss Worthing crisply. "Aunt Eulalia was right there with you."

"Then why . . . ?"

"Listen, Mary Ellen." The older woman leaned forward and gestured energetically with an upturned hand. "We have this rather . . . odd," she took up the word again, "odd situation, all of which is more and more unlikely under any examination whatsoever. No, I am *not* going to tell you our reasoning yet. But can't you see that you and Stephan did, in fact, have the most patently obvious motive for murdering your cousin?"

There! Miss Worthing sighed. The word itself has been spoken. And now she watched—unhappy with herself— as the implications of what they had just been discussing were slowly manifested to the younger woman's mind.

It was always a source of amazement to her, too, how often people persist in willful blindness, and then wake up horrified, as though the kind of poisonous direction in which things had been heading had never occurred to them. That in spite of logic, of proof, in spite of the most incontrovertible evidence staring them in the face, they nonetheless grow still and appalled at the word being put to it—as though in this disagreeable chore of descrying villainy alone, humankind still possessed the power of Adam to create the reality by naming the act.

"Murder!" Mary Ellen whispered, her eyes wide. "I don't see how it's possible."

"Don't you?" Miss Worthing asked and stood up. "Perhaps that's just as well for now. But you can, if you are so inclined, help us."

"How?"

"We have to continue to pretend that the actions undertaken by you and Stephen were, albeit at his insistence, the proximate cause of your cousin's death. That there may in fact be a measure of culpability in those actions we cannot for a moment ignore." Miss Worthing held up a hand to forestall comment. "Nevertheless, there are a few other ideas that have occurred both to my aunt and to me. It is imperative that these be examined sensibly."

This extremely formal speech seemed strangely to comfort the young woman. She shook her head, held it high, and replied in much the same manner. "I entirely agree, I only ask that I . . ." Her voice faltered. "I would like to tell Steve," she finished quite simply.

"That, I'm afraid, is out of the question," said Miss Worthing sharply, and then unexpectedly smiled. "At least, I hope you'll keep this under your hat."

After a moment, Mary Ellen nodded her agreement. "It's horrible," she whispered.

"It always is, my dear," Miss Worthing replied more gently.

"But let's go to the police." Mary Ellen suddenly jerked her head up. "After all, it can only be one of . . ."

Miss Worthing breathed a brief prayer for patience. "Under other circumstances, that would, of course, be the best idea. Under these, it's a terrible one."

"Why?"

"Because if we got a herd of flat-footed policemen in here right now, even supposing they would listen to the vagaries of a mob of old women—and yes, my dear, that is exactly what they would think of us—any chance of garnering enough information to find out what really happened would in all likelihood be lost forever. Judging from what little we do know, this whole taradiddle was done very cleverly indeed."

For a few interminable moments, Mary Ellen said nothing. She sat very still and stared at her hands clasped on the table in front of her, her left forefinger absently rubbing the right.

What was she thinking, Miss Worthing wondered, hoping that her intuition had been right. Was Mary Ellen, too, going back over the events of the preceding days and finding all not, perhaps, as it had seemed at the time?

"Okay," whispered Mary Ellen presently. "I'll be all right." Then, suddenly, she smiled. "You know, I don't know if you're right or not . . ."

"And no more do we," muttered Miss Worthing beneath her breath.

". . . but if you are, I somehow feel better about Uncle Rudy if we can do something about it. Is there anything I can do now?"

"Indeed there is," Miss Worthing began after a moment's thought. "First of all, I want you to describe to me everyone who was in the house and what they did all day long the day your cousin got sick."

"Do you mean from the time the pneumonia started?"

"No, from the time he first took ill."

"In other words, when he was stung."

Miss Worthing nodded.

"I can't seem to think." Mary Ellen frowned. "Paul—Dr. Becay was here most of the time. He . . ." She blushed. "He's been spending a lot of time here lately."

"I know about Paul Becay's 'attentions,' shall we call them?" Miss Worthing smiled.

"Your aunt?" Mary Ellen asked wryly and, when Miss Worthing nodded, added, "She doesn't miss much, does she?"

Miss Worthing gestured for her to continue.

"Helmut was here, of course . . ."

"Was he the one to suggest the singing?"

"Yes."

"And furthermore he gathered the posy from which the . . . the insect, we'll call it, crawled forth."

"Yes," Mary Ellen agreed, frowning, "but what does all this have to do—"

"I don't know yet," Miss Worthing interrupted. "I'm still just gathering data."

"And that's all—unless you count poor Harvey."

"What about your cousin?"

"Steve?"

"No, Lawrence."

"But he didn't get here until after Uncle Rudolf already had pneumonia."

"When did he come?"

"I don't remember. Steve fetched him from the airport. We called him up and told him Uncle Rudolf had been stung."

"When was this?"

"Right after the stinging. Paul suggested it. Uncle Rudolf was already out of danger, but Paul thought it would be a good time to get them back together again, and Larry seemed pleased enough to be home."

"Where was he?"

"In Las Vegas."

"I dare say he would be glad to get home," Miss Worthing commented dryly.

The catechism went on for another quarter hour, until Miss Worthing, utterly at sea in a mass of unconnected facts, stood up, shaking her head.

"Well, dear," she sighed, "if you think of anything else—Wait a minute! There was a nurse, wasn't there?"

"Miss Martinez. We'd had her before."

"Through the registry?"

"Yes."

"I think that will be all for now, my dear. Thank you for your help."

"Help!" Mary Ellen snorted. "How have I helped?"

Miss Worthing laughed. "I'm quite sure I don't know. I'm afraid I have one of those dreadfully disorganized minds that shuffles all the interesting bits away and then mulls over them until something yells, 'Bingo!'"

"'Bingo!'" repeated Mary Ellen unhappily, "and one of us is a murderer."

"Do you have the number of the registry?" Miss Worthing asked rather sharply.

Mary Ellen's head snapped up. "Of course." She gestured with the paring knife. "It should be there beside the telephone. We used to . . ." Her voice suddenly trembled again. "We had to use it quite often."

Miss Worthing memorized the number and went to the swinging door. "I'll call from the living room. I noticed another phone in there."

"What should I do?" asked Mary Ellen almost plaintively.

"Finish peeling those miserable vegetables and try to recall everything about what went on here, day before last."

chapter
FIFTEEN

Stephan and Lady Fairgrief sat in a long, companionable silence in the desolation of the rose garden, her ladyship thoroughly bundled up inside a cocoon of shawls and lap rugs, Stephan huddling against the chill inside a thick sheepskin jacket. He stared out across the valley, his face drawn and lean as though he had lost considerable weight. His coloring was high and mottled. He looked, in fact, about to drop.

Did he suspect, she wondered. Or did he know? Oh Lord, she prayed, let it not be the children. But, she said stalwartly to herself, she had been right there with them. But *was* she right, her conscience asked for perhaps the hundredth time. Of course, there were those other things . . .

Poor Rudy! Was there no way we could have saved you?

And the voice to which she had long grown accustomed to listen attentively quietly told her, "No."

"I first met him in Vienna," she said softly.

Stephan said nothing, but something in his attitude told her he was listening.

"It was such a long time ago . . . although not really. Between the wars? I think so. It must have been. I can't remember," she said, vexed with her uncertain memory. "He was so flattered when Arthur took an interest in his career, not knowing, of course, how very flattered Arthur felt in knowing him."

"They were great friends, weren't they?"

She nodded in her blankets, suddenly not quite trusting her voice and thoroughly detesting the task Matilda had assigned her.

"He never planned to be a singer," Stephan said suddenly. He laughed quietly. "I guess it runs in the family."

"Mary Ellen?"

"Yes," he replied. "In a lot of ways, she's a lot like Dad."

"At least she's not a budding scientist," she observed with some asperity. She had lived too long not to perceive that the cult of progress was not without drawbacks.

Stephan cast an affectionate glance at her across the gulf of years between them and then turned back to regarding the valley spread out below.

"What you're thinking isn't true at all, you know. Dad always said his scientific training and the basic scientific approach is what made him a great artist."

"How so?" her ladyship asked with disbelief.

"He analyzed everything. He was always inquiring into the whys and the hows. He tried to teach us to be that way, too. That's why"—he shook his head—"I'm not too sure . . ."

She held her breath for an excited moment. He'd guessed. He too saw its unlikelihood. Instead, he only shook his head again, this time as though trying to clear away distracting thoughts.

"Helmut," he finished with a flash of contempt, "thought that Dad's approach was all nonsense."

"What would he know?" Lady Fairgrief asked with matching acid.

"That's what Dad used to say." Stephan suddenly laughed. "But he always gave Helmut a hand anyway."

"Why?"

"That's easy enough. When Dad was first starting to get ahead as a singer, Helmut used to cover for him at the laboratory in Vienna or in their field work."

"Your father worked with Schmidt?"

"He worked *for* him. He was Dad's doctoral mentor."

"You're joking! How did he get into music?"

"He's a Jew," said Stephan, "and I gather he spent the first months after the *Anschluss* being hunted from pillar to post till Dad was able to get him smuggled through the lines to Britain. It must have been horrible for him. Dad always said he was never the same afterward. Anyway, when the war was over, he wanted a complete change, and for the most part the university no longer even existed. I guess you can't blame him and Dad felt he owed him something. Apparently, he'd always been one of those enthusiastic amateur musicians the Germans are always turning out, so Dad got him a job as the chorus master here in Jolliston and he's gradually . . ." His voice hesitated.

"Smarmed his way up?" she concluded for him with a chuckle.

He nodded.

"You don't like him, do you?"

"He's an asshole. Sorry, your ladyship"—he grinned at her—"but that's precisely the way I feel about him."

She waved the crudity aside. "I wasn't necessarily asking for a description," she said dryly. "Is he any good?"

"Oh yes. He's a reasonably good administrator and he could charm the skin off a snake. He has all that Mittel Europischer flair in spades."

Her ladyship chuckled. "I had a maid once who was from"—she waved her hand again—"I don't remember now, some Slavic country. All fire and ice and *Bozhe moy,* twenty times a day. She finally ran off with a footman who wanted to be in the music halls. . . ."

"Anyway," Stephan continued, "Helmut should be happy now."

"Why is that?"

"Because Dad never got the chance to sign a new codicil to his will."

"What?"

"Yes, he and Helmut had gotten into some pretty fierce disagreements lately . . ."

"He told me."

". . . and so Dad was going to lard his bequest to the opera company with all kinds of stipulations. He never did."

"Rudy did say something about that," said Lady Fairgrief. "But he never said what kind of stipulations?"

"Well, Helmut has this typical Viennese thing about 'the New World.' Americans can't sing and all that tripe. Dad was very up on American artists and, well, it got pretty hot there on occasion." Suddenly, Stephan snickered. "Dad even threatened," he informed her gleefully, "to complain to the Equal Employment Opportunity Commission in Washington."

"What did he leave the company?" Lady Fairgrief suddenly asked.

"About a million and a half, I believe," the boy replied coolly. "It will help the endowment fund quite a lot."

Her ladyship gasped. That Bessermann had been rich, she knew, but such riches . . . "What about the rest of you?" she asked.

Stephan smiled and pulled his jacket closer around him. A wind had begun to rise. "Oh, you don't have to worry about us. That bequest to the company is going to go a far piece to reducing taxes on the estate."

"Pity," she observed tartly.

"I beg your pardon."

"Just that, a pity. It might be better for you and Mary Ellen to have to make a living."

"That is probably true," Stephan rejoined rather hotly, "but in today's competitive market what's wrong with a little cushion to ease the way?"

"I'm not certain I believe in cushions," she replied. "They may make it too easy not to get off your . . ." She cleared her throat and glared at him. "Are you going to try?" she demanded.

"We have to." He laughed. "We can't stay here."

"Why ever not?"

"Because Dad left the house to you."

For a very long moment, Lady Fairgrief was not quite sure she had heard him properly. "What?"

He nodded. "It is—believe it or not—entailed to me and my children. He insisted on putting it in his will, even though it's really not legal. But then when you showed up in San Francisco, he changed his will so that you would have a lifetime interest in the house and an adequate income to keep it up."

"How much?" she asked breathlessly, quite indifferent to the way such a question would sound.

"I think it will work out to about forty-five thousand a year."

There was a curious feeling in the pit of her stomach and she wondered, briefly, if she were going to have another heart attack. But there was a sudden burning in her eyes and before she really knew what she was doing she was crying quietly, somehow more shocked by this than even her poor dear Rudy's death. Death, after all, sooner or later comes to all. But this extraordinary kindness, this tactful rendering of much needed assistance, made all the more bountiful for spanning the silence of the grave . . .

"I don't know what to say," she finally gasped. "And you must stay here, with me."

Something in her voice made him look more closely at

her. He noticed her curious color. "Tante Lally, are you all right?"

"No!" she replied almost angrily, "Of course I'm not." Tears continued to course down her cheeks but quickly and fiercely she wrestled her feelings under control. Dimly, she remembered that there was a purpose to this conversation and that, like it or not, she had to get a grip on herself. After a few unsuccessful starts, she asked, "Was Helmut Schmidt himself a legatee?"

"Token things, scores and such. He's done quite all right for himself." Stephan grinned again. "Dad had been thinking about leaving the house to the opera company as a workshop center, but thought you and poor Harvey could put it to better use."

"Oh dear, I hope the Jolliston Lyric will forgive me."

"I don't know about the kids in the company but you've put Mary Ellen and me onto the streets." He laughed at her fussing.

"Stephan"— she glared at him—"I will not hear this."

"Oh well," he chuckled. "It is entailed."

"Now that"—she suddenly frowned—"seems to be a very old-fashioned thing indeed."

"That was Dad all over," he said and quickly turned his face away from her. "Dad," he repeated quietly. "I'll never be able to say that again."

Above the distant hills, clouds were piling into the stratosphere. "It's going to rain soon," she said. "I remember clouds like that when I was a little girl living here in the valley." She fetched a short sigh. "I do hope I last the winter. I'd like to see one more spring in this place where I began."

"We'll keep you warm, Tante Lally," he said, stooping over and tucking the rugs more tightly round her legs.

"What about Larry? What about Mary Ellen?" she asked suddenly.

"What about them?"

"The will."

"Why are you so interested?"

"I'm afraid I may be cheating them," she lied superbly, not altogether certain it was a lie.

"Listen," he said urgently. "We three have an equal share in everything, when everything else has been taken care of. In fact, everyone is a residuary legatee of everyone else. Dad thought it was the best thing to do. Oh, he did threaten to cut Larry off, but I never really thought he would do it. Besides," he said more soberly, "he never got the chance. So the terms of old will still stand. You and Harvey were to live on here for the rest of your days, with the house eventually coming, well, basically to the three of us again. There were some odds and ends, but I only remember the main things Dad told me about. There were some small things for the gardeners and the day help. Oh yes, and Paul, of course."

"What do you mean?"

"Well, with Dad's allergies and what not, Paul virtually danced attendance on him for the last five years or so and he's spent a lot of time over here besides." He flushed deeply and looked away. "He's to be the executor of the estate, too. He's a pretty good businessman whereas none of us is. He can at least have that."

"But not Mary Ellen?"

He smiled at her as a sudden gust of wind in the trees sent a cloud of dead leaves snowing down onto the gravel. "You are a witch, aren't you," he said pleasantly. "Come on, it's getting on and the wind's up."

The wind is indeed up, Lady Fairgrief reflected rather crudely to herself. "Good," she said aloud, "I want some tea."

I also, she concluded grimly, want to talk to dear Matilda and find out if she remembers what a tontine is.

chapter SIXTEEN

Miss Worthing peered sourly around the vastness of the living room. No doubt it was convenient—even pleasing—when great numbers of people were gathered for rehearsals or voice lessons; there was space aplenty for sounds to grow and mix.

At the moment, however, empty and silent, it was rather an eerie place to be, like a vacant theater or an empty church at night. One always felt that someone might be watching from one of the darker, more hidden places. . . .

Quickly dismissing such morbid fancies, she dialed a number. It seemed to take forever before the telephone at the other end was answered by an almost *basso profondo* female voice.

"Jolliston Nurses' Registry," it barked.

"Yes," Miss Worthing began rather hesitantly. "I would like some . . . ah, some information, please?"

"What kind of information?" The voice was gruffly cautious.

"Actually, I need the name and address of one of your nurses."

"We don't ever give out that kind of information" replied the voice peremptorily.

"Oh, I know you don't *ordinarily*," Miss Worthing said, dropping without hesitation into her dithery old lady routine. "But this is quite a *special* case."

There were inquiring noises down the wire.

"Yes," Miss Worthing breathed loudly into the mouthpiece, "I'm afraid it's poor Mr. Besserman. You do know he died last night?" Allowing the dragon on the other end no time to react, she rattled on, feeling thoroughly ashamed of herself. "Yes, it was *quite* sudden and—well, I understand that he *always* had the same nurse, a Miss Martinez, was it not?"

"Yes," the voice replied after a moment.

"Well, we, that is, the *family* would like to ask her to come to the funeral and wake, and"—she blushed furiously at her utter mendacity—"of course, afterward there will be the reading of the will . . ." She left the sentence to dangle most suggestively.

"Well," the voice expostulated, "in that case, will you hold the wire a moment?"

"Of course," Miss Worthing uttered sweetly and in the ensuing silence muttered a prayer for forgiveness.

"Do you have you a pen?" the voice returned.

"Yes."

"Good. Write it down because I'm sure I couldn't do this again."

"Go ahead, please." Miss Worthing, pencil poised, controlled an impulse to snap.

"It's Miss Consuela Martinez, R.N., 1485 Loma Linda Drive."

"Here in Jolliston?"

"Yes."

Miss Worthing repeated the address. "Is there a telephone number, please?"

The voice supplied the number.

"Thank you very much," said Miss Worthing gratefully, "very much indeed, Miss . . . ah . . . Miss . . ."

"No names, please. I only hope it's worth Miss Martinez' time," the voice replied shortly and hung up.

For a few moments, Miss Worthing stood staring into space, trying to order her thoughts. Finally, she picked up the receiver and dialed again.

"Hello?"

"Miss Martinez?" Miss Worthing asked.

"Yes."

"I understand you treated Mr. Bessermann in his recent illness."

"Yes, I did." The nurse sounded as though she might be crying. "I just heard the news on the radio."

"I'm very sorry to trouble you, but, you see, Lady Fairgrief told me how you . . . felt."

"Thank you, thank you very much, but, please, who is this?"

"My name is Matilda Worthing. You may have heard of me."

There was a long silence at the other end of the wire. "You don't live in Jolliston and not hear about you, Miss Worthing." The nurse's voice was sharp with suspicion. "What's wrong?"

"I was rather hoping you could tell me. Perhaps I could come to see you?" she suggested diffidently.

Again there was that pause. "At my house," the nurse said quickly, "after ten," and immediately she hung up.

"Goodness," Miss Worthing said out loud, "now that's interesting."

She recradled the receiver. Then—as she turned to go back to the kitchen—she noticed that the portieres over the terrace doors were moving.

"The wind must be up," she muttered and went to close the French doors.

They were, however, already closed and when she stepped out onto the terrace there was no wind blowing, though farther up the hill, in the poplars around the rose garden, the tops of the trees were moving in a fitful breeze.

There was no one in sight.

Back inside, she heard voices in the library raised in brief argument. She knocked and entered.

"Excuse me!"

Lawrence Bessermann and Helmut Schmidt were painstakingly ransacking the shelves. Vast piles of music were spilled over the table and various opera scores were stacked on chairs. Larry was standing at the large central table, a score open in front of him, wiping his hands with a handkerchief. Schmidt was on a ladder, a large folio opened on the top step. A window giving onto the side path was open. Both men turned to her with some impatience, their faces red and excited.

"So sorry," Miss Worthing again dithered deliberately, "but we were wondering if you would like some coffee or tea?"

"Thank you," Larry responded unhelpfully and returned to a score open on the table before him. Schmidt merely glared at her and turned back to the shelf.

Miss Worthing closed the library door behind her and for a moment considered. Someone had listened to her conversation but those two ninnies seemed to be too involved in what they were doing to leap out a window and stalk around.... Nonsense, of course; Larry's hands were dusty from handling all those filthy old volumes.

She returned to the kitchen, where Mary Ellen, who was standing at the door to the breakfast room, greeted her. "Oh, *there* you are, Miss Worthing."

"What?"

"I heard someone in here. I thought it might have been you. There isn't anyone there."

Involuntarily, Miss Worthing glanced around the room. The door on the landing of the back stairs was open. With a click of her tongue, Mary Ellen ran lightly up the stairs and pulled it to. "I do wish people would remember to keep that door closed," she said with a small frown as she came down again. "It's hard enough to keep that barn of a living room warm."

"Was it open all this time, dear?" Miss Worthing asked sharply.

"No, I closed it when I came down."

"Is that the only connecting door between the front and back stairs?"

"No, of course not," Mary Ellen gestured. "There's one on each floor."

"Did anyone come in here?"

"No, I told you I thought it was you. Why?" she suddenly asked, in a frightened voice.

"Nothing, my dear, nothing." Miss Worthing tried to become dithery once more. "Just an old woman's fancies." She took Mary Ellen's arm. "Let's finish dinner."

Mary Ellen shook her hand away. "You're not a fanciful woman, Miss Worthing," she said shortly. "What's going on?"

"Mary Ellen," said Miss Worthing with severity, "don't complicate things by asking unnecessary questions."

"I'm frightened."

"Of what?"

Mary Ellen shrugged. "I don't know," she said and sat down at the table.

"Now," Miss Worthing instructed, putting a kettle on the stove, "I'm going upstairs for a few minutes. You stay here."

Upstairs, it was very quiet. A thick carpet ran the length of the hall, absorbing any sound a footfall might make. As quietly as she could, Miss Worthing started at one end of the hall and worked her way down the entire length, opening door after door. She was annoyed that people no longer had those old-fashioned keyholes, which made for such admirable snooping. She was also fully satisfied that there was only one person on the whole floor, and he appeared to be sleeping. In the attic there was nothing but a great deal of dust and the mummified remains of a bat. She went back down to the second floor and once more considered the fact of Paul Becay, stretched out on his bed, fully clothed and to all outward appearance in a deep slumber.

An idea occurred to her, and though admittedly it was a little absurd, she reckoned any port in a storm and all that. Slipping into the room next door to Becay's—the room in which Bessermann had died—and taking the water glass from the stand next to the bed, she carefully placed it against the wall and applied her ear to it.

She was rewarded by the rhythmic light snoring of the doctor. Feeling uncommonly silly, she replaced the glass on the table and then, suddenly, exclaimed, "Drat." A trail of ants was weaving between the bureau and the bed.

Getting down on her knees she lifted up the bedclothes and peered into the darkness under the bed. The object of the ants' labor was a small lump, just under the bed. Acting on a sudden speculation, she wrapped her hand in her apron and, reaching out, swept the thing toward her only to feel a thrill of quiet elation. The lump was the bodies of two honeybees. The ants' depredations were already well advanced but there was quite a bit left of the insects. Shooing off the ants, she wrapped the remains carefully in a tissue and put it into the pocket of her apron.

* * *

Somewhat later, Miss Worthing ordered Mary Ellen back upstairs to take another nap. The younger woman had grown increasingly moody and irascible and Miss Worthing felt she could not promise that *she* wouldn't start throwing things if there was just one more sigh.

Presently, Stephan and Lady Fairgrief appeared, the latter loudly demanding hot tea. In short order, her ladyship was sipping at a steaming cup. Stephan watched her and shook his head.

"I wonder what God gave you for kidneys," he said and then laughed at the expression on her face.

"My kidneys, young man," replied the old woman austerely, "though it grieves one of my generation to mention them, are in marvelous shape precisely because I drink so much tea. It is, after all, as effective as embalming fluid." She cackled at the expression on his face. "You should try it."

"No thanks." He grimaced. "I'll stick with beer."

"Bad for the liver," her ladyship muttered.

"But oh so good for the nerves." He smiled, opening the refrigerator and extracting a bottle. "Anyone know where Larry is?" he asked after swallowing hugely.

"He's in the library, with Herr Schmidt," Miss Worthing replied, peering around the pile of vegetables and hoping she had got everything.

"Oh Lord," he said and dumped the rest of the beer in the sink. "I forgot we were going to discuss the music for Dad's . . ." He turned away, opened the cabinet beneath the sink, and threw the bottle into the trash where it clinked against something else.

"I suppose," Lady Fairgrief observed waspishly, "that Herr Schmidt is planning to turn Rudy's obsequies into the *Götterdämmerung*."

Stephan nodded unhappily. "'Scuse me, please," he said softly and went through the swinging door.

Neither of the women spoke for a long while. The house was strangely huge and silent around them, as though no one really lived there and had not for a long, long time.

"What did you find out?" Miss Worthing finally asked, setting her cup down.

Lady Fairgrief finished the last drop in her own cup and held it out for more. Miss Worthing poured.

"That perhaps," the older woman said very soberly, "we have been deluded."

Her niece looked at her sharply but said nothing.

"We are trying to discover if Rudolf was murdered and if so, by whom, aren't we?"

Miss Worthing nodded.

"Then we have to have the right motive, am I not correct?"

Miss Worthing considered for a long moment and then firmly shook her head. "No. It's too easy to make a mistake relying solely on such an intangible as motive, or at least that's what I've always been led to believe. It seems that it's far better, procedurally, to attempt to discover the *quibus* and *quo modo* first . . . The mo—"

"Matilda," her aunt interrupted. "What *are* you talking about."

"Sorry, dear." Miss Worthing chuckled. "They're just two old Latin phrases that mean nothing more than 'by what means.' And as I was about to say, motives will frequently be uncovered when you find out the how."

The old lady's eyebrows went up quizzically.

"Well, you see . . ." Miss Worthing had the distinct feeling that she was getting into a thorough muddle explaining something she herself understood perfectly well. "It's just that so often, in a crime of this sort—assuming a crime has been committed—usually there are so many people who had some motive sufficient to bring them to the act."

Her aunt nodded. "I'll say," she said bitterly. "Everyone in this house."

"Even you?" Miss Worthing smiled at her aunt.

"Even me," said Lady Fairgrief quietly and put her cup down.

The two women regarded each other intently for a moment. Finally, Miss Worthing leaned forward and put a hand against the teapot; a ring she was wearing clanked melodiously against the china. She stood up. "I'm going to get some more hot water," she said, peering into the pot. "Then I want you to tell me what Stephan told you."

Her ladyship nodded and pulled her shawl tightly around herself. She stared down at her clasped hands, gnarled and twisted with rheumatism and age, and tried to marshal the thoughts and ideas that had crossed her mind while Stephan and she had chatted in the garden. To her horror, a part of her was sorry now that she had ever cried foul in the first place.

"I've meddled again," she muttered aloud. "Why am I always meddling?"

She expressed her sudden doubts to her niece when Miss Worthing turned around with the boiling kettle. The younger woman, after stirring the pot and pouring more of the brew into her aunt's cup, began to pace up and down the kitchen flags, her lower lip pinched between thumb and forefinger, her face unusually severe.

"You could be right," Miss Worthing finally conceded. "And God only knows that there are aspects of this thing that make no sense at all—at least at the moment. But I can't help but feel that, at the moment, the preponderance of evidence is on our side.

"Look." She swirled around to face her aunt, held out a hand, and then, interrupting herself, laughed. "Do you know, I'm committing the unforgiveable—trying to extrapolate without sufficient data." She resumed her seat across from her aunt. "What did Stephan tell you?"

When Lady Fairgrief had finished a recitation of the

substance of her conversation in the garden, Miss Worthing sighed. "This is awful," she muttered.

"Oh dear," her ladyship cried and clutched at the handles of her chair. "I was afraid you would say that."

"But, my dear Aunt Eulalia, it not only doesn't change anything. Indeed, this information adds a few piquant points which definitely want examining. You know, we may *be* silly, deluded, or meddlesome. Make your choice. But I really don't think so. There is no question that, had you not been here or gotten me involved, this whole thing would have been utterly passed over and one more great singer would merely have gone down into the dark.

"But!" Miss Worthing held up a closed fist and raised her index finger. "One: There's the bee in the posy. A bee! In November. Two." She raised another finger. "And this is really most intriguing. There's the second sting on the face. Think about that.

"Thirdly, there's that pneumonia and, yes, I'm going over to speak to Miss Martinez tonight.

"And fourthly"—she put her hand into her apron pocket, withdrew the tissue, and unfolded it—"I found these under Rudy's bed."

"No!"

Miss Worthing nodded. "Fifthly," she added grimly, after putting the tissue back into her pocket, "Harvey is dead, to all intents and purposes by his own hand."

"I don't believe it for a minute."

"Neither do I. He was a convert to Catholicism of the most disagreeable kind; he was just one step short of a fanatic."

Miss Worthing ceased to count points on her fingers and, leaning both elbows on the table, propped her head between them, "and that, damn it all, is where we stand."

"What's wrong with it?"

"Because that's where it all falls apart. Five people, six

if you want to count you, which frankly I think is absurd . . ."

"Good of you," observed Lady Fairgrief dryly.

"Oh, think nothing of it," her niece replied as tartly. "So let's say five people, each with something to gain, and all of them, Lord love 'em, with excellent motives and superb opportunities, and all that remains is the demon of how and I can't for the life of me—"

"Matilda," the old woman spoke sharply. "Drop it. I've seen you get like this before. Your mind will give it to you when it's ready."

Miss Worthing's shoulders slumped and she smiled ruefully. "You're right, of course. There are some things I do have to attend to this afternoon. Tell me, would you mind awfully if you went to bed?"

"Heavens no, I'd rather like a nap. But get me some sherry. In fact, bring me about ten ounces of sherry. Then I won't bother anyone till supper."

"Ten ounces of sherry and I'm not altogether certain I'd bother anyone ever again."

The old woman grinned. "Oh well, old livers are sound livers."

"That"—Miss Worthing got up and swung her aunt's chair around—"is a truly appalling pun. Come on"—she unlocked the brake—"let me get you installed and then I'll bring you your beaker of sherry."

chapter
SEVENTEEN

Three quarters of an hour before dinner, Miss Shaw returned from San Francisco. She took one long look around the kitchen, clucked like an angry hen, and donned an apron.

"Really, Mattie," she expostulated. "Nothing's done. What have you been doing?"

Miss Worthing relinquished the kitchen chores with relief. She went straight to the sideboard but then hesitated somewhat guiltily as she hefted the nearly depleted decanter. Finally, she poured herself an almost ostentatiously small sherry and went out into the darkening house to light lamps and rouse people for dinner. Upon opening the library door, she felt almost physically struck by the hostility vibrating in the air. Stephan and Schmidt were at opposite ends of the long central table glaring furiously at one another. Paul Becay stood languidly draped against the bookshelves, cigarette negligently held in his fingers, a bored expression on his face as he looked from one combatant to another.

Schmidt sat—the score of something orchestral in front of him—glaring at Stephan, his fingers tapping out an impatient rhythm on the polished walnut surface of the table. They all started when Miss Worthing cleared her throat loudly.

"What *is* it, Miss Worthing?" Schmidt snapped at her.

She looked at Schmidt for a brief moment with the kind of loathing detachment one brings to bear upon a particularly repellant curiosity and announced in her most frigid voice that dinner would be in half an hour.

"Do you know where Lawrence is?" she asked.

"He said he was going for a walk," Stephan said angrily. "Do you know what he and this—"

"No, Stephan," Miss Worthing interrupted, her nostrils pinched in distaste, "nor do I want to. I merely want to announce dinner. If you see your brother, inform him so. Thank you." Without another word, she faced about and shut the door firmly behind her. Once outside, she leaned against the door and fought to regain control and calm, annoyed and more than a little astonished at the extremity of her own reaction to what could only be called their hopelessly vulgar behavior.

"All this squabbling and carrying on," she muttered to herself, climbing the stairs to rouse Mary Ellen. "That overage hippy Lawrence Bessermann seems to think that the only thing that matters is to put on a good *show*"— she winced at the word, and then recognized the aptness of it—"a good show at his own father's funeral and as for Schmidt . . ."

With a vast effort of will she dismissed the little man from her thoughts and knocked on Mary Ellen's door. There was no response. "Mary Ellen," she called softly and opened the door. She instantly recoiled. The room reeked of gas. Quickly inhaling a deep breath in the corridor, she rushed to the bedroom casement.

Mary Ellen was collapsed in front of the window in her nightgown. One small pane was broken, through which a fresh breeze barely trickled into the room.

Quickly, Miss Worthing threw the casement open and slung Mary Ellen across the sill. Then, grabbing another breath from the open window, she rushed to the gas valve near the door and turned the loudly hissing thing off. Quietly, she also closed the door.

In a few moments, the smell of gas had appreciably lessened in the room. Mary Ellen lurched to her feet and staggered into her bathroom where she was violently sick. Miss Worthing sat down on the edge of the bed and waited for her to come out.

Presently, Mary Ellen emerged from the bathroom, her skin ivory pallid, her black hair stuck limply to her forehead. She leaned groggily against the lintel, gasping for breath. Miss Worthing went to her and helped her to stagger back to the bed and lie down; she watched as Mary Ellen swallowed and sucked air into her starved lungs. Mentally, the older woman was raging at herself.

"Fool that I am," she muttered to herself angrily as she watched the young woman closely for any signs of poisoning. "I should have seen that this might happen." She groped about in her mind for memories of wartime nursing and what to do for gassing, but Mary Ellen seemed to be all right. "How do you feel?" she asked.

"I think I'm okay now," Mary Ellen said raspingly after a moment. "I just need air and a few minutes."

She opened her eyes and looked at Miss Worthing's quite fierce expression. With a soft cry of "oh no," she sat up and flung her arms around Miss Worthing's neck and cried with all the abandon of a child, while Miss Worthing, in turn, tried awkwardly to try to comfort this woman upon whom all the tensions, responsibilities, and burdens of that unhappy house had fallen. Wisely she said nothing, merely patting Mary Ellen's heaving shoulders, waiting for the storm to end, and grimly staring into the dark.

"It's true then, isn't it?" Mary Ellen asked in a very small voice.

"I'm afraid so," Miss Worthing agreed and presently stood up.

Mary Ellen lay back on the bed, watching the face of the older women, who, most unexpectedly, smiled.

"Why are you smiling?" Mary Ellen asked.

"Not because of anything particularly amusing, my dear," replied Miss Worthing crisply. "But whoever did this has both made an enormous mistake and angered me, yes, angered me very much. I think a little light begins to glimmer. . . ."

She went to the window and took another deep breath, exhaling slowly before turning back to Mary Ellen. "I have to ask you something."

The younger woman nodded. "I thought you might," she whispered. "'Do you remember anything at all, Miss Bessermann?' the prosecuting attorney asked, without taking his eyes off the accused."

Miss Worthing chuckled softly. "Not half bad, my dear, but that isn't quite what I had in mind. On the other hand, do you? Remember anything?"

Groggily Mary Ellen sat up, swung her feet over the side of the bed, and put her head into her hands. After a moment, she looked up. "I dozed off pretty quickly this afternoon," she began doubtfully, "but I do sort of remember a click, like the door shutting, almost waking me up . . ." She shrugged. "That's about it."

"How did you get to the window?"

Mary Ellen gave a little laugh. "Uncle Rudolf saved me," she said simply. She got off the bed and stood next to Miss Worthing, taking several long deep breaths. Then she turned and saw the expression on Miss Worthing's face. "No." She laughed. "I didn't see his ghost, but I dreamt that I was back in Uncle's room, you know . . . God!" She ran a hand through her hair. "Can it really only be last night? Anyway, Steve was yelling for him to breathe. Suddenly, I couldn't either. Oh, yes, and Lady Fairgrief was there, too, pointing at the window, so I went to open it."

Miss Worthing silently uttered a brief thanksgiving to the god of singers and took the younger woman's hand. "Help me," she said.

"How?"

"You mustn't tell anyone about this."

Mary Ellen opened her mouth, drew breath to protest, and then, changing her mind, nodded. "Yes, I think I can understand that."

Miss Worthing went to the door. "Dinner is in twenty minutes," she said and chuckled. "I know I sound like a heartless old woman, but do try to eat something. You must appear as though nothing has happened."

Mary Ellen gestured her agreement and Miss Worthing went to arouse Lady Fairgrief. Halfway down the stairs, she heard the doctor's voice raised sharply in anger.

"I've had quite enough." He stood at the door of the library and yelled back into the room. "I'll attend to your natterings after supper if you're still at it."

He was stalking toward the dining room doors when Miss Worthing called him. "Dr. Becay?"

He glanced up and gave her a half smile. "It's a crazy family. I wish I knew now why I ever became a throat man. I'm prescribing a drink for myself."

He went into the dining room, from which presently she heard the pleasant sounds of bottles being moved about and ice cubes tinkling in crystal. For a longish moment she stood at the foot of the stairs wondering if she could possibly get away with what she had in mind. After a moment, she shrugged, made a devil-may-care gesture to the empty living room, and sailed into the dining room in full dither.

"*Dear* Dr. Becay," she twittered, laying a hand on his sleeve, "would you mind giving me a hand with my dear old aunt?"

"Your aunt?" He hesitated, glass halfway to his mouth.

"Yes, old Lady Fairgrief."

"But doesn't she have Maude?"

"Ordinarily, of course. But poor Maude had to go to San Francisco. *So* sudden. Something *terribly* important, I'm sure, so I'm here to help." She lowered her eyes and her voice. "With the *funeral*, don't you know, and my poor old aunt . . ."

"Your aunt?" Becay repeated. She noticed with extreme annoyance from beneath her fluttering eyelids that he was eying her in an unpleasantly speculative manner. "Are you Matilda Worthing?"

Miss Worthing acknowledged the fact with a flutter and prayed that she was reading the expression flickering across his face to mean that he had dismissed her completely.

"Your aunt's in the library. Your friend got her up." He turned back to the business of alcohol.

A short time later, Miss Worthing presided over the preprandial cocktails in the hope of smelling something out. None of the men had bothered to change, and Lady Fairgrief's stiff black shantung and jet earrings and choker seemed somehow incongruous and bizarre. Miss Worthing had changed into a navy-blue silk with white, coin-sized polka dots, a dress she thoroughly detested. It did, however, help to keep up the harmless old granny routine.

Unfortunately, any advantage she had hoped to gain by Mary Ellen's entrance was completely thwarted by Lawrence and Stephan. It was one of those consummately stupid accidents, which, for all that, are intensely annoying.

Stephan and Lady Fairgrief had been discussing something rather quietly and Stephan had bent over, the better to hear. Behind Stephan, Miss Worthing handed Lawrence a rather overfull martini glass. Stephan straightened, jogging Lawrence's elbow, and his drink promptly spilled down Miss Worthing's dress just as Mary Ellen entered.

With an abrupt, savage gesture, Lawrence threw the cocktail glass into the fireplace, where it smashed loudly. He whirled round just as Stephan started to stammer an apology. Before either of them said a word, Lady Fairgrief snapped at them. "Lawrence! Stephan! Control yourselves!"

At the door, Mary Ellen, looking almost austere in black satin, caught her lower lip in her teeth. Becay began to move to her side, but stopped when he caught Stephan's eye. Schmidt, stiff with disapproval, handed his glass to Miss Worthing. "Would you pour me another, Miss Vorzing?" he said in an abnormally loud voice.

"Can't you see she's soaked?" Lady Fairgrief eyed the man unmercifully. She turned her attention to her niece. "For goodness sake, go change, Matilda," she ordered and then snickered rudely at Miss Worthing's dabbings with a damp rag. "That's only going to make it worse. Mary Ellen can take over."

In her room, Miss Worthing confessed herself to be both amused and annoyed by the whole contretemps. Annoyed for her patently infuriating inability to see anyone's face when Mary Ellen walked in of whole flesh, but amused too. "This murder," she chided herself, "will be solved by logic and dull routine. Not by adventitious good luck."

And then, too, there were the tensions in the house, which was normally so placid. "No, that's not right. Had it really been placid then none of this would be happening."

Yes, of course. All those tensions roiling now so close to the surface had, of couse, been there a good amount of time. Those youngsters, for instance; or worse, those two fighting over Mary Ellen like two dogs over the same bitch. . . . And now if a man—or woman, she remembered sourly—had already done death, it was not going to be that great an effort to do it again in anger or even in spite.

Not for the first time she found herself fascinated by the mystery of evil. No, that wasn't right, for none of these people was evil. Regardless of the fact that murder, a cold-blooded and heartless one at that, had been done; in spite of that most appalling of sins—all of the people here were, if not good, certainly not evil. For how often did one actually come face to face with genuine evil? To be sure, there was spite, and envy, and negligent indifference to be found every day and everywhere. But the giant repudiation of the good by a Hitler or by a Stalin—those were merely the obvious landmarks in a landscape of pettiness, meanness, and dispirited malice.

Engaged in these perspicacious if depressing thoughts, she changed into her tweeds and went down the back stairs and out to the garage before joining Martha in the kitchen.

"You've changed," Miss Shaw observed, glancing up from adding something arcane to a serving dish of vegetables.

"I had to," Miss Worthing said and explained what had happened in the dining room. "And so," she concluded, taking the bowl of vegetables and heading toward the door, "I think we had better stay out here; it will look better. Although," she added sourly, "I dearly would love to know what's going on in all those minds."

Miss Shaw followed in a billowing crimson velvet muumuu, bearing the meat on a serving platter. They deposited the food on the table, laid rather haphazardly with odds and ends of silver, announced dinner to the nervous group at the other end of the dining room, and beat a hasty retreat through the service room into the kitchen.

They had barely sat down to their own plates of food when Mary Ellen burst through the door. "You can't possibly eat out here," she cried, and took the ladies' plates virtually from beneath their lifted forks.

"But we can't obtrude upon you at such a time," Miss Worthing protested.

"Obtrude?" The girl gave a slightly hysterical giggle, causing Miss Worthing to look sharply at her. "You must be joking. You and Miss Shaw are the only normal people left in this house." Still holding the two plates, she turned, and, without another word, left the kitchen. Feeling both rather vexed and yet relieved, Miss Worthing and Miss Shaw followed after.

chapter EIGHTEEN

As soon as they emerged from the service room into the dining room, Miss Worthing understood precisely what Mary Ellen had meant.

Stephan's high coloring had gone angry and mottled. He made no pretence of eating. Rather, he was speaking in a voice that was cold and immensely controlled, which gave him rather a pedantic air.

"Our father would have been horrified and shocked at the very suggestion of operatic music in church," he was saying. "He had, as you may recall, very fixed ideas about that kind of thing."

Schmidt was glaring at Stephan much as he had earlier in the library. "Then perhaps you can tell us," the little Austrian asked venomously, "vat ve can do. The chorus and orchestra have all been prepared."

"What?" Miss Worthing was startled into asking.

"Of course," Schmidt deigned to reply. "I sent Larry to my house this afternoon for the *partiture* und I called principals from here."

Miss Worthing frowned but before she could say anything further, Schmidt turned back to Stephan. "It would hardly be fair to have all those people show up tomorrow morning for the funeral and then there be no point to it."

"I don't give a damn."

"You mean," Lawrence asked, "like you didn't give a damn about what happened to Pop?"

"Fat lot you cared," Stephan suddenly flared at his brother. "Off playing all those years with that goddamn rock band when you know what he wanted."

"I didn't kill him," Larry countered nastily.

"Both of you, stop it," Becay said urgently. With a hand at Mary Ellen's wrist, he concentrated on his watch as he counted her pulse. "Mary Ellen," he said almost severely, "I think you had better get some rest." He stood up to assist her.

The young woman's eyes were half closed. She really should not have chosen to wear that black gown, Miss Worthing thought, almost with annoyance. It only accented the pallor of her skin and the dull listlessness of her usually shining hair.

Stephan smothered an oath and lurched to his feet, but Miss Worthing and Miss Shaw, after one brief conspiratorial nod, intercepted both him and Becay and, gathering Mary Ellen up, hustled her out.

"Take her up to her room," Miss Worthing murmured at the foot of the stairs and hurried back to the dining room to resume her place. She picked up her wine and tipped a wink to her aunt.

Lady Fairgrief returned the merest ghost of a smile. She toyed absently with the food on her plate. So even she is upset, Miss Worthing reflected, and suddenly spoke up. "Why don't you do the Verdi *Requiem*?"

"It's two hours long," Schmidt snorted.

"I wasn't suggesting"—Miss Worthing's eyes narrowed as she skewered the man with a glance—"that you do the whole thing, but you could do parts of it."

This time, Schmidt did not speak. Lawrence Bessermann snarled something into his wineglass, but Stephan spoke up in the unnaturally loud tones of one voicing an unpopular opinion. "It was one of Dad's favorite things."

"But the church," Schmidt objected. "Would they let us do it?"

"Herr Schmidt," Miss Worthing observed tartly, "you must have had your head buried these fifteen years or more."

"What do you mean?" he asked truculently.

Everyone at the table at least began to look interested.

"We could do a low Mass with incidental music," Stephan answered and thumped the table.

Miss Worthing nodded. "Of course. Since the liturgical changes," she explained to the table at large, "whatever else one might think of them, at least Rome is rather more lenient about what music can and cannot be performed in the churches."

Schmidt had a faraway expression on his face and was nodding rapidly. "*Ja*," he finally said, "I do remember reading something about that." He suddenly turned to Lawrence. "You were trained as basso, *nein?*"

"I haven't done that kind of singing for years." Lawrence frowned.

"*Ach.*" Schmidt waved a dismissing hand. "You know the score?"

"Of course."

"So?" the Austrian snapped. "You and Mary Ellen will sing *Lacrymosa*." He directed his attention to Stephan. "Und you will do *Ingemisco*," he ordered like a drill master. "Then"—and he seemed to withdraw inwardly for a moment—"we will get Kathryn Anderson up here from San Francisco, and we can do the *Kyrie* and the *Recordare*. *Ja?*"

He glared round at everyone as though daring them to contradict him. Lawrence shrugged and Stephan slowly nodded.

"I hope Mary Ellen can sing in the morning," Stephan muttered.

Schmidt stood up, food forgotten. "So sorry." He

poured and drank down a glass of wine. "It must all be done tonight. Lawrence, come with me. We will go get the *partiture*."

Lawrence too stood up. "Sure. It probably is the best idea since we can't do the kind of music Dad really loved," he said bitterly and glared at Stephan.

Presently, the four people remaining in the dining room heard them go out the front door, Schmidt nattering away a mile a minute.

It was a long time before anyone said anything. Miss Worthing was feeling an acute social embarrassment. Why had she made that suggestion after what she had done just before dinner? Even though her little activity in the garage had been a bit late. Furthermore, she was quite furious with herself for not having anticipated it.

She stared fixedly at her plate, until even the sound of silver on crockery sounded so preternaturally loud that she put her fork down and prepared to leave the table. Then, out of the corner of her eye, Miss Worthing suddenly saw that her aunt was almost quivering with anger.

"What kind of people are you, Stephan?" the old woman asked in a whiplash voice. "Your father has been gone less than a day and you and your brother and your cousin behave as though it had all happened so long ago you can't even remember it."

"You're not being fair," the young man said loudly, the blood once more rising in his cheeks. "I know Dad is dead, that is to say, I'm trying to realize it. It's not easy, you know, damn it all . . ." He suddenly threw his hands up and they thumped down upon the table. "I don't know what the hell I'm trying to say."

Becay had been watching Stephan with a quite unreadable expression. Now he turned to face Lady Fairgrief. "I think that what he means is that the shock still hasn't worn off," he explained to the old woman. "He said he hasn't 'realized' it yet. That's an excellent word, Steve. It's not all that uncommon a reaction."

He said this with the kind of lightly ironic tone with which he might have lectured a classroom of recalcitrant interns. He picked up his wineglass and held it toward the light. Without looking at her, he continued to address Lady Fairgrief. "And one does assume, Lady Fairgrief, that *all* of Rudy's friends want his obsequies to be appropriate to the man and to his station."

Oh fiddle, Miss Worthing thought to herself, but felt a grudging admiration for Becay's masterful play of precisely the gambit that might give pause to one of Lady Fairgrief's generation and sensibilities. She risked glancing at her aunt and, sure enough, the old woman was rigid.

"Please, Matilda," said her ladyship woodenly, "would you please take me to my room. I am most bitterly ashamed of myself."

Stephan rose. "Sit still, Miss Worthing," he instructed, and knelt down next to Lady Fairgrief's chair. She turned her head away from him. "Please, Tante Lally," he said gently, "I understand. I don't think, though, that you altogether understand the . . . well, the bizarre way we sometimes live."

The old woman turned her head round and looked into the beseeching countenance of the young man. She reached out with her hand and briefly caressed his cheek. "I am more sorry than I can say for having spoken as I did. I was trying to remember just now that when my dear Arthur went I was scarce able to believe it true for weeks and months thereafter." She suddenly smiled, though it was a bleak smile indeed. "I sometimes forget how much the world has changed. When I was a girl and someone died, even if it was someone not so very close to you, you made a pretence that you were stricken with grief even if"—she made a vague gesture with her hand—"as sometimes was true, you felt not a thing in the world." She chuckled and looked down at the still kneeling Stephan. "I think you're probably right to do this your way. After all"—she turned to the others, her smile still charming even in the wreckage of her once great beauty—"Queen Victoria died eighty years ago. I suppose it's time that even I left her to sleep in peace."

Stephan stood up. "Do you still want to go to your room?" he asked.

She nodded. "Yes. I've eaten as much as I can and I need to rest."

When they had left, Miss Worthing was plunged into thought while Becay slowly swirled his wine around in the glass, occasionally sipping at it. After a moment, Becay uttered a barely audible chuckle and set his glass down. "You must think that we're all mad," he said lightly.

Miss Worthing regarded Becay quietly for a space and then, with deliberation, put her fork down and leaned forward over the table. "Did you sleep all afternoon?" she asked.

If Becay was surprised at the question, he gave no indication other than a slightly raised eyebrow. "Of course. I was totally exhausted."

"I can imagine you would be," she commented.

"So is everyone else in this house," he added rather coldly. "That's the reason they're all at each other's throats."

"That may be one of the reasons," Miss Worthing muttered beneath her breath.

"Pardon?"

"Nothing, Dr. Becay. I'm sorry if I was rude."

"Not at all, my dear woman," he said in a tone of voice that meant she had been very rude indeed. "Was there a reason I shouldn't sleep all afternoon?"

"Of course not," Miss Worthing dissembled. "As you say, you must have been exhausted."

They were spared further conversation by Miss Shaw rolling back into the room on a wave of crimson.

"She's gone to sleep," she said, sitting down and beginning to eat with good appetite. "This pot roast was a waste." She held up a forked piece of beef. "No one's eaten more than a bite."

"Not so, Miss Shaw," Becay said with a smile. "I enjoyed it thoroughly."

"Well, I've done," Miss Worthing said firmly and stood up. "You finish, Martha, and I'll clear."

Stephan returned and, after once more sitting down, stared at his plate with evident distaste. "I don't think I want to eat anything," he said moodily.

"You should eat something," said Becay matter-of-factly. "Tomorrow will be a busy day for you."

Miss Worthing was busy piling dishes and, after mouthing a few morsels, Stephan added his to the top of the stack. "I'll take them out, Miss Worthing." He smiled at her. "And I'll wash them. You two have done enough for one day."

Miss Worthing gratefully surrendered the hateful chore, sat down again, poured herself another glass of wine, and chatted amiably with Martha as the other woman continued eating. After a while, Stephan came back into the dining room to fetch the serving dishes.

"Was my aunt all right?" Miss Worthing asked him.

He glanced at the clock on the sideboard. "Yes, fine. She just asked if you would go in to put her to bed at ten. What's wrong?"

Miss Worthing had turned in alarm to look at the clock. It read 9:45. "How did it get to be so late?" she exclaimed and stood up.

"Ladies," Becay suddenly called from the other end of the dining room. "Would either of you like an after-dinner drink?"

"Thank you, Dr. Becay," Miss Worthing said quickly, "but perhaps"—she glanced down at Miss Shaw, who

175

nodded—"a green chartreuse for Miss Shaw and I wonder if Aunt Eulalia would like something . . ." She looked questioningly at Stephan.

"She likes an amaretto after dinner," he replied. "Pour me a cognac, Paul, would you," he said over his shoulder and disappeared into the service room again.

With a silver tray bearing a pony filled with the garnet-colored liqueur, Miss Worthing let herself into Lady Fairgrief's room. Her ladyship was reading the Bible, a fact upon which Miss Worthing commented with some amusement. "I've brought you your booze to read the Bible by."

Lady Fairgrief pursed her mouth and lowered her lorgnette. "I am merely reading the lesson for the day—an old-fashioned and, I am sad to report, utterly neglected exercise. Is that amaretto?"

"Yes, Aunt Eulalia."

"Lovely. But I think you'd better put me to bed first," she said, and laid the Bible down.

Miss Worthing set the tray down on the bureau, assisted the old woman in changing her nightdress, and then hoisted her into her bed. She finished hanging the stiff silk gown and went to fetch the liqueur, but her aunt indicated that she was not to. Instead, she said, "Sit here a moment," patting the mattress.

Rather gingerly, Miss Worthing sat down.

"Well?" her aunt asked and no explanation was needed.

"I don't think there can be any doubt at all."

"For certain?"

Miss Worthing hesitated the briefest moment. "It's quite simply really. Mary Ellen was gassed this afternoon."

"What?" Her ladyship was outraged. "Tell me what happened.

"So that's why she was so bleached out at supper," she

observed a few minutes later, after Miss Worthing had told her of the episode. She indicated that she would like her liqueur.

"Here you go, Aunt Eulalia." Miss Worthing handed her the glass and bent down to kiss her. "Have a good night," she said and turned to go.

"How extraordinary," she heard her aunt mutter behind her and then, surprisingly, sneezed violently.

She turned around. Lady Fairgrief was frowning. "What's wrong?"

"It smells odd," the old woman replied and started to take a sip.

"Stop!" Miss Worthing ordered loudly.

"What is it, Matilda?" her aunt asked, somewhat confused.

Carefully and gently, Miss Worthing took the glass from her aunt. A most horrible suspicion had entered her mind and, with great caution, she too sniffed at the glass. Then, her mouth a grim line, she took the card that marked her aunt's place in the Bible she had been reading and covered the pony with it. The card, she noted, in grisly apposition had the Ten Commandments written out on it. She opened a closet and put the tray on the top shelf.

"What is it, Matilda?" asked Lady Fairgrief anxiously.

Miss Worthing came out of the closet, her eyes blazing and her nostrils pinched in anger. "Does anyone else drink amaretto?" she asked.

"Not that I know of," her ladyship answered. "I think Rudolf bought the bottle for me when he decided to get together a small house party to welcome me, disaster that it's been. Why?"

"Because, dearest Aunt Eulalia, unless I am very much mistaken, that bottle's been tampered with."

"How?"

"Aunt Eulalia," Miss Worthing replied with some asperity, "what fairly common chemical could be slipped into amaretto and, as they both smell of almonds, be hardly noticed before the"—she hesitated a moment and then plunged on—"the execution of the deed."

Lady Fairgrief's brow wrinkled a moment in thought and then, with a little cry, she shrank back into her pillows. "Cyanide," she whispered, her eyes wide and startled. "Someone's tried to kill *me*—with cyanide?"

"What could be better?" her niece asked. "The stuff is so very volatile that it vanishes—even from a body—within days after death, unless you're specifically looking for it. And it would look exactly like a coronary."

"And at my age . . ." Lady Fairgrief left the phrase unfinished.

"Just so," agreed Miss Worthing. "I'm going to leave that glass in the closet for now and I'll try to sequester the bottle, too.

"I'm going to lock you in tonight, Aunt Eulalia," she said at the door. "You should be perfectly all right. There is, at least, one thing we do know now."

Lady Fairgrief looked up with worried eyes.

"That we weren't wrong, that there has been murder done." Miss Worthing answered the unasked question. "And there may be murder still being done." She clicked off the overhead light. "I'll come for you in the morning," she said and shut and locked the door behind her.

chapter
NINETEEN

In the dining room, Miss Worthing found the others engaged in sporadic, desultory interchanges over liqueurs. Eyeing the amaretto bottle very much askance, she poured herself a pony of crème de menthe—the same thing, she noticed, that Becay was drinking. After one brief look at the clock, she joined them at the table, listening to the inane conversation for the few agonizing minutes it took to empty her glass.

She beckoned to Stephan and went into the kitchen. He joined her as she finished rinsing out the tiny glass and put it into the drainboard. "What's up?" he asked.

"I want you to go up to your room—it's right across the hall from Mary Ellen's, isn't it? Good. Well, go up there and read or something, but do contrive to keep an eye on her door, would you?" She hesitated for a long moment and then added, "And yourself, too."

She fetched her coat from the kitchen closet where she had put it earlier. The young man took it and held it for her. "Okay," he said. "But why?"

"Because she's almost totally exhausted, physically and emotionally."

Suddenly, almost before she realized what she was doing, she rounded on him. "Don't any of you realize the responsibilities that poor young woman has had thrust on her?" she demanded quietly but fiercely. "First, your father expected her to be the world's best housekeeper and you and your brother all let her take on herself the lion's share of any work to be done around here or at the opera company—" She cut her tirade off as Stephan's face flushed.

"I know," he admitted, his expression suitably penitent. "We haven't treated her very well."

"Men!" she grumbled, peering into her wallet to make sure she had her driver's license with her.

"But I promise you, I intend to make it up to her."

"Good," she commented, "it's about time." Then, abruptly, she laughed and—rather gently—put her gloved hand to his cheek. "You can start by going upstairs this very instant."

"Where are you going?" He smiled back at her.

"I have an errand to run and I'm a whole hour late."

He nodded briefly and ran up the back stairs.

In the dining room, Miss Shaw was still comfortably lolling in her place, swirling chartreuse in an oversized balloon glass. Becay, however, was gone.

"Where did he go?" Miss Worthing asked in a sharp voice.

"He said he was going into the library." Miss Shaw looked up, startled. "He said he wanted to read before going to bed."

"Martha," Miss Worthing said, after considering a moment, "go in there. Keep an eye on him and . . . well, anyone else who comes along. Try to do it unobtrusively but don't let them out of eye or earshot until I get back."

"The nurse?" Miss Shaw raised an enquiring eyebrow.

"Yes," Miss Worthing replied and headed for the front door.

She drove down the long drive to the front gate, keeping an eye peeled all the way, and frowning when she reached it. Dimly, at the back of her mind, something was nagging at her, some connection a part of her had recognized and was just not communicating to her conscious mind. After a few moments, as she loitered at the gate and peered either way down the road, she dismissed it.

"At least," she said aloud to herself, as was her habit when alone in an automobile, "the Mayhew case was brutal and straightforward. Not that anything like that should ever happen again. This is much too small a town to have so many bodies lying about. Nasty business, but at least there weren't the infernal blind alleys there seem to be here."

These rather scatty ruminations were suddenly interrupted as she turned onto the main road and found Schmidt and Lawrence Bessermann walking back toward the house.

"Ah ha," she said to herself, and pulled over. "What's happened?" she sang out.

"Our brakes have been tampered with," Lawrence shouted in his anger.

"Some vun tried to kill us," Schmidt chimed in with equal outrage.

Lawrence turned swiftly toward Schmidt. "Shut your goddamn mouth," Miss Worthing barely heard him mutter savagely to Schmidt.

"Well, boys," she said cheerfully. "Climb in and I'll take you back to the house. You can call a garage from there, okay?"

The two men got into the car and as they drove back up to the house were totally silent except for the seething intake and outgo of breath.

"What happened?" prompted Miss Worthing.

"We were right at the top of Vallejo Hill," Larry's voice rasped in the darkness beside her. "I put my foot on the damn brake pedal and it went all the way to the floor."

"Most distressing," Miss Worthing murmured in shocked tones.

"I had to drive into a tree to stop us."

"Vindshield is shattered," Schmidt protested.

"Something else could have been smashed, Herr Schmidt," Miss Worthing couldn't help pointing out, "if Larry hadn't thought to drive into a tree."

They pulled up in front of the house. Both men were out of the automobile like a shot.

"'Something else' is us," Miss Worthing overheard Schmidt growl as they climbed the steps to the veranda. She felt, briefly, a small stirring of conscience and contrition. Perhaps, she reflected, she should have read that car-repair manual more closely. She had planned to have their brakes give out before they left the main gate. Probably, she thought blithely, she hadn't cut far enough through the hose. Oh well, all's well and all that, but she just couldn't let anyone leave the house tonight.

Of course, it was very likely they might try to get another car. But—she chuckled to herself—she would trust in Martha's pertinacity and their own considerable shaking up to prevent that. As she coasted out onto the road and then, shortly, nosed down Vallejo Hill, she observed with a certain rueful satisfaction that the car was indeed smack against a tree.

Besides, she reflected, there seemed to be some barely controlled animosity raging among the several men in that house. Under most circumstances, she would have had precious little patience with it; under the present ones, it could only be to the good.

* * *

Loma Linda Drive was a street in one of the few really suburban parts of the valley, an area of pleasant but rather small houses with postage-stamp plots of grass and minuscule gardens behind. Not too long ago, they—

Miss Shaw and Miss Worthing—had even thought of buying one. Then—to her everlasting satisfaction—Miss Worthing's childhood home had most unexpectedly come on the market, and they had snapped it up. Unfortunately, it was getting to be a bit much for two elderly women to manage and for the last two years there had been a constant wrangle going on between them as to whether or not they should try to get some help.

Try, of course, is the operative word, she thought to herself as she parked in front of number 1485.

There were no lights on in the house.

"Now that's strange," she muttered as she walked up the path, her footsteps loud in the crisp night air and the tangible silence of the surrounding countryside. The yard was thick with dried fall leaves, stirred and scattered by the persisting wind. They scurried around her ankles with vague rasping whispers and loudly crunched under foot. Their most likely source—two tall sycamores obscuring the roof of the darkened house—reached nearly naked branches into silhouette against the eastern sky, where the moon had just begun to rise.

She knocked.

There was no discernible answer.

After waiting a few minutes, she rang the doorbell and heard, faintly within, a melodious chime. Suddenly, a light shone in the fanlight above the door and she heard the chain being put up. The door opened a crack revealing a bulky shadow against the bright light in the tiny foyer.

"*Si?*" a voice said very softly.

"Miss Martinez?" Miss Worthing asked.

To her surprise, a sob greeted the question. "No," the voice answered tearfully. "She is dead."

"What?" said Miss Worthing. "But I had an appointment with her tonight."

"She . . ." The voice dissolved.

"See here," said Miss Worthing strongly, "can I come in? I would like to ask you some questions."

"Police here all day askin' me questions."

"Please, it's very important."

After a moment of hesitation, the door closed, the chain was slipped off, and the door opened wide. Miss Worthing stepped into a very pleasant entry hall barren of any furniture or furnishings but a needlepoint hanger and floors of oak burnished to a dazzling shine. A heavy, small Mexican woman, her hair white, her face a road map of wrinkles, dressed in a faded blue cotton dress, let her in.

"I am Consuela's sister," the still weeping woman explained. "I live here, too." She led the way into the living room, also spartanly furnished but with hundreds of photographs on the walls.

"Patients?" Miss Worthing wondered silently, and said aloud, "Please, Miss, Mrs. . . ."

"I am Mrs. Baca," the other woman said. "Will you sit down? Coffee?"

"No, thank you, Mrs. Baca. But I would like to know what happened to Miss Martinez."

"She got a call to go to the hospital this afternoon—" Mrs. Baca began.

"What time was that?"

"It was around two, I think."

"And?"

"When she got to the hospital, they said she was mistaken, that they had not called her. That, anyway, is what the police tell me. She went out to wait for her bus and when she crosses the street, this car, it seemed to come out of nowhere, they say, and . . ." The woman began to sob anew.

"But who did it?"

"We don' know. They drive away."

"Did anyone see the car?"

"No—they . . . they couldn't . . . wouldn't . . ." She began weeping afresh.

"Hit-and-run?" Miss Worthing muttered in extreme exasperation and shook her head. Really, this was beginning to look like the last act of Hamlet. "I won't trouble you any further in your grief, Mrs. Baca." She stood up. "I'm very sorry."

In her car, Miss Worthing felt considerably shaken. By far the nastiest part of this whole taradiddle had been the merry slaughter of the innocents caught up into a maelstrom that was none of their doing, and then swept out ruthlessly and relentlessly as though they were so much unwanted dust.

Which was precisely the moment it struck her.

"But he couldn't have done this?" she murmured to herself. "It's plain ridiculous. He was the only one who *couldn't* have done it. Oh ye pigs and little fishes of the Lord, help me now."

* * *

Miss Shaw and the men were all in the library when she returned to the house. "Indeed yes," Miss Shaw was rattling on. "We've been buddies since the Great Depression. We went into business, then, don't you see. Rather a daring thing to do, actually, but we did have a lovely time of it eventually, but, oh Lord, those first years . . . Well, thank God we needn't ever go through that again. Of course, I always thought I might get married but, you know, running a business, and gentlemen in those days didn't much care for women who . . ."

Listening outside the door, Miss Worthing was grimly amused. Miss Shaw had certainly taken her at her word. However, it was high time she got in there. When Miss Shaw began to talk of marriage, it was a sure bet that even she was running short of conversational topics.

She swept in. "Martha, really. I believe you're chattering their ears off," she gushed, smiling vaguely around at them. She doffed her coat and draped it over the arm of a chair. "Now would any of you like a cup of nice hot cocoa before retiring. The funeral is tomorrow afternoon and I'm certain you will all have things you have to do in the morning."

"Would anyone like a sleeping pill?" Becay asked, his bleary eyes looking disinterestedly about.

Schmidt snorted and addressed Miss Worthing. "A cup of cocoa would be lovely, kind lady."

A considerable change in attitude since last the man had addressed her. "You're staying, Herr Schmidt?" she asked.

"*Ja.* Mary Ellen asked me to stay. I vas going to call a taxi, but . . ." He shrugged. "Iss best. I vill be here first thing."

"Indeed," she murmured, picking up her coat and, in handing it to Miss Shaw, dropping it to the floor. Miss Shaw and Miss Worthing both bent over to retrieve it.

"Anything?" Miss Worthing whispered.

"Not a damn thing," Miss Shaw replied, picking up the coat and waddling out of the room.

"I'm going to have a Scotch and soda," Becay suddenly said and got up. Schmidt and Lawrence Bessermann scowled at him and, putting their heads close, began a murmured conversation. "After that," the doctor continued, glaring briefly at the two of them huddled together, "I'm going to bed. Good night, everyone," he said loudly. Frowning at the two men at the other end of the library, he bowed slightly to Miss Worthing and left the room.

Miss Shaw returned bearing a tray of filled mugs and thick slices of plain cake. Lawrence and Schmidt both took mugs and thanked her. Miss Worthing, too, accepted one and, slowly sipping it, began to browse around the library, peering at the titles of the books on the shelves.

"It's always such a pleasure to see someone else's library," she said to no one in particular. "One can usually tell so much about a person that way."

Schmidt nodded and, cake in hand, made a gesture that included the whole room. "Iss true here," he said unclearly, his mouth full.

"You can certainly tell a few things about your father," she said to Lawrence, who sat moodily staring in front of him as he sipped his cocoa. "First, not only can you tell that he was a musician, but a singer. Look here." She beckoned to Martha, who cheerfully toddled over, mug in hand. "The scores could have been in the library of any musician, a coach or conductor, as well as a singer. But look here." She pointed to a shelf of fragile-looking volumes. "These are all singers' memoirs or biographies of—oh look!" She removed a small octavo. "It's, my goodness, an original of Lamperti." She returned it to its place almost reverently and continued around the room and on up the circular iron stairway to the gallery, peering at the small hand-lettered cards indicating subject locations: apiculture, botany, chemistry, geology, horticulture. She peeked over the metal balustrade at the others. "Goodness, your father certainly kept up his interest in science," she exclaimed.

Lawrence looked up at her as she slid her hand around the upper shelves, head tilted back, gazing up at the titles of the upper volumes, dim and uncertain in the inadequate light of the gallery.

"He sort of had to." He tried to smile and did not succeed too well. "He needed to keep healthy."

Again she turned about to peer down at the young man and caught the tail end of some message flash between him and Schmidt. Interesting, she thought, and once more turned her attention to the shelves. Carefully she took down a volume.

"Someone certainly takes good care of this room," she

commented admiringly. The book was free of any accumulation of dust.

"I think Mary Ellen has someone in every few days to do the whole place," Lawrence said, climbing the circular stairway himself and drifting a hand across the books. Suddenly, he laughed. "God! Leave it to Pop to include music theory in the science section."

"I think you should all go to bed." Miss Worthing smiled at him. "I'll lock up." She descended the narrow iron staircase and began to turn the locks on the windows. Her hands came away grimy. Their daily help was not perhaps as thorough as she might have been. She tutted at the sight and Lawrence laughed.

"We don't usually lock the windows," he said. "There's nothing in here to interest most people."

Without thinking, she took a tissue from a pocket to clean off her hands. Then—suddenly—she stopped and stood stock still, a rather foolish smile lighting up her face. She had not infrequently bemoaned the fact that her mind moved like an iceberg, most of it beneath the surface. When, however, the surface was finally broached and all the clarity of noon shone on the structure that had slowly been abuilding, there was no other joy in the wide world to match it.

"What is it?" Larry asked, descending the stairs.

"Nothing, Larry." She smiled at him. "Nothing at all. It's just I've forgotten something for tomorrow." And with no more ado, she turned and left the room.

* * *

After a while, Miss Shaw found her friend sitting in the kitchen drinking cup after cup of tea so strong it would have taken the paint off a wall. "What on earth are you doing?" she enquired.

"There's a thousand things to do." Miss Worthing looked up. "First of all, go upstairs and see if Stephan is still awake."

"And?"

"If he is, ask him if there's either a microscope or a hand glass in the house."

Miss Shaw peered bemusedly over her glasses. "Got it?"

Miss Worthing nodded solemnly. "Yes, Martha. I believe I do."

After Miss Shaw had departed on her errand, Miss Worthing rummaged about in her purse for a while and came up with a small memorandum pad and her ancient fountain pen. From her apron, which hung on the back door of the utility room, she took the tissues that held the bodies of the bees she had found earlier and, with almost tender care, placed them on the table. In a drawer she found a flashlight and turned it on briefly to check the batteries, expecting the baleful glow such things usually had. For a change, it functioned beautifully. She waited for Miss Shaw, drinking another cup of the vile brew she had made. The powerful stimulant was coursing through her and she felt the same kind of disagreeable anxiety she remembered as her main emotion the night she and poor Alfred Mayhew had shot it out in Rodeo Lagoon in the Marin headlands.

Miss Shaw came back with a small wooden box. "It's Stephan's microscope he had in high school. He said it's not very good, no more than about four hundred X, but at least it's something."

With a grunt, Miss Worthing set up the scope and put the flashlight down beside the instrument to shine into its mirror. Carefully, she put first one bee and then the other on a slide and, with a toothpick, turned them about this way and that while she squinted into the inadequate eyepiece, all the time muttering to herself.

Presently, she straightened and looked at her friend. "I'm afraid," she said in an almost confessional tone, "that I've been gulled by almost wholesale misdirection. Our only hope is that it's been largely, as I suspect, unintentional. Also," she sighed and shook her head, "the truth as I see it now is so very unlikely indeed."

"How so, Mattie?" Miss Shaw asked. Pouring herself a cup of tannic acid, she settled back to watch and listen.

"Here." Miss Worthing took her pen, uncapped it, and opened the memo pad. "Let's look at the thing chronologically, or at least logically," and she wrote:

> MS and MW are invaded by hiveless bees (!!!)
>
> Arly Lloyd reports two hives torn up by vandals. What person in his right mind would do so?
>
> Stephan and Rudolf perform, Rudy is playing and Stephan singing. They switch places (as, of course, would happen). A bee (??) emerges from an autumn posy gathered by Schmidt. Stings Rudy 2X (!!!)
>
> Rudy recovers after a lung intubation.
>
> The next day to sign new codicil.
>
> A day later is down with pneumonia. Pneumonia!!! Did Maude get it all right? Important query.
>
> Rudy dies in less than 24 hours of apparent heart failure! From pneumonia???
>
> Inheritances.
>
> MW finds the bodies of two dead honeybees under the bed Rudy died in.
>
> Mary Ellen is gassed.

> Consuela Martinez is run over in the middle of the afternoon, the same afternoon Mary Ellen is gassed.
>
> That very evening, Aunt Eulalia is proffered cyanide.

"You're joking!" Miss Shaw exclaimed.
"Not in the least," replied Miss Worthing shortly and returned to her memorandum.

> There is no dust on the books in the library, but there is on the window frames.

"There . . ." Miss Worthing began, and then frowned savagely. "Oh dear, no! There's one more thing:

> I'm forgetting poor Harvey. How could one forget poor Harvey (except of course, one always did). Harvey? Suicide?

"And there it is. Why Harvey?" Miss Worthing sighed and capped her pen. "It isn't *the* key but it's definitely the only one that's going to open this particular door."
"How?" asked Miss Shaw. Lumbering to her feet, she peered into the pot by the sink. "Do you want any more of this foul stuff?" she asked.
Miss Worthing chuckled. "By all means make another pot of it. You and I are going to be up all night long, my dear. How?" Miss Worthing returned to Miss Shaw's unanswered question. "By knowing who could do each of those specific acts. That's what has been plaguing me. Come with me," she commanded, standing up and hefting the flashlight.

"Where are we going?" demanded Miss Shaw.

"Only to the library, Martha. Nothing silly."

The room was eerie in the light of the waning moon, which shone through the enormous windows. As the two ladies once more ascended the iron staircase, their footsteps sounded hollow, reverberant, and huge, no matter how carefully they tried to tread.

"Now look at this." Miss Worthing flashed the light on one of the handwritten cards. She muttered under her breath as she searched the volumes. "This one seems likely," she said and handed the flashlight to Miss Shaw. "Now hold that steady," she said and opened the book. "It looks old enough.

"*Die Bienehalten,*" she read aloud, turning to the copyright page, which simply read: *1934, Wien.*

It was one of those grotesquely academic tomes so characteristic of a certain type of Teutonic scholarship, a compendium of overwhelmingly learned articles on the rather whimsical craft of beekeeping. She read down the table of contents, and with a small satisfied grunt, snapped it to and put it back on the shelf.

"And to think it's been in front of me the whole time," she muttered.

"What has?" Miss Shaw asked, but her companion was already halfway down the stairs.

Back in the kitchen, Miss Worthing picked up the telephone and dialed a number. It continued to ring for a long time at the other end.

"Mattie," Miss Shaw remonstrated with her. "It's one-thirty in the morning."

"I know." Miss Worthing chuckled. "I do hope George won't be too angry with me."

"George Lorris?" Miss Shaw exclaimed.

Just then the other telephone was picked up and a sleepy voice said blearily, "'lo?"

"I want to speak to Mr. Lorris," she said. "Tell him Matilda Worthing is calling."

There were confused mutters at the other end of the wire. Finally, another voice came on saying sharply, "What *is* it, Miss Worthing?"

"George, sorry to bother you at such a hour but you are the district attorney. I thought I'd better get on to you instead of Sam."

"What is it?" George Lorris repeated more sharply still.

"Come over to the Bessermann house." There were thunderous protests. "Immediately," she continued. "There's something I think it's high time you knew about."

chapter
TWENTY

The morning of Rudolf Bessermann's funeral dawned high and clear. The air was ripe with the smells of yet another Indian summer day but the weather forecast had warned of snow before nightfall.

When Mary Ellen descended the stairs that morning, her pallor had, if not gone, at least not deepened, and the listlessness of utter fatigue had been replaced by her usual efficient step. Only the tightly drawn skin around her eyes indicated the pressure under which she still labored. She wore a plush emerald-green dressing gown and had obviously tended to her hair. Her face was still shiny and newly scrubbed.

Halfway down the stairs, she stopped in surprise. All the furniture had been waxed and polished until it gleamed in the sunlight streaming through the front windows. The rugs all looked as though they had been swept within an inch of their life and not a speck of dust was visible anywhere.

It was the flowers, though, that were most wonderful. Scattered all about the room were floor vases of autumnal chrysanthemums, earth-colored and sober, while on the coffee table, an enormous bowl of luxuriously scarlet roses seemed almost to dominate the huge room. It was the vases of cala lilies on the piano and the end tables, however, that vied for pride of place.

"Where on earth did they come from?" She bent to admire the lilies. "They are so outrageously out of season." Her question was answered in the kitchen. Miss Shaw and Miss Worthing were seated at the table, their hair done up in dusters and clothed in dilapidated, threadbare cotton housedresses, which, once upon a time, had been blue but were faded to a dingy, disreputable gray. A pot of coffee sat between them as they propped their heads on their hands, weary and red of eye, drinking from steaming mugs.

"Have you two been at it all night?" she exclaimed, startling Miss Shaw into a faint squeak of alarm.

Miss Worthing uttered a weak giggle and earned a nasty glare from Miss Shaw in return. "There was," said Miss Shaw presently, having regained her composure, "a great deal to be got through."

"It's beautiful," said Mary Ellen gratefully. "And those flowers! Where did you get them?"

"I got them last night in San Francisco," Miss Worthing said rather blandly. "A dear friend of ours has a shop in the Embarcadero Center. They are lovely, aren't they?"

Miss Shaw slewed around to stare in amazement at Miss Worthing, who was being very careful not to catch her eye.

"Would you like some coffee, Mary Ellen?" asked Miss Worthing, ignoring her friend. "Or tea? There's both and a big breakfast spread. In fact"—she giggled weakly again—"we prepared enough for the Seventh Fleet. There are going to be a lot of people here."

Mary Ellen sat down. Once more weariness seemed to overwhelm her. "Yes, there are," she said. "The entire funeral party—chorus and everything—is meeting here before going to the church." She broke off and, remembering herself, arched an eyebrow at them. "And you two haven't even been to bed yet," she protested.

Miss Worthing got up and came around the table. Gently, she laid a hand on Mary Ellen's shoulder. "I'm afraid there's rather more to it than that," she said gently.

Mary Ellen said nothing. For a long moment—her posture gone suddenly rigid—she sat staring directly in front of her. "It's so beastly," she finally whispered.

Miss Worthing sighed and concurred. "I know, dear, but . . . well, I thought you had better know. It will all be over shortly."

"I'm not sure I believe that," Mary Ellen said flatly. But before Miss Worthing could think of anything to say to that, she added, "But I will be glad when this nightmare is over. Two days of total . . ." She caught hold of herself and shook her head as though refusing to allow entry to the thoughts swirling round. "I can't let myself mourn yet. Not yet." She looked up at the two women and frowned slightly. "I feel as though it all has to end before I can, before I dare, allow myself to cry for Uncle Rudy and poor, dear Harvey."

Miss Shaw made a small grunt of approval.

"And you're absolutely right," Miss Worthing agreed firmly. "None of us felt we could mourn until we had done our jobs."

"And you did have to do your jobs?" asked Mary Ellen bitterly. There was no reply. The two elderly women merely looked at her calmly. After a moment of facing that dispassionate regard, she nodded once and then again. "I'm sorry," she said softly, "that was stupid. We all have to do our jobs. I have to do mine this morning." She stood up. "Is there anything I can do?" she asked simply.

"Go wake up everyone and tell them to get themselves together."

Mary Ellen seemed to think this was funny. "They'll all be up already," she said with a wry smile. "They have to warm their voices up in"—she glanced at the clock—"within the next half hour if they're to be ready by one o'clock." She glanced from Miss Worthing to Miss Shaw and back. "And then?" she asked.

"Just leave everything to Martha and me."

Mary Ellen turned around and went out without another word. Miss Shaw waited until her friend had once more sat down and poured herself another cup of coffee before speaking. "What, may I ask, were you doing in San Francico?" she demanded. "I thought you went to Hector Velasquez for those flowers."

Miss Worthing tutted and sipped coffee. "I went to fetch Maude. Aunt Eulalia will need her this morning and I expect to be very busy."

"I do wish you wouldn't drive that kind of distance at night," her friend said severely. "You know your eyes are not very good."

"Good enough," rejoined Miss Worthing tartly. "Besides, you were busy here."

"Lord knows." Miss Shaw sighed heavily and stood up. "What next?"

"Feed me!" said Lady Fairgrief in a demanding voice as she was pushed through the doorway by a very well-rested-looking Maude.

"Good morning, Aunt Eulalia!" Miss Worthing exclaimed, giving her aunt's cheek a peck. "How do you feel this morning?"

"Fit as a fiddle and rarin' to go," the old woman exclaimed heartily.

"My lady!" Maude reproved mildly.

"Oh, stuff," her ladyship sputtered. "I clean forgot you weren't in the picture." Before her maid could be reasonably expected to ask the logical question, she waved her hand dismissingly. "But don't ask what picture 'cause I won't tell you."

Miss Shaw caught Miss Worthing's glance. "Lady Fairgrief," Miss Shaw said after mastering herself, "you're just in time to be of great service."

"Ah." The old woman breathed satisfaction.

Miss Worthing chortled. "Martha and I have to go and don our funeral rags," she explained. "We want you to stay in here and keep an eye on things."

"Good." Her ladyship nodded vigorously. "I'm hungry anyway and Maude is here to protect me." She patted the arm of her maid, who beamed back at her.

Miss Worthing yawned mightily and stretched. "Oh, what I wouldn't give for a nap," she groaned and then brightened. "But there's a murderer to catch . . ." She twinkled at them.

Maude gasped. "My lady!"

"Quiet, Maude!"

". . . and I have a few necessary traps to lay," Miss Worthing concluded after the interruption.

She and Miss Shaw departed as they could hear the house come alive above them. Lady Fairgrief finished her meager breakfast and loitered over coffee.

First, Stephan rushed in wearing only a towel. "Whoops," he shouted, catching sight of the old woman, "'Scuse me, Tante Lally, but I'm in a hurry." He scooped up a sausage and rolled it between a piece of toast, sloshed coffee into a cup, and drank it straight off. "Where's Mary Ellen?" he asked, munching his improvised sandwich.

"In the library, I believe, laying out scores."

At that moment, however, Mary Ellen's rich mezzo-soprano began a slow, sustained vocalization from the living room. Stephan wolfed the last of his sausage and toast and washed it down with more coffee. "Lord, I've got to vocalize, too," he said, rushing out, coffee cup in one hand, his slipping towel clutched in the other.

Upstairs, Miss Shaw and Miss Worthing finished their hasty ablutions, which at least had the virtue of helping to awaken them slightly. The two ladies donned the severe navy suits they always wore to funerals and met in the hall. Miss Worthing held something wrapped in a piece of tissue paper. "You go on down, Martha," she murmured quietly. "I have to do something first."

Miss Shaw waddled off down the hall. Miss Worthing waited at the turn in the hallway and watched as Becay sauntered out of his room in immaculate mourning clothes and went downstairs. From inside the shower at the head of the stairs, Stephan's voice was raised above the splashing of the water.

Suddenly, she heard Lawrence's voice yelling at him. "How long you gonna be?"

"Till I'm cleaned up and warmed up."

"Hurry up then. I have to vocalize, too."

Downstairs, Lady Fairgrief could not help overhearing this shouted exchange. "Do they always vocalize in the shower?" she asked.

Becay looked up absently from his newspaper. He was steadily working his way through a sizeable breakfast. "It's some kind of tradition in the family." He smiled, taking a sip of coffee. "Rudy used to do it, and somehow all the kids picked it up from him."

Above them, Stephan's voice was rising to the B flat of the *Ingemisco*. It cracked halfway up the brutal passage. "Damn," he shouted, "damn, damn, da-a-a-a-mn," vocalizing on the open syllable.

Lawrence came in wearing an eye-searing bathrobe and laughed at Lady Fairgrief, whose lorgnette had gone up in astonishment at the fluorescent paisley gown. He picked up a few pieces of bacon, put them onto some toast as his brother had done, and poured coffee. "Is there any tomato juice," he asked, looking around.

"I'll bring some out," Miss Shaw said from the kitchen.

Lady Fairgrief put her cup down to say something to

Lawrence, but refrained when she caught him looking with peculiar malice at Becay, who flushed and retreated behind the newspaper.

Miss Shaw lumbered out of the kitchen with a water tumbler full of tomato juice. "I brought you a big one. You singers have such quirks."

"You're quite right." He smiled tightly. "This is mine." Nodding to the ladies, he went out, his bathrobe an incandescent train behind him. As he ascended the stairs, he met Miss Worthing coming down. He muttered a brief greeting to her and continued his way up the stairs. Miss Worthing hurried down the rest of the stairs and disappeared into the library. Presently, Lawrence's incredible basso was rattling the tiles in the shower.

"Lord, what a horror," Miss Shaw muttered.

"Eh?" asked her ladyship, who could hear nothing above the din.

The noise was quite astonishing: Lawrence, a bass, was in the shower; Stephan, a tenor, was in his bedroom, apparently with the door wide open; and Mary Ellen, a mezzo-soprano, was in the living room. The overall effect of three people vocalizing in three different keys was precisely that of cats brawling violently at three in the morning.

Suddenly, Becay stood up and threw his paper down on the table, his face gone pasty white. "Christ, what a family!" he swore violently, stalking to the door, where he turned. "I'll be in the library if anyone cares." He almost collided with Miss Worthing, who was just coming out of the library. He stood aside as she passed and then closed the door behind her.

Mary Ellen was playing softly through the *Recordare* section of the *Requiem* and humming. She had changed into a severe black crepe with a form-fitting square-necked yoke. Under ordinary circumstances, it would have managed to be both virginal and alluring. At the moment, however, the midnight black only accentuated the lack of all color in her skin. She glanced up and smiled at Miss Worthing. "There was a man here to see you, Miss Worthing," she said.

"Oh?"

"Yes. Tall, sandy-haired, good-looking."

"Oh yes." Miss Worthing smiled happily. "I was expecting him."

"He's with Miss Shaw in the kitchen." The young woman cocked her head to one side, looking curiously at Miss Worthing. "I sent him around the back way."

"Splendid."

"Who was he?"

"Now don't you fuss," Miss Worthing began. "You just go on prac—" She was interrupted by loud, violent, and *basso profondo* swearing. "Now what on earth is all that?" Miss Worthing exclaimed.

From upstairs, they could hear Stephan bang on Lawrence's door. "What's the matter, Larry?"

There was a moment of silence, then Lawrence's voice yelled out, sounding a bit shaken. "Nothing's wrong. I thought my diamond studs had been stolen in Vegas."

Mary Ellen's eyes went up and she shook her head in exasperation. "Excuse me, Miss Worthing," she said, forgetting the visitor. "I do have to finish here." She gestured toward the score.

Grateful for the interruption, which had spared her yet another difficult explanation, Miss Worthing trotted happily into the breakfast room. She peered briefly into the kitchen and nodded at the man seated there, a cup of coffee in hand. Then, with a small sigh of intense satisfaction, she stood by the cupboard and idly buttered a piece of toast.

chapter
TWENTY-ONE

Presently, Stephan came downstairs dressed in a simply cut, three-piece black suit with a modest pearl- and black-striped four-in-hand. His hair was still wet and plastered into place. He looked very young.

He stood for a long moment gazing across the living room at his cousin, who was now singing the lovely words and heart-breaking melody of the *Lacrymosa*, her dark, warm voice richly colored.

She glanced up and caught his eye. To his deep surprise, she blushed and looked back at the score.

"Mary Ellen," he said urgently, striding across the room. "What's wrong with you?"

She shook her head without looking up. "It's just so awful," she said sorrowfully. "Uncle Rudy's been dead barely two days and here we are"—she looked up at him—"vocalizing and wondering whether we're going to perform well."

He sat down next to her on the piano bench. His arm automatically went round her waist, but she stiffened and shrank away. With a muffled oath, he whirled round on the bench. "I don't believe you," he said.

She found herself able to say nothing whatever, lest she say everything. A bitter shame rose up inside of her like bile. At the same time, a voice at the back of her mind kept repeating over and over, "you mustn't cry, it's bad for the throat; you mustn't cry, it's bad for the throat; you mustn't . . ."

Suddenly, Stephan threw himself back against the piano, his elbows awakening a loud and jarring dissonance on the keys. He turned and looked briefly into Mary Ellen's face, which she held half turned away from him, taut with conflicting emotions. Unable to do more, he stood up and took one of her hands, limp in his gentle grasp. He turned it over and kissed the palm. "I'll go now," he said quietly. "If we seem so very brutal, remember that Dad would have wanted us to be pros."

She nodded dumbly and stared into the face, which, in spite of everything, was the face she loved best in the world. He swallowed, turned, and stalked back toward the stairs.

"I'll be in my room," he said without turning around. "Send someone for me when the rehearsal begins."

Above him, Lawrence—rather absurdly dressed in mourning clothes with his mop of hair all anyhow—came tripping down the stairs. He was visibly seething with some barely controlled emotion. He stared briefly at his unhappy brother and swept the rest of the way down the stairs. He carried a pair of moleskin gloves, which he was impatiently slapping into the palm of the other hand. "Mary Ellen," he said peremptorily. "Have you seen Paul?"

His cousin continued to hold her head in one hand, an elbow resting on the stand of the piano, while she tinkled out a small and maddening tune with one finger, singing words in a small voice: "He is dead and gone, Lady; he is dead and gone. By his hat and—"

"Mary Ellen!"

She looked up. "I'm sorry, Larry. What is it?"

He looked sharply at her. "Are you all right?" he asked. "You won't screw up the performance?"

Her face clouded angrily. "Do you mean your father's funeral?" she demanded sharply.

His lips tightened. "I asked if you had seen Paul."

Not trusting her voice, she jerked her head toward the library. Without another word, he opened the door and went in.

Mary Ellen went back to plucking out her little tune. In the doorway of the breakfast room, Miss Worthing—who had missed none of what had transpired—calmly munched her toast and glanced at the clock. "Five minutes," she said to herself and checked to make certain the small pin she had stuck in the lapel of her suit was still there holding an inconspicuous piece of hat feather.

Suddenly, out front, there was the sound of automobiles. Mary Ellen sat up, patted her hair, and tried to get a grip on herself. She stood and found Miss Worthing at her elbow.

"Hurry." The older woman was urgent. "Get out there and stall them. Give me fifteen minutes. It's a lovely day. Get Martha to send out coffee. Tell them . . . oh, tell them anything but don't let them in."

She hurried the younger woman to the front door. People dressed in black and navy were pouring out of cars, their faces studiously composed into that faintly self-righteous expression they wear for someone else's sorrow. It seemed almost too beautiful a day for such unhappiness. Here and there a sluggish wasp bumbled along and birds were singing in the spruces near the drive.

"Good," Miss Worthing murmured to herself. "Even the weather is with me." High over the western rim of the valley, though, clouds were piling higher and higher. With only a fleeting regret for the last of the summer weather, she turned to go in.

Mary Ellen went down to speak to the choristers and Miss Worthing dashed back to the kitchen. "Quick, Martha, fill up a large urn of coffee and take it out. Mary Ellen's already out there. Maude, give Martha a hand and you, Aunt Eulalia, you stay put. Understood?"

Without waiting for a reply to her commands, she turned on her heels, crossed the living room to the library, paused for a moment, and then threw the doors wide open and walked in, shutting them behind her.

The two men were standing at either side of the table. Lawrence was rigid, his back to the open windows. Across the table, Becay had one of his hands on the back of a chair and was pounding the table with the other. Both were clearly in a towering rage. They turned toward her.

"What *is* it, Miss Worthing?" Lawrence snapped at her with unconcealed impatience. Becay uttered a foul oath and flipped open a cigarette case.

"I'm so sorry, gentlemen," she dithered at them. "But I seem to recall leaving my prayer book in here." She looked vaguely around as though expecting it to appear in the air in front of her.

"Can't you get it later?" the doctor asked in an acid tone.

"But Mary Ellen says the others will be here soon," she flapped at him. "I just thought I'd nip over now and . . . Oh!" she exclaimed, "there it is."

The small volume lay on the floor in front of one of the open windows.

"Lawrence, dear"—she blinked—"would you be so kind?" She peered at him through her thick lenses as she scuttled toward the book.

With ill-concealed annoyance, Lawrence turned around and bent over. Beside him—and with her body hiding her movements from Becay—Miss Worthing whipped the pin from her lapel and let the tiny feather drop on Lawrence Bessermann's neck.

"What was that?" he yelled.

"Don't move," she said quickly, her voice pregnant with worry. "There's a wasp landed on your neck."

"Oh sweet God," the young man yelled, his voice rising in fear. "Get it off! Get it off!"

"Hold still," she cried, "I'll get it," and with her hand swiped at his neck. The pin, concealed in the palm of her hand, struck precisely the point where the feather had landed.

Lawrence screamed. "It stung me! Oh God, no!" He jumped up, almost knocking Miss Worthing over, his hand clasped to the back of his neck. "I'll die," he wailed. "Christ, somebody get a doctor." He ran toward the door.

"But Dr. Becay's here already," she cried, and restrained him with a surprisingly strong grip.

The man's face collapsed in terror while he tried to shake her hand away. Out of the corner of her eye, she saw Becay's eyes open wide. "Do you think I'd let him kill me, too?" Lawrence shrieked at her. "After what he did this morning?"

"Shut up, you fool," Becay shouted.

"Oh God, get a doctor." Lawrence threw off her hand at last and dashed to the door.

"What's the matter, Larry?" Miss Worthing demanded in a strong, commanding voice. "Afraid you'd die of a lipid pneumonia, too?"

Both men stared at her. Becay began edging his way around the table, his eyes blazing. Lawrence yanked the door open. "Mary Ellen!" he yelled.

"Do you think I'll let you get away with this, Miss Worthing?" Becay asked quietly.

A male voice from the doorway checked him. "That's far enough, Becay."

The doctor jerked his head up to see Lawrence struggling in the grip of Sam Marshall, the sheriff. The tall, sandy-haired man to whom Miss Worthing had nodded earlier in the kitchen, stepped around the struggling men into the room.

"Hello, George, Sam," Miss Worthing greeted the two of them affably.

"Get me a doctor," Lawrence wailed, writhing to get out of Marshall's grip. "I'll tell you everything."

Becay's expression disintegrated into pure loathing as he glanced from Miss Worthing back to Lawrence. "You stupid shit," he snapped and jammed a cigarette into his mouth. "Well, I hope you don't think I'm going alone?" he asked calmly, but his hands trembled as they lit the cigarette.

"I'm dying!" Tears of terror were streaming down the face of the younger man.

"Oh?" Becay suddenly turned on him savagely. "It's been over two minutes. Got any symptoms?"

"Very astute of you, Doctor," Miss Worthing said, confronting Lawrence with the pin. "This is your wasp," she said acidly. "Now get a grip on yourself. Sam?"

Marshall let go of Lawrence and took a folded piece of paper from his back pocket. With a snarl of rage, Lawrence launched himself at Miss Worthing. Marshall grabbed him again.

"I'll do it, Sam," the district attorney said, and took the paper. "You're both under arrest. I have a warrant here signed by a qualified judge. You are charged with three counts of murder and three counts of conspiracy to commit murder. You have the right to remain silent . . ."

The ritual was got through and the two men were led out of the library just as Stephan once more came down the stairs. "I heard the people out front. What's going on?"

"Go into the breakfast room, Stephan," said Miss Worthing gently. "Lady Fairgrief will explain."

Instead, he followed them outdoors, where the crowd had been considerably swelled by the arrival of the orchestra. Little swirls of people eddied round them and it seemed almost like a choral scene in an opera as the crowd parted before the principals, who came face to face with Schmidt in conversation with Mary Ellen. Upon seeing them, the little Austrian's voice slowly faltered and came to a dead stop. He began backing away.

"What's the matter, Herr Schmidt?" Miss Worthing's voice rang out in derision. "You look as though you'd been stung."

Becay began suddenly to laugh maniacally. "God, you've even found out about him, too? Stow it, Helmut," he growled as the Austrian tried to protest. "The old broad's got us dead to . . ." His voice cracked. "Dead," he repeated dully.

"I don't know what you are talking about," Schmidt blustered.

"Don't you?" Miss Worthing asked mildly. "Herr Doktor Helmut Karl Schmidt, Professor of Apiculture or, of course, *Bienenzucht*, as they would have said in Vienna. Wonderful article on hive behavior in 'Beekeeping.' Yes, it was published in Vienna in 1934. Rudy had a copy in his library. Your part was unquestionably the cleverest of all." She gestured to the waiting deputies, who roughly thrust the three men into a Black Maria and drove away.

"There *was* somethin' goin' on here," Marshall groused at her.

"Sam." She raised an eyebrow at him and shook her head. "You wouldn't have believed me if I'd told you."

Behind her, Mary Ellen had finally given way. Her sobbing was audible and wracking.

"No one is going to ask you to perform now," Miss Worthing said gently.

Stephan nodded and continued to stroke his cousin's hair as he led her back inside.

The chorus principal approached her very hesitantly. "Excuse me, Miss Worthing," he asked, "but what do we do now."

"Something simple and appropriate, Harry," she replied crisply.

"The *Ave Maria?*"

"Saccharin, but acceptable."

"Well Kathy is here from San Francisco. We could do the *Vergine degli Angeli,*" Harry suggested tentatively.

"Conducted," she asked wryly, "by you?"

He tried to look elsewhere.

"No matter." Miss Worthing chuckled. "That will do. In fact," she said quietly after a moment, "that will be lovely. 'The Virgin of the angels,'" she quoted softly, "'will cover thee with her mantle, and the angel of the Lord shall stand steadfastly beside thee.' Yes, Harry, do that."

He pranced away to tell his fellows.

"It's done now, Rudy. It's done," she murmured and, turning about to look toward the mountains, slowly blessed herself. "And may the souls of the faithful departed, through the mercy of God, rest in peace."

chapter TWENTY-TWO

Early next morning, Miss Shaw was cheerfully scrambling enormous quantities of eggs and frying equally numerous rashers of bacon. The perfume of coffee was rising to the upstairs regions. Presently, bodies were audibly moving above, and smiling to herself, she added an iniquitous amount of butter to a skillet and, when it had melted, slowly poured the eggs into it.

"Martha, my dear," Miss Worthing said as she came in looking very well rested indeed, "thou art a miracle of grace." She peered into the skillet and chuckled. "So delicious, but enough cholesterol to kill one." She sighed in deep satisfaction.

Miss Shaw laughed and continued to turn the eggs slowly. "It's all a myth, you know. Besides, we're much too active for it to matter," she added illogically and turned the golden mass onto a platter. Butter ran out the sides; she carefully blotted the excess before covering the gorgeous things. "Mary Ellen said Louis Quinn would be coming over this morning."

Miss Worthing nodded. "Yes, there's to be the reading of the will."

The two ladies regarded each other for a moment and sighed. "Money!" breathed Miss Shaw. "So troublesome," agreed Miss Worthing.

"And such a bother," Miss Shaw added with an edge on her voice, "if you haven't got any."

Miss Worthing blinked her accord over a steaming cup. "It smells heavenly in here." Mary Ellen entered with a Chinese robe of black silk wrapped around her. Her eyes were a trifle red around the rim, but clear and sparkling.

"She's young yet," Miss Worthing conceded to herself, "but she'll recover now. Maybe one day she'll be as strong as him."

For just then, Stephan, too, came in and, after first kissing Mary Ellen's neck and taking her coffee cup out of her hand, said playfully, "Thank you. Just the way I like it," and made a remark about the cooking aromas.

Miss Shaw put her hands on her hips with a spatula sticking out to one side. "Well, is everybody just gonna stand around smelling it?" she asked. "Doesn't anyone want to eat any of it?"

Later, after everyone had finished breakfast, Miss Worthing and her aunt lingered over a final cup of coffee. "Those two are awfully brittle this morning," Lady Fairgrief said severely to her niece. "What's to be done?"

Miss Worthing stood up and began to stack the dirty dishes on the table. "I'm not altogether certain that there is anything to be done," she said thoughtfully. "They've lost their father and now their brother.... It can't be easy on them."

"Do tell," her ladyship muttered sarcastically.

Suddenly, Miss Worthing sat down again next to her aunt. "Stay with them, Aunt Eulalia," she said fervently. "Stay for a long time. They'll need you."

The older woman pursed her lips and nodded thoughtfully. "I think you may be right. Last night, Mary Ellen was hinting that they would like to get married here in Jolliston, and, in spite of Rudy's bequest, this is their home. Besides, I think those two are going to feel strangely ill at ease in the world for a while."

"I wonder what they'll make of themselves now." Miss

Worthing began to speculate, but the front door bell rang. "That must be Louis," she said, and wheeled her aunt toward the library.

* * *

". . . And so," the lawyer concluded, folding up papers, "the estate will have to remain under the probate court until after the criminal trial." He spoke with consummate delicacy. "If, of course, there is a trial. Nevertheless"—he regarded the assembled over a pair of half spectacles—"should there be any need for living expenses, I'm sure Judge Manning will make no fuss. Any questions?"

There were none and the lawyer rose.

"It's exactly as I suspected," Miss Worthing sighed. "But at least Steve and Mary Ellen will be comfortable for the rest of their lives. And now"—she too rose—"I want to go home."

"Hello, everyone." George Lorris startled everyone by walking in and skipping his hat onto the table. Mary Ellen uttered a brief little cry. Her hand caught at Stephan's and Lorris immediately looked sheepish. "Sorry," he muttered and glanced at Miss Worthing.

Quinn cleared his throat. "If that is all?" he said and looked round the room.

Mary Ellen saw the lawyer to the front door. When she came back she paused for a moment in the doorway, took a deep breath, and caught and held Stephan's eye. A charge like electricity seemed to pass between them; both straightened and stood taller. Covertly observing them, Lady Fairgrief felt a shock of pure joy go through her. The cure had begun.

"I know it's ridiculously early," Mary Ellen suddenly announced in a determined voice, "but I'm going to bring out the sherry." She looked gravely at Lorris. "It will help some of us," she said and smiled wryly, "to keep a

212

steady keel. As painful as it might be, there are a few questions I want to ask."

"Hear, hear," Stephan said quietly and fervently.

Everyone but Lorris took a glass of wine and then settled themselves comfortably around the shining walnut table. Light streamed through the windows. The portieres had been pulled back to reveal the back lawn, that vast expanse, covered with a thick virgin fall of snow upon which the sun shone brightly and blazed reflectively from the surface, which was marked only by the three-toed prints of birds.

"Now, Mr. Lorris," Stephan began, taking up a position in front of the fireplace. "How did you know that my father had been murdered? I was there. I was there all the time and I could have sworn it was . . ." His voice quavered slightly. He swallowed sherry and finished the sentence, "that he died naturally."

"It was meant to look that way," Lorris replied. "In fact, in a way, it was natural." Lorris looked toward the other side of the table. Lady Fairgrief, Miss Worthing, and Miss Shaw were all sitting quietly but he noticed that their eyes were gleaming and Lady Fairgrief's nostrils were quivering like those of a thoroughbred at the starting gate. He flushed and reached for a cigarette. "But I really think," he said, "that we ought to let the person who really did the legwork tell you." He bowed to Miss Worthing.

Rather wishing she felt less like an after-dinner speaker, Miss Worthing muttered, "Too kind," which for some reason sent Lady Fairgrief into gales of laughter.

"Just like Florence Nightingale," the old woman cackled.

Miss Worthing peered over the rims of her glasses at her aunt, saying nothing, two spots of color rising in her cheeks.

Stephan looked from one to the other. The heat from

the fire flushed his own features and a lock of hair falling into his face had been caught and plastered against his forehead by some slight perspiration. Mary Ellen stood up and took his arm. They stood together almost hieratically, their eyes flickering about the room.

Miss Worthing took herself in hand. "The question was"—she cleared her throat and plunged into the tale—"how did we know that murder had been done? Frankly, we didn't. Not, that is to say, know. On the other hand, when Aunt Eulalia reported to me the events leading up to poor Rudy's death, we could not see how it could be anything else."

Lorris suddenly looked pained.

"No, it's true, George, and for one very simple reason: Rudolf Bessermann was a singer."

Mary Ellen and Stephan looked at each other before looking questioningly at Lady Fairgrief.

"Of course," she answered their unspoken question. "The possibility occurred to me that very night." She shook her head ruefully. "Perhaps had I been smarter, poor Harvey and that poor nurse would still be alive."

"The nurse?" Mary Ellen exclaimed. "Did they kill Miss Martinez?"

"I'm afraid they rather had to, my dear," Miss Worthing said and leaned forward. "One, Harvey. Two, the nurse—and both because they knew something that could hang the three of them."

"What did they know?" Stephan asked. "We all knew the same things about what was going on. We were there."

"Not always, you weren't," Miss Worthing said, beginning to pace back and forth. "Harvey made a very shrewd guess that your father didn't die of pneumonia."

"He didn't?"

"No, Stephan, he died of another bee sting." She resumed her place at the table.

214

Mary Ellen covered her face.

"Then Harvey was right," Maude gasped.

Stephan looked to Lorris, who nodded. "We even have the bee, or rather bees," he said.

"Where?" asked Stephan incredulously.

"Miss Worthing found them under your uncle's bed. The autopsy was finished this morning and I'm afraid two bee stings were found in the tuck of his collar bone. Besides which I'm told his lungs were very near total collapse."

Miss Worthing suddenly looked sharply at Lorris. She seemed almost about to say something and then, abruptly, to change her mind.

"Were the bees Miss Worthing found . . ." Stephan began.

"We don't know that yet. There are still some tests to be done. But finding them there under the bed was a real bonus."

"It was a lucky accident," Miss Worthing said quietly. She was frowning at her hands folded on the table in front of her. "Of course," she added absently, "I should have been looking for them by then."

"Why?"

"Because of what your brother did the night of your father's death," she answered vaguely.

Stephan slammed his hand down onto the top of the table. "For the love of God," he exploded, "do we have to pull everything out of you?"

Miss Shaw nodded a ponderous agreement. "I quite agree. This is driving us wild, Mattie. Pull yourself together and tell the story."

* * *

"As I've said," Miss Worthing began, "it was very difficult at first even to conclude that a murder had been done. When, however, we put the whole thing together, it had a rank smell. That was why Lady Fairgrief first blew the whistle.

"She called me at four-thirty in the morning, right after poor Rudy died. It was rather fortunate that she called me, too," she said and chuckled.

"The thing, oddly enough, that sparked her curiosity was the simple fact that Rudolf Bessermann, one of the greatest heldentenors of the century, died of complications of pneumonia."

"There was more to it than that, Matilda," her aunt interjected.

Miss Worthing held up a hand. "I know, Aunt Eulalia, but I want at least to try to do this as logically as I can.

"A heldentenor," Miss Worthing continued, "is quite a remarkable physical phenomenon. Of literally heroic strength, much of the power lies in an unbelievably strong respiratory apparatus—well-aerated lungs, a diaphragm so powerful it is a visible ridge of muscle. Most singers with chest *colds* have no trouble getting rid of any accumulated fluids that could collect and lead to pneumonia. Had Rudy had emphysema even—which is not unknown among singers—it would have been a different story. But he was a hale and hearty seventy with the general health of a man twenty years younger. Why he could still sing like a god! And this man died of pneumonia?

"Now earlier that very day, Lady Fairgrief had occasion to scold her maid, who had not been there when she wanted to get up that morning. Maude, in fact, was having a cup of tea and a jaw with Miss Martinez in the kitchen."

Maude flushed and started to speak.

"No, Maude, please. It was a good thing you did so, else we might never have been the wiser.

"Miss Martinez told Maude that she wasn't certain Becay was a very good doctor. Now that's absurd. The man is a very well known, if elusive, specialist. Naturally,

Maude asked why Miss Martinez thought as she did. The reply was that one should not—among other things—intubate, or catheterize—to use a perhaps more familiar word—someone's lungs using petroleum jelly as a lubricant."

"Good God!" Stephan exclaimed.

Miss Worthing nodded grimly. "Of course. The lungs are completely incapable of throwing off the grease, the oils, what-have-you. The fluids collect to fight and you have, presently, a lipid, or fatty, pneumonia. It is always fatal."

Nothing was said for a few minutes as this sank into their minds.

"But then why the bee?"

"I think they were worried about lucid intervals."

"The codicil that never got signed!" Stephan shouted.

"Precisely. Schmidt wasn't going to take any chances. More fool he. If he had waited, no one would ever have been the wiser, in all probability. But their actions that night, pointless—even uncharacteristic—made Harvey suspicious and, when Lady Fairgrief told me, made me jumpy, too.

"Harvey told Maude in the kitchen that night that it was a bee sting—another bee sting that sent his beloved master into the dark. But Harvey was drunk and he'd been rather a poor excuse for a valet for a long time anyway. Stars, he was so old he was half ga-ga."

Lady Fairgrief harrumphed.

"Anyway," Miss Worthing continued, slightly red in the face, "Maude dismissed the whole thing as a senile fantasy. Then, on the way back to her post, she thought she heard someone in the pantry. She dismissed that, too.

"But someone else didn't dismiss Harvey's raving. Someone who knew that, drunk, Harvey was no problem, but when Harvey sobered up—and remember, he had laid Rudy out—Harvey was going to be big trouble indeed.

"So Harvey was roused during the night just long enough for one of them to tell him to drink his milk and he would feel better in the morning.

"It had to have happened that way. Harvey was an almost repellently fanatical Catholic. Suicide would have been unthinkable. But who could have done it? Becay was tending Aunt Eulalia's heart attack and everyone else was in the library."

"No, they weren't," Stephan said abruptly. "I was, but Schmidt and Larry both went to get a drink from the dining room, and Schmidt came back alone."

"So agreeable to have one's theories proven correct," Lady Fairgrief murmured. "It must have been Larry."

"That's right, ma'am," said Maude. "Don't you remember that I told you when I went to the kitchen that night to get a cup of tea, I heard Mr. Larry swearing something awful and saying he was going to get a drink."

Miss Worthing nodded. "Just so. Although I didn't know it, I knew it had to be someone like that because who else would Harvey have so trusted?"

"But if it was suicide . . ." Mary Ellen began.

Lady Fairgrief looked at her rather scornfully. "Now really, my dear!" she said with a click of the tongue. "Do you really think a man like Harvey would commit suicide?"

After a moment, Mary Ellen shook her head.

"Besides," Miss Worthing picked it up again, "as I said, they'd already behaved most strangely."

"What do you mean?" asked Mary Ellen.

"Well, my dear, why didn't *one* of them shut the window when they came pouring into the room to stop you and Steve? It seems such a simple thing. First of all, why did *both* rush to the bedside? Why did *both* fuss at poor Rudy so? The room was like a meat locker, wasn't it?"

Both Stephan and Mary Ellen nodded, their eyes glued to the floor.

"Then what *were* they doing?"

"And then, do you know what kept putting me off from that line of inquiry? Larry was as allergic to bee venom as his father and Schmidt, bless my stupidity, always had struck me as an incandescent booby."

"But he was—" Stephan began.

"I know," he was interrupted. "Now. But you know 'apiculture' and 'agriculture' are unfortunately very similar words and when you told Lady Fairgrief that he had been your father's *doktorvater*, I expected that it had been in music. The other shoe didn't really drop until I was in the library and realized that your father's scholarly background was in bugs, not music.

"But I'm getting ahead of myself.

"Anyway, after Harvey's death, I was quite convinced that poor Rudy had been murdered and by Paul Becay. So I called Miss Martinez to go see her. Someone overheard me. That's fairly obvious by now. But who? Schmidt and Larry were in the library. They could have overheard. But when I looked in, Schmidt had his nose buried in a score and Larry was dusting his hands off. The logical conclusion was that they'd been in there poring over mounds of dusty books."

"But they're not dusty," Mary Ellen said.

Again, Miss Worthing held up a restraining hand. "I know. Again, now. Those books aren't dusty. But the window locks are."

"Oh really." Mary Ellen frowned and muttered something about "that woman."

Miss Worthing grinned. "In any case," she continued, "I assumed they'd been too busy to overhear. What, of course, they'd done is overheard me on the telephone to the nurses' registry asking for Miss Martinez' number. Then, because that door really is quite thick, Larry probably scootched out a window and listened outside on the terrace.

"Then, Lord save me, when I went back into the kitchen, Mary Ellen said she'd heard heard someone go up the back stairs. Only Becay was upstairs. Immediately, I settled on him. Which was precisely when things began going haywire.

"Becay was in the library with Steve, my aunt, and Schmidt when Mary Ellen was gassed. Only Larry was unaccounted for and he says he was taking a walk. Fiddlesticks.

"Then, God save us, at supper Schmidt informed us Larry had gone to get the orchestra parts for the music they'd selected that afternoon. I cut their brakes before dinner so no one would leave. But I was too late."

"And so, when I got to Miss Martinez' house and found out what had happened, it began to come to me that the three of them must all be involved."

"Larry and Schmidt may both have had motives, but Becay?" Miss Shaw objected. "A doctor? They make plenty of money."

"What kind of practice can a man have," Lady Fairgrief asked with some asperity, "who dances attendance on one patient—and his heiress, I might add—and then drops everything to attend a house party for an old dragon. Does he have any other patients?"

Lorris grinned. "Not a whole lot."

"Indeed," Miss Worthing nodded, "but as executor of the estate with a handsome legacy to boot—and he still had a sufficiently good enough idea of himself to think he had a chance at winning the hand of the heiress— why, he would be doing quite all right. And it was needed?" She made it a question to Lorris, who nodded.

"There! Is that all, then?"

A storm greeted this.

"No," Stephan's voice rose above the rest. "You said you were the right one for Lady Fairgrief to have called."

"Oh yes, of course." Miss Worthing smiled. "That was why I said that Schmidt's part was the cleverest of all. Who suggested a musical cocktail hour?" She held up a hand to indicate the rhetorical nature of the question. "Who was it who gathered that lamentable posy of autumnal foliage? Who knew—as anyone who knows singers would know—that if Stephan started singing, Rudy would, too?"

"Schmidt, of course," Lady Fairgrief suddenly snapped. "But why were you so fortunately placed to know anything? Although," the ancient woman added somewhat more reasonably, "we have done rather well for ourselves."

"Because, dearest Aunt Eulalia, that very morning, while Martha and I were—fortunately for us—inside after a morning in the garden—and, incidentally, I was weeping buckets over your letter—a swarm of bees descended on us. A swarm of bees!" she repeated. "In November! But it wasn't a swarm, not really. There was no queen anywhere and they were confused and angry. Later, I found out that the man who owns the lot next to us—who is Jolliston's leading beekeeper, let me remind you—had had two hives ripped to shreds. A queen bee is, besides being the stupidest creature in the hive, the only bee that can sting twice."

Mary Ellen blanched. "That's what he was trying to say," she said.

"What?" Lorris asked sharply.

"When he was stung. He was lying on the floor and Paul and I were trying to help him breathe. He kept choking out 'k-k-an . . .' I thought he was trying to say, '*Kann nicht atmen*,' I can't breathe. Instead he was trying to say '*Königin.*'"

"Which is the German word for queen," Miss Worthing said quietly. "And so," she concluded, "I put a bee in Larry's bedroom this morning and, although I hadn't planned it that way, Schmidt and Larry both assumed that Becay had cut their brakeline. As a result, all three of them were so suspicious of the others that it was a snap to set up my little scene in the library. It was a good thing it worked too because it was a pretty dicey setup."

A grin appeared on Lorris's face.

"Well, it was, George, and you know it." Miss Worthing glared at the district attorney. "With the setup they had, they could so damnably easily have gotten away with it." She ticked off points on her fingers. "An expert to get the thing to which Rudy was desperately allergic. An unscrupulous doctor to do precisely the wrong thing at the wrong time. A supposedly loving son to lend"—she snorted grimly—"artistic verisimilitude, *and* hold his father pinned to the bed while Schmidt applied the insect and Becay created a necessary tongue lashing as a diversion. Neat, that was. But, you know," she added thoughtfully, "it must have given them a horrible turn to come into that room and find the three of you there. And so, they didn't do what any normal person would have done—just close the window." She shook her head. "Apart from the pneumonia itself, it was the first detail really to hit me—two little corroboratory incongruities, without which, you know, we might never have caught on."

"God," Stephan whispered. "We stood right there and watched it happen."

"Yes," said Miss Worthing softly, and peered over the tops of her glasses. "You were right there."

EPILOGUE

For a few minutes there was only silence, unbroken but for the clink of cups in saucers, or the gurgle of the decanter as someone poured more sherry into a glass. Then, abruptly, Mary Ellen went round to Lady Fairgrief and, kneeling down, had a brief whispered conversation with the old woman, who presently smiled and patted her arm.

"I'm going for a walk," Stephan suddenly announced.

"And I'll come with you," said Mary Ellen quickly, standing up. In a few minutes, they were seen crossing the lawn swaddled in heavy overcoats.

"Mr. Lorris?" Lady Fairgrief broke the thoughtful silence still attaining in the library. "Will it stick?"

"That's very hard to say, ma'am," the man replied after a moment. "Most of the evidence is circumstantial. We do have Larry's rather stupid remarks, and we do have those bees—Lord, that was stupid. We do have the coroner's report on the lipid pneumonia. Of course, we could try to put Maude on the stand—"

"George," interrupted Miss Worthing thoroughly scandalized, "that would be hearsay."

"Yeah, but three people are dead. The judge just might allow it. It is"—he glared at her—"a somewhat unusual case."

He stood up to go.

"But even if we can't make murder one stick, we have a very pretty conspiracy case and the fact that there are three bodies lying around. Well . . ." He picked up his hat and shrugged himself into his coat. "Be talking to you," he said genially and left.

The four women—Miss Worthing, Miss Shaw, Lady Fairgrief, and Maude—continued to sit in a comfortable silence in which not a little smugness was mixed. Suddenly, Lady Fairgrief nudged her maid. "Maude! I want a martini."

"Oh your ladyship!" exclaimed Maude joyously, rising to her feet. "How wonderful!"

Miss Shaw and Miss Worthing exchanged a mystified glance.

"I only have them once or twice a year," her ladyship explained. "I'm only supposed to have them on the highest of red-letter days. This," she observed firmly, "is the reddest of red-letter days."

"What on earth can you mean?" her niece asked.

For an answer the ancient woman gestured toward the window. Silhouetted against the sky at the top of the garden, Stephan and Mary Ellen were very close. "I think that when they come back down, they're going to tell us they're to be married as soon as it's decent."

"How do you always seem to know these things?" Miss Worthing enquired with some irritation.

"Because, my dear Matilda"—Lady Fairgrief grinned malevolently—"Mary Ellen was just asking me to think about how many servants I thought I would need to keep this place up."

"Servants?"

"Of course! To take care of me!"

Miss Worthing said nothing. It had briefly crossed her mind to invite her aunt to stay with them. The Bessermann fortune, however, put her own into the small time and the house, after all, was Aunt Eulalia's for the rest of her life. It would be better this way.

"You know," her ladyship continued, "I bet you anything that those two are going to go off to Europe where they should have been years ago, get into those arenas that count, and finally make a commitment to themselves and their careers."

She spoke with a fierce satisfaction and, as always, Miss Worthing found herself full of wonder at her ancient relative. To be ninety-five, if she were a day, and still looking forward with such undiminished relish. . . .

When, presently, Mary Ellen and Stephan came back in, their faces shining with cold and relief, they did indeed announce what the good lady had predicted. Voluble congratulations rained down upon them and in the flurry of good wishes and gratitude, Miss Worthing and Miss Shaw betook themselves home.

"What do you say we attack that attic storeroom, Martha?" Miss Worthing suggested as they got into their automobile.

"Sounds great to me," replied Miss Shaw stoutly, as she let in the clutch and began her usual cheerful babble. They were, in fact, nearly half way back to Jasmine Avenue when she noticed her companion's total silence.

"Mattie, what on earth's the matter with you? You haven't said a word since we left the Bessermann's."

"Haven't I, Martha?" Miss Worthing asked quietly. "I'm sorry. I was just thinking that I hope my aunt never finds out."

"Finds out what?"

"Martha, pull over."

Miss Shaw obeyed. They stopped at the edge of a winter-sere cornfield, from which a flock of crows rose protesting raucously as the car pulled to the side of the road.

"You mustn't breathe a word of this, but those two—

Mary Ellen and Stephan? They agreed to kill Bessermann themselves."

Miss Shaw had trouble taking this in. "What of it?" she eventually asked. "I've wanted to kill a lot of people, too."

Miss Worthing smiled. "So've I. No, Martha. It kept bothering me why Mary Ellen and Stephan were both so pointlessly upset during the whole investigation. And then, today, they're so . . . Well, so preternaturally happy. I'm not terribly certain that either of them is really all that distressed that poor Rudy is gone."

"He did rather put them through the hoop."

"True, and murder's been done for a lot less than that. But damn it all, Martha," she said with sudden intensity and turned and looked at her friend. "They're singers, too. They knew as surely as Becay must have known—and I'm very curious as to whether he'll say anything about it—that they were risking collapsing the lungs. Do you remember what Aunt Eulalia said, that they went into a huddle and argued before they agreed to help Rudy try to breathe? And the autopsy did show that the lungs were nearly through. Do you remember how white Mary Ellen went last night at supper when Larry said at least *he* hadn't killed Rudy . . ." Her voice trailed off and she turned to look out the window of the car.

"What are you going to do?"

"I'm not going to do anything." Miss Worthing shrugged. "As it happens, they didn't kill him."

"They tried," said Miss Shaw simply.

"Yes, but it was a question, I suspect, of seizing the moment. Besides which, what good would it do? There would be this pointless hullabaloo in a courtroom about motivations and intentions and were they conscious of what they were doing, etcetera, etcetera. And then there's that old business that if a man were falling from a fourteen-story window and someone shoots him, is the one who shoots guilty of murder? The law, of course, says he is. Doesn't this seem to be something like that?

"Schmidt did put the queen bee in that posy, Becay did use grease on the intubation unit, Lawrence did hold his father down while Schmidt applied another bee. God, Rudy never had a chance!

"And so, dearest Martha, neither the remote nor the proximate cause, as they say, had anything to do with Stephan or Mary Ellen. They just, as I said, seized an opportunity."

"But he asked them."

"And they should have refused. And furthermore," Miss Worthing added almost angrily, "my blessed aunt should have kept her mouth shut. It was all the encouragement they needed." Then, suddenly, and completely unexpectedly, she chuckled.

"What's the matter now?" asked Miss Shaw rather irritably.

"I'm going to be very, very careful from now on," Miss Worthing replied, a grim smile on her face. "If someone is out to get you, by golly, you'll be got. And, God only knows, Rudy wasn't that bad a man. But if I ever take to laying down the law like a Teutonic field marshal, please, dearest Martha, remind me what happens to them."

Miss Shaw, massively shaking her head at the enormities of humankind, watched the crows circling round the cornfield.

"Ah well," said Miss Worthing as lightly as she could. "There's nothing for it now. Let's go home."